A HOLIDAY COLLECTION

Very Merry Wingmen

DAISY PRESCOTT

Give and Take was previously published in 2015

Olaf's Christmas Carol was previously published in *Love, Laughter and Happily Ever After* in 2016

Wingmen Babypalooza was previously published in 2017

Cover Design: Juliane Burke/Heart to Cover Design
Editing: There for You Editing
Interior Design: Jenn Beach PA

Print ISBN: 978-1-7330712-3-9

A NOTE FROM DAISY

Characters from the *Wingmen* and *Modern Love Stories* books gather together to celebrate the holidays in these festive tales of love and community.

All previously published Wingmen holiday stories and newsletter exclusives are in a single collection for the first time.

Very Merry Wingmen is a collection of holiday shorts starring everyone's favorite wingmen on Whidbey Island, including:

Give and Take
Olaf's Christmas Carol
Wingmen Babypalooza
Olaf's Christmas Miracle
A Dan & Roslyn bonus scene
A John and Diane bonus scene
A Tom & Hailey bonus scene
A Carter & Ashley Thanksgiving bonus scene
An Erik & Cari Christmas bonus scene
A Jonah and June Holiday bonus scene

Happy Holidays!

❄

May your love be merry and bright.

GIVE AND TAKE

CHAPTER ONE

JOHN

Hailey opens the small crate hidden under a blanket in the cargo area of her SUV. "He's a Labradoodle."

A tiny brown dustball of a puppy stumbles out and blinks at us. I pick him up and cradle him in the crook of my arm. The pup snuggles into my flannel shirt and softly nibbles the cloth. "Are you sure? He looks kind of small for eight weeks."

"I'm sure. The breeder said he'll get big, bigger than a normal Lab."

I examined the puppy's tiny paws. "Not sure about that. Aren't you supposed to be able to tell by the size of the feet?"

"I thought that was for penises, not dogs." She blurts out and blushes.

"I think it works for both." I need to change the subject. No way am I talking about penis size with Hailey.

As if he knows we're talking about him, the brown fluff ball barks. The sound is a squeaky yip.

"What are you going to name him?" I let him bite on my shirt with his sharp teeth. Those things are like tiny razors.

"I figured Tom could name him, but I'm partial to Gus."

"Just don't let him name the dog after his boat. One Master Baiter is enough." I scratch the top of the dog's head.

"Knowing him he'll pick something like Carhartt or Stihl. He's pretty predictable." She tugs her knit cap down over her short hair against the chilly breeze off the bay. December at the beach is quiet and beautiful, but also cold and damp. Most of the houses are empty this time of year.

"How long do we get him for?" I pull my shirt free from the puppy's mouth. He nips at my finger, but doesn't draw blood. Maybe they should name him Sharky.

"I want to surprise him after the Sip 'n Stroll. I don't think I can wait any longer than that."

This weekend is the annual holiday event in Langley. It's a draw for locals and tourists alike. Back in our wingmen days, Tom dubbed it the Sip 'n Troll when we'd set up at The Dog House tavern to share holiday cheer. Those days are, thankfully, long over. I think I can speak for both of us when I say our lives are better off now. Way better. Whole different world.

Nodding, I say, "I can keep him here until the weekend. I'll put his crate upstairs in the spare room so Babe doesn't bother him." My Lab might not approve of a new dog in the house. Poor guy doesn't realize just how much his world is going to change in a few months.

"Thanks, John. I know how much Tom hates surprises, but he's been hinting about a dog for months. It was either this or another fish."

"The one he got at the fair last summer didn't last a weekend. Are you sure he can handle a mammal?" Poor fish was half-dead before we even finished the lumberjack competition. Tom was ridiculously proud that he won it for Hailey, he bragged to all the kids surrounding him at the duck pond game. Never mind it was a kids' game to begin with. The man wanted a fish, he won a fish.

"Poor Orca." Hailey frowns and pulls down the sleeves of

her sweater, tucking her hands into the thick wool. "Now that we're living together, I'll be in charge of keeping nameless here alive."

The puppy lifts his head at her voice and squirms in my arms. "They're both lucky to have you."

Hailey and I don't spend much time together without Diane or Tom around, but I like her. The two women have become close friends, and whatever she does to manage Tom seems to be working. He's never been happier.

"Likewise. Honestly, I can't believe I'm living with Tom Donnely."

"A year ago if you told me, I never would've believed it. Maybe if he was renting out a room." I scratch my beard and give her a smile. "He's not making you pay rent is he?" Tom inherited his land and built the house himself. He doesn't have a mortgage and other than property taxes has no expenses other than utilities. But he can be cheap too.

"I tried to pay him once for a tank of propane. That didn't end well." She rolls her eyes at my best friend's stubborn nature. "He's oddly traditional when it comes to being a man and providing for his woman."

"That doesn't surprise me. He takes after Pops more than he'll admit."

"We all miss his grand-dad. Sometimes I like to think Clifford's ghost gave Tom the kick in the ass he needed. Is that terrible of me?"

"If anyone could come back and haunt us, it would be Clifford Donnely." I hand the puppy back to her. She nuzzles his head with her nose before putting him into the crate. Nameless burrows into the blanket and closes his eyes.

"How's Diane feeling these days? I haven't spoken to her since last week."

"She's good. Eating, sleeping more. Otherwise the same." I don't mention we've entered the crazy horny stage of her pregnancy. Now that she's not throwing up anymore, all she wants to do is eat and have sex. If it weren't for her giant boobs, I'd say she was turning into a super horny teenage boy.

"Look at you, John Day, married man and dad to be." She grins at me. I've known Hailey most of my life, and despite the events of the past year, it's tough not to see her as little Lori Donnely's tough-as-nails tomboy friend.

"I could say the same thing about you, Hailey. Well, not the married or pregnant part ..." I let the last part trail off. I don't really want to discuss my best friend's sex life with his girlfriend. Ever.

She slowly blinks her eyes and shakes her head. "No on both the last two. We're not really going to talk about sex, are we? Please say no."

"God, no." I take a step back. "Nope. Don't ask, don't tell."

She closes the crate door and picks it up by the handle. "On that note, I'm going to head home." She hands me the crate and a bag of puppy food. "I was never here. We never had this conversation."

I nod and settle the bag under my arm, holding the crate with the other hand. "What conversation?"

With a wave she walks to the front of her car.

It's a good thing she's leaving. Our conversations should never involve penis size or sex lives. Plus, I'd gotten too close to blowing Tom's plans for the weekend by bringing up marriage.

Christmas has exploded all over Langley. As I pull into a parking spot on Second Street, I note that every storefront is covered with holiday greenery and festive decorations. Some windows are painted with winter scenes, including a pod of Orcas wearing Santa hats at the music store, while others have enough mistletoe draped everywhere to poison the entire town.

The holiday stroll doesn't officially start for another hour, but I told Diane I'd meet her early. Christmas carols play through the speakers hidden under the buildings' eaves as I make my way down the path to her Pilates studio. She bought the business from Traci this fall. Once the baby comes, she'll need someone else to take over her classes for a while, but having her own business makes her happy, and I love anything that makes her happy.

I pause outside the building and think about how casually I just thought about the baby. My baby. Our baby. After the shock wore off, I slowly adjusted to the thought that in a few months, I'm going to be a dad. Me. With a kid. Hell, we have years before he'll be a full blown kid. Baby.

By the way, baby is a four letter word. I've said a lot of four letter words over the years, but baby has become my new favorite.

Smiling at what a huge softie this whole pregnancy has made me, I shake my head and open the door to the studio. Diane sits on a mat on the floor, stretching. Her belly protrudes enough she can no longer reach her toes. With her dark hair pulled back, the mirror reflects her cleavage as she leans forward. It's my favorite part of her ever-changing body.

She catches me staring and sits up, grinning. I swear she leans back on her hands in order to push out her chest, and tease me further. "You are so predictable, husband of mine."

I walk over and stand in front of her. The view is even better from this angle. Her workout tank cuts low, giving me a spectacular eye-full.

"Are you going to stand there ogling my boobs, or will you help my fat ass off the floor?" Her cheeks are pink from exercise. Or the tightness in my jeans. She is almost eye level with my fly and I'm certain she can see how she affects me.

Still. Every day.

Always.

I extend both my hands and lift her up. Fat ass? Never.

I pull her to me and remind her how beautiful she is. My hand cups her head as the other supports her back, dipping her slightly as my lips find hers. I moan a little when she weaves her fingers into my hair and tugs. Her strong grip on my bicep tells me she is as turned on as I am right now. If it weren't for the fact the glass doors are unlocked and all the lights are on, I'd take this much further right now. Forget the holiday stroll. Why didn't I lock the door when I came in?

Her stomach rumbles. Loudly. It sounds like a motorcycle revving. Or a bear growling.

I break the kiss because I'm laughing.

She tightens her hand on my arm and pulls me back down with her fingers in my hair. Her moan is of frustration.

"Ignore the monster demanding food. Kiss me!"

I peck her lips. It's all I can do because now I'm smiling and chuckling, and there is no way I can kiss her properly.

Her lips pout, full of disappointment. "You're laughing at a poor pregnant woman."

"I'm laughing that your stomach sounds like a bear. It's my husbandly duty to feed you and worry about your ankles swelling." I glance down to make sure her ankles aren't swollen. From this angle, I can't even see her ankles because of her belly.

"They're fine. I'm fine."

Her stomach grumbles again. This time it's a low rumble. The mountain is angry. I pat her bump. "We'll stop and get you a snickerdoodle at the bakery."

"Mmm … I do love those." She stretches up on her toes to give me a soft kiss. "You're the most wonderful husband ever."

I run my hands down her side and over her hips, which have also become more curvier in the last couple months. "I do what I can."

"Let me change and I'll be ready to go. What time are we

meeting Tom and Hailey?" She steps away and heads toward the changing room.

I glance at the clock on the wall. "We've got about fifteen minutes before we said we'd meet them.

She stops walking and gives me a slow smile. Her tongue runs along the edge of her top teeth.

I can't believe I'm turning this down. "We don't have time."

"We have plenty of time."

I close my eyes to this temptress and exhale. On a normal evening, we'd have plenty of time for something fun, but not tonight. Not for the surprise I've arranged. There isn't enough time for Diane to shower and get ready. We can't show up smelling of sex. Not tonight.

"Are you turning down some hanky-panky?" Her mouth drops open in disbelief.

Staring at her inviting lips reminds me of the wood I'm half sporting since the kiss a few minutes ago. We wouldn't have to have full out sex …

I've about convinced myself to offer a compromise, when cold air hits my back from the opening of the front door.

Should've locked it.

"There you are," Hailey exclaims as she walks into the space. A knit hat covers her hair and a puffy coat makes her look like she's wearing a sleeping bag. After unwrapping her long knit scarf, she stops, her focus bouncing between us. "Oh. Am I interrupting something?"

Beard burn has deepened the pink on Diane's cheeks. Her hair is mostly out of its ponytail. She looks thoroughly kissed. Blushing deeper, she dashes into the small changing room and shuts the door. "Be right out!"

Hailey stares at me.

I rub my hand over my beard again.

"I was totally interrupting something! I'm so sorry." She focuses on the window instead of meeting my eyes. "It's cold and I'm early, so I thought I'd grab Diane and then meet up with Tom, but you're here already, and Diane's not changed yet, so she's not ready, but you're wearing your jacket and I'm not sure even what's going on, but the look you two were giving each other could melt metal, and now I'm babbling. So this is awkward."

I don't know if she breathed at all while she said all that. Pretty sure she didn't.

"It's fine. You didn't interrupt."

She meets my eyes. "I don't believe you, but okay."

We stand there awkwardly for a minute.

"I dropped off the puppy at your house on my way over here. I also let him out, so he should be fine for a couple of hours."

"Thanks for taking him. I owe you."

Luckily, Diane's a fast changer. She exits the room wearing those black leggings she lives in these days and a big sweater.

Hailey makes a cooing sound like a dove when she sees her. "You got bigger this week. I think you popped."

Is popping a good thing?

Diane doesn't appear so sure. "Suddenly, I'm huge." She rubs her belly and smiles down at her hand. Some weird pride or other emotion lodges itself in my throat at seeing her loving expression.

Huge softie. But I'll deny it if anyone asks or comments.

"Where's Tom?" I need reinforcement. I need my wingman. I stare out the glass doors. All I can see is a reflection of the three of us. It's only five o'clock, but it's completely dark out already.

"He's running late, but said he'll find us." Hailey smiles at Diane, reaching out to touch her belly. "Can I feel?"

"Sure. Sometimes the baby kicks after I've been stretching. I don't think she likes it."

Hailey's eyes widen. "She?"

Diane nods. "Well, this week I think she's a she. John's

being old fashioned and doesn't want to know the sex until the birth."

"I'm convinced he's a boy." I cross my arms. Boys I can handle. Little girl? I'm not ready for that. I know too much about guys like Tom and me to be able to survive raising a girl.

The two women give me sympathetic frowns, but amusement flashes in their eyes.

"What?"

Diane flattens her expression. "Nothing, honey. Girl or boy, you're going to be an amazing poppa."

My neck prickles in embarrassment. This is too much.

"I'm going to stop by and check on Olaf at The Dog House before this thing starts. You know how he gets cranky when there's going to be a big crowd and a whole hullabaloo."

"Right, Olaf gets cranky." Diane nods. "Sweet of you to check on him. We'll catch up with you in a bit."

"Okay." I rub my neck. "Good. I'll text Tom and tell him to meet me there."

I give her a quick peck on the cheek and nod goodbye to Hailey.

Their heads are together in whispered conversation before the door closes behind me.

I need a beer and some testosterone.

I text Tom.

He replies in a few seconds that he'll meet me at The Dog House.

I laugh at my best friend. He knows me well.

CHAPTER TWO

TOM

"Hey, Tom." Erik Kelso is setting up a bar stool outside the front door of The Dog House as I cross the street. His Santa hat droops over the left side of his head. He resembles an oversized elf.

"Pretty cold out here for sidewalk drinking." I stop next to his perch. The forecast is for flurries and the damp night air is cold enough for snow. "Or is Olaf carding tonight?"

"Ha, when was the last time Olaf paid for a bouncer?" Pointing above our heads, he gives me a grin. Hanging over us is a ball of mistletoe. I step back and away from its shadow. All along the street, balls of greenery and mistletoe decorate the doorways. Some shops even have chalkboards outside to tally kisses. I have to give the guy credit for the stool.

"Nice," I tell him.

He holds up his fist for a bump. "I figure why try to work the entire street, when I can sit here comfortably and wait for the ladies to come to me. Carter is pissed he didn't think of it first."

I look around for the other Kelso brother, but don't see him inside at the bar.

"Carter's down the block at the pizzeria. We decided to divide and conquer."

Resembling big yellow puppies, the two of them could be John and I a few years ago. I hate to admit it, but their game might even be better than ours. I never thought to set up a stool under a kissing ball. That's horny guy genius at work right there.

"The women won't know what to do with themselves." I bump his fist, giving him his deserved props.

"Speaking of women, does Hailey have any clue what you're planning for Christmas?"

I shake my head. "So far, nope. You guys coming over tomorrow to help me? The girls are scheduled to head over to Seattle to go shopping for the day. I figure we can get the framing up while they're gone. It's all loaded on the flatbed over at the farmhouse."

As weird as it might seem, I'm liking, hell, even enjoying, living with Hailey. Sharing the house and especially my bed with her has been easier than I imagined.

However, sharing a shop space between a welder and a carver has been less than ideal. My barn is big enough for the two of us, but wood and sparks aren't a great mix. So I'm building a small shop for her. That way she can listen to all the Backstreet Boys music she wants.

She'd kill me if I told anyone she still loves '90s boy bands, but I don't think people would be shocked if they found out. The new shop will be pretty small, under a thousand square feet, but vented and all open for her torches. She can still store stuff in the barn.

"So what's the plan for tomorrow?" Erik asks.

"We're loading up the framing on the flatbed in the morning. I poured the foundation a couple of weeks ago when she and her mom went on a girls' weekend. It's been covered under a tarp so she doesn't get suspicious."

"She's not suspicious about a tarp in the yard?" He gives me a doubtful look.

"I threw a bunch of carvings and stumps on it and then covered those with another tarp."

He nods in support of my genius. "You're a duplicitous bastard, Donnely. How'd you ever get a hot babe like Hailey?"

"Big word. You studying to pass your GED?"

"Ha ha. I graduated college. I'm just saying you being all monogamous is pretty strange." He lifts his pint glass to take a swig.

Smug asshole. I flick the bottom of the glass, causing it to over tip, spilling a thin stream of beer down the front of his jacket.

He sputters and wipes at the beer. "Hey! What was that for?"

I shoot him a dirty look. "That's for suggesting I'd ever cheat on Hailey."

His eyebrows furrow and his mouth hangs open a little. "I'd never do that. You aren't that stupid. And even if you were, I'd be first in line to console her."

I swat at his head. "There's going to be no need for you, or anybody else, to console Hailey. She's mine and I plan to keep it that way. For a long time. Forever. Got it?"

He holds up his hands. "Got it. Damn, you're so sensitive these days. You and John both are whipped hard."

"You should be so lucky." I laugh and cuff his shoulder before opening the door.

"I'm trying to get lucky. Why do you think I've got my stool here?" His chuckle fades as I enter the bar.

Olaf grumbles hello and puts two pint glasses on the old wood bar. "That kid's going to be trouble tonight."

"You didn't have to serve him. Or give him the stool." I knock on the window to scare Erik. He bounces off the stool and it tumbles over. Flipping me the bird, he straightens up and resumes his seat.

Olaf's laughter turns into a cough. "Eh, he's better out there in the cold than in here where he bothers me. At least I don't have to listen to him."

I sip the foam off of the pint he pours for me. Outside, more people pass by on the sidewalk, their cheerful voices carrying through the glass.

"Damn revelers," Olaf mutters.

"You seem in fine holiday spirits, tonight, O." I spin on my stool to observe him. For as old as he is, and he's got to be in his sixties now, he's still pretty spry. Or maybe ornery is the word I mean.

"Bah humbug." He scowls. "There's going to be caroling later. If people want to sing, that's fine, but standing outside someone's place of business and singing at them feels like harassment. If I wanted to hear all those women singing off-key, I'd go to church. You see me in church on Sunday, Tom?"

I raise my eyebrows. "Can't say that I have, O. Then again, I'd have to be there to see you."

"That's my point exactly."

My gaze flicks left to right as I try to figure out his point. That we're both sinners? "Not following you."

"All this fuss and cheer. I don't need it." He gestures at the strand of multi-colored lights in the window and the faded paper Santas taped to the walls in a couple of places. It's not exactly a holiday wonderland in here.

"Nice kissing ball outside, O," John says as he sits on the stool next to me.

Olaf practically spits. "They hung that up this morning without my permission. Now that Kelso boy has taken up residence underneath it for the night. Probably going to nurse that one beer and scare away my paying customers, too."

John faces me with an alarmed look in his eyes. His beard twitches as he fights a smile. "Olaf seems to be in a good mood."

I nod, struggling not to laugh. "Where are Hailey and Diane?"

"They'll be here in a bit. I left them at the studio, cooing over babies." He takes a long pull on the beer O set in front of him.

We both silently drink our beers and stare out the window past the colorful lights.

John breaks the silence. "You get the ring from your grandmother?"

"Yeah. It's in my glove box." I even locked it just in case. "I had to swear Gramma to secrecy. She wanted to tell my mom. Mom would tell Lori and there wouldn't be any point in trying to surprise Hailey."

"I almost mentioned something at the studio."

"What the hell, dude?" I stare at him. "You what?"

"Calm down. I didn't. Hailey walked in on Diane and me … not full out, but you know, and I got flustered."

"Dude."

"I know, I know. It's serious business. I'm still kind of surprised you're doing it so soon." He takes a swig.

"If Pops taught me anything, it's that life is short. Why wait if I know this is forever?"

John spins his own wedding ring around his finger. "I understand. Completely."

"You're on schedule for Diane's surprise?" I ask.

"Should be. I got a text from Maggie that she was at SeaTac about an hour ago. She and Gil were driving up from Portland for the weekend. Turns out, she's picking up more friends who have a flight around the same time, so they're taking two cars. It all worked out perfectly. "

"That's pretty cool your neighbor was willing to help you out, considering."

He arches his eyebrow. "Considering?"

"What a crush you had on her and how she flirted with you."

"Yeah, that's ancient history. I owe her big time for renting to Diane."

I nod in agreement. Movement outside the window catches my eye. "Speak of the wife …"

Diane is waving at us, while Hailey chats up Kelso. With a jolt, I notice MY girlfriend is standing directly under the kissing ball.

Oh, hell no.

I bolt from my stool, leaving it rattling behind me as I rush the door.

CHAPTER THREE

HAILEY

Strong arms wrap around me from behind, pulling me off my feet and spinning me onto the sidewalk. I squeal and thrash about until Tom's voice whispers against my ear.

"If anyone is going to be kissing you tonight, tomorrow, or any other night for the foreseeable future, it's going to be me. Me. No one else." His breath warms my ear and cheek. He sets me down, turning me to face him.

Before I can ask him what the hell is going on, his lips crash onto mine. His mouth is demanding, claiming. I can't breathe, but I don't dare stop kissing him. Not that I have a choice. Oxygen is overrated.

My body responds to him. I press myself closer, wishing I didn't have this puffy jacket creating a down version of bubble-wrap between us. My hands go to his face, anchoring him to me. His arms wrap around my waist.

"Well, that mistletoe seems to be working." An older woman's voice breaks through the sound of my blood pumping in my ears. I break away from Tom's mouth. I can feel the heat from his beard on my cheeks and chin. I look up to see we're standing underneath a ball of mistletoe.

"That was one helluva kiss you two. I'd say get a room, but you're already living together." Erik's sporting a smug smile. I forgot he was sitting here. Diane's studying the greenery above the chocolate shop next door, avoiding our make-out session.

Tom's arms are still around my waist. We're blocking the entire sidewalk and the door to the bar.

"Was it the mistletoe or did you miss me?" I try to pull away, but he tightens his hold.

"I missed you." He gives me a peck on the mouth. "Missed you." He kisses me softly. "So much."

I arch back so I can see him. "And?"

He slowly blinks at me. It's his innocent look. For when he's up to no good or has done something he thinks will piss me off.

With a slow exhale, he releases me, but grabs my hand in his. "Kelso looked like he was going in for the kill with you standing under the mistletoe. I couldn't let that happen." He glowers at Kelso, who gives him a wolfish grin.

Part of me wants to be mad. I don't need a man getting all territorial over me like a dog toy. On the other hand, when Tom gets jealous, he gets this look on his face that I find ridiculously hot. Like he's about to drag me back to his cave. I'll never admit to him that I like it. Or how much it turns me on. Never. He's ego is big enough already.

"Tom …" I try to pull my hand back.

"Hailey …" He pulls me closer. I try to resist. I do. I step back and dig in my heels. He's stronger than me and when I give in, I fall into his arms. "I can't help it. I don't trust those Kelsos." He leans down to kiss me, but I sense him eyeing Erik behind me.

A group of a dozen carolers surround us, singing enthusiastically and very loudly, forcing us to move out of their way.

"Here We Come a-wassailing,
among the leaves so green.
Here we come a-wandering,

so fair to be seen.
Love and joy come to you,
and to your wassail, too..."

Diane shelters herself in the doorway of the shop next door. Only the ball on her knit hat is visible. I can barely make out the top of John's dark head in The Dog House's doorway. Erik on his stool, Tom, and I make up a strange audience trio.

Tom backs us up so we have the window behind us. Our legs hit the bench below it and we sit down. Might as well. There's no escaping the hoard of singers.

My eyes meet his and we widen them in a silent conversation.

He leans toward me and whispers in my ear, "What's a wassail?"

Without turning my head, and with a forced smile on my face, I whisper back, "I have no idea, but it's both a noun and a verb."

Thankfully, the song comes to an end. Sadly, we never learn the definition of wassail.

We clap and smile, and clap some more. Amongst the brightly dressed revelers, I spot Sally in a Christmas sweater with Rudolph and his red nose blinking on her chest. Next to her is Sandy, in an equally bright holiday sweater, covered in three-dimensional, sparkly tinsel. Both are outdone by Connie's sweater. Her chest is covered with a puffy Christmas tree, complete with ornaments hanging off of it and strings of lights, which are also blinking. Combined, the blinking and sparkling could give someone a seizure. What's a word for beyond tacky?

"Happy Holidays!" they shout at us in over-zealous merriment. I grip Tom's hand. Honestly, I'm a little afraid right now.

Tom flinches beside me.

We wish them the same. John squeezes past Erik to join us.

"Oh, John. We didn't see you there. Where is that lovely

wife of yours?" Connie cranes her neck to look around him, as if he's shielding Diane behind him. I wouldn't blame him if he did.

"Oh, look John, you're under the mistletoe." Sally purrs, slinking toward him.

You've never seen a man move so fast. I nearly choke on my laugh.

"Hailey." Erik points above my head. Damn mistletoe is everywhere. I give Tom a quick peck. He isn't expecting it. I get mostly cheek and beard.

"Where is Diane?" John scans the crowd.

"She's over there." I point to the empty doorway. "Or she was."

A few seconds later, Diane appears with a waffle cone in her gloved hand. It looks to be a triple scoop of chocolate ice cream.

With a sheepish smile, she greets us. "I got hungry waiting for the singing to finish. I wasn't sure how long it was going to last. And John promised me a cookie earlier, so I had sweets on my mind." She licks the cone and closes her eyes in pleasure. Opening them again, she asks, "Anyone want some?"

We all decline.

"We wanted to let you know we started a pool on the baby at the bank," Connie chirps with delight. "People have to guess the date, time and the sex, since you won't tell us."

"We have another one going at the grocery store." Sandy adds. "A dollar a guess. We're up to thirty-five dollars so far, and it's only been up this week."

John grumbles and walks over to Diane. "You're betting on my baby?"

Diane's hand on his arm stops his grumbling. "Oh, that's sweet. Please don't feel hurt, but we're not telling anyone the sex because we don't know it."

"And I think it's actually called gender now." John's voice is calm like he's talking to young children.

The three women murmur and smile at him in return. There's a flurry of oohs and aahs when Diane pats her belly.

It's a little disturbing. I wonder if she feels like a prized heifer these days. I wonder if I'll feel like a cow when I'm pregnant.

If.

I mean I'm not planning to get pregnant right now. I wasn't like Lori growing up–always counting the number of kids I'd have.

If.

Tom and I haven't even been dating that long. Yes, we're living together. Yes, I love him. But we're not ready for kids. Not like Diane. She was ready the second she and John got married. Maybe even before then.

Although, little Toms running around would be really cute. Floppy blond hair and his dimples in a pint size person? Adorable.

But that's a long way off. Like marriage. We haven't even talked about getting married. I mean I'm not opposed to it, but he's just getting used to having a serious, adult relationship and a girlfriend.

There's no rush.

If, not when. I'm barely thirty. We have plenty of time for us before we start thinking about kids.

Tom squeezes my fingers. I glance up at him. His eyes hold so much love for me. Reflecting the Christmas lights all around us, he's the most handsome man I've ever known. Growing up, he was the cutest boy I'd ever seen. I never believed he could be mine.

Okay, maybe when we have kids.

For now we'll have the puppy. That's a good place to start our little family.

The carolers finally move down to the next group of shops, leaving the four of us on the sidewalk. Erik's disappeared, too.

"Shall we stroll?" Diane breaks off a piece of the cone.

John leans over and steals a big bite of her ice cream.

"Hey!" She moves it away from his mouth. "No stealing from the pregnant girl."

"Let's mosey." Tom holds out his arm for me to take. It's an old fashioned romantic gesture. Totally unexpected from him and completely sweet. I tuck my arm with his and he holds my hand.

John and Diane lead the way down First Street. Diane finishes off the ice cream in record time and starts talking about finding mulled cider. We step into the street to avoid the crowd trapped by a boisterous rendition of "Up on the Housetop," complete with noisemakers and sound effects.

"Diane!" A woman with shoulder-length blondish red hair calls out from the other side of the carolers. She's wearing a giant plaid scarf the size of a blanket.

"John!" Now she's walking toward us. A really handsome older guy with salty-gray-brown hair follows her. He has the whole hot professor look going for him in a blazer and jeans.

CHAPTER FOUR

MAGGIE

"Maggie!" Diane rushes over to us, not looking either way when she crosses the street. It's a little worrisome.

I know it's tiny Langley. Most nights you could lie down in the middle of any street and not get run over, but I don't think John could survive if anything happened to her. Especially now that she's pregnant.

I've never seen a man more ridiculously excited about having a baby, but in a stoic, classic John way. He smiles more and laughs more. He's always watching her to make sure she's okay.

Now that John's happily married and starting a family, Gil has warmed up to him. He doesn't even frown when John's name comes up anymore. As if there was ever any real competition there.

Diane hugs me while John says hello to Gil. Clearly, Diane hasn't spotted her big surprise behind us yet.

John and I wave at each other. He cocks his head in question and I jerk mine back to answer him.

"So what brings you to the island?" he asks innocently. Too innocently. He might as well be whistling in nonchalance.

Diane stares at him, clearly suspecting him of something. She studies me and then goes back to staring at him. "You two are acting odd. What are you up to?"

Beside me, Gil chuckles. I elbow him.

He rocks back on his heels. "I've never been to the Sip 'n Stroll, so I demanded some holiday cheer after turning in my final grades. Maggie agreed and suggested we spend Christmas on the beach this year."

Diane nods, but her eyes still hold doubt.

"You are the worst surprisers in surprise history!"

Diane's eyes widen at the voice shouting behind us.

"Surprise!" Quinn shoves me out of the way. "Look who's here!"

I stumble, but Gil steadies me. After all this time, I should anticipate Q's exuberance.

"Quinn!" Diane bounces up and down twice before she's enveloped by our mutual friend. "What are you doing here? Is Ryan here?"

"We're here." Ryan walks around Gil, carrying Lizzy in his arms. The toddler's bundled up like a pink Eskimo, complete with miniature shearling boots to her knees and faux fur trim on her parka. She twists in his arms, suddenly shy around strangers.

Ryan's dressed in all black like a typical New Yorker. His hair is a little bit more salty at his temples under his hat. His dark eyes crinkle at the corners when he smiles.

Quinn is dressed as a lumbersexual from Brooklyn. It's kind of funny to see him standing next to John. Both men are wearing flannel, jeans and boots. John's boots are scuffed from work while Quinn's are perfectly polished. John wears a thick Carhartt coat. Quinn is in a navy cashmere peacoat. Even his knit cap sits at a jaunty angle, leaving his blond hair mostly exposed.

Lumbersailor? I'll have to ask him if seamen is the new fashion trend. Or would that be lumberseamen? I laugh to myself. I'll have to share that with Selah later. I'll even give her permission to use it in one of her books.

"How long are you here?" Diane's eyes well up with tears.

Oh, boy. This is only part of the surprise. I told Quinn and John that shocking a hormonal woman is never a good idea, but they didn't listen. I hope she has tissues.

Ryan hands off Lizzy to Quinn. She reaches out her arms and says "Da-dee" as he takes her. Ryan gives Diane a big hug. "We're here for a week. New York misses you."

"Oh, I've missed you two so much. Happy Chanukah!"

Ryan beams at her. "Thanks for remembering us Jews. We're multi-denominational when it comes to Christmas. Our house is definitely on Santa's list, much to my mother's displeasure."

"Fine with the husband, but not Santa?" Gil chuckles.

"She's all about the grandkids."

Diane rubs her hand down Lizzy's back. "Of course she loves Little Lizzy. Well, not so little anymore."

"Speaking of not so little anymore." Quinn points at Diane's belly. "You're huge."

Only a gay man, well no, only Quinn, can get away with saying such things to a woman. Ever. He knows he can get away with it, too. Blunt is part of his charm.

"If you were blue, you could play Violet Beauregard in a production of Willy Wonka." He laughs at his own joke.

"Stop. I'm not that huge." Diane giggles.

"You polished off a triple scoop of ice cream and didn't even share," Tom says. I recognize him and his girlfriend from John's wedding last summer. I make the introductions all around.

"Quinn's one of my oldest friends," I explain.

"By old, she means we met as children. Toddlers, really."

It's my turn to laugh. "We met in college and we've earned these wrinkles."

"Wrinkles?" Quinn gasps. "Never!"

"Ryan's an amazing dermatologist," Diane tells her friends.

A driver honks his horn at us. I realize we're standing in the middle of the street. We move out of the way in a big clump, chatting all at the same time. Diane is now holding Lizzy's hand as we stroll. Lizzy still has her head tucked into Quinn's shoulder, but she holds a tight grip on Diane's finger.

"Do you think Ye Olde Carolers know the Wham Christmas song?" Quinn asks as the singers break into "Jingle Bells."

"I'd take some Mariah Carey over another round of 'Silent Night'." Diane suggests.

"Oh, I only like her song that was in *Love, Actually*," I say. "It's–"

"Your favorite movie." Gil and Quinn finish my sentence.

"Oh, I love that movie," Hailey agrees. "'God Only Knows' is a great song, too."

We run through a list of our favorite songs and scenes in the movie, becoming instant friends.

John taps away on his phone, oblivious to the conversation. I feel my phone vibrate in my coat pocket and take it out. I respond to his text, fighting a smile while I do it.

"Look at all this bearded goodness!"

The voice can only belong to my other best friend, Selah. I lift my eyes to spot her dark hair a dozen feet away. She's staring at John and Tom like she's a sailor and it's fleet week in NYC. Standing beside her, Kai, her fiancé, is sporting a nice level of George Clooney style scruff. They got engaged this past summer, but I suspect they might be one of those couples that stays engaged for years. Or elope, and not tell anyone. I covertly eye their fingers for wedding bands, but find none. I love weddings, but who am I to talk? Gil and I have no plans to get married.

"Damn. It's a real live lumbersexual convention right here on the sidewalk." Selah purrs.

John visibly bristles at her words.

"Oh, Paul Bunyan, I don't mean you. You're the real thing. All seven feet of you." She teases him good-naturedly.

Even Hailey and Diane laugh at her nickname for John.

"Why didn't I come up with that one?" Hailey mumbles to her friend.

"Holy cats, you've procreated." Selah's eyes focus on Diane's belly. "You lucky, lucky woman."

Diane looks up at John and back at Selah in confusion.

"We haven't met. I'm Selah, the obnoxious friend." She sticks out her hand.

"Oh, I've heard all about you." Diane shakes her hand and adds, "All good things."

Selah's laugh is deep and throaty. "Then you haven't been talking to Quinn."

I observe our little group. Selah's right about the facial hair. Gil has started growing his winter beard. He'll shave it before the spring semester starts. Along with Kai, Quinn sports more scruff than usual. Only Ryan is clean-shaven. I guess beards are taking over the world.

Selah hugs Ryan and gives Quinn a half hug so she doesn't squish Lizzy. It's the closest ever Selah's come to holding her. I laugh as Lizzy lets go of Diane's finger to grab the fringe on Selah's cape/poncho. Despite her overstated dislike of children, Selah smiles and tickles Lizzy's nose with more fringe, causing the girl to giggle and lean in for more.

"When did you arrive?" I ask Kai. We might all live in Portland, but we rarely find time to get together. Kai spends a lot of time in Africa and travels the world for his non-profit work, taking Selah with him when she's not teaching.

"Yesterday. Selah finished her grades and we drove up in the evening."

"Are you settled in the house?" I'm happiest when my little cabin on the beach is filled with my favorite people.

"We are," Selah says. "We even brought a tree with us

over on the ferry. Kai strapped it to the top of the car like he's a Norse God. I swear he lifted the thing with one arm."

She may notice other men, hell, we all notice good looking men like John and Tom, you'd have to be blind not to, but her heart is firmly held in the hands of Kai. He might even give the island guys a run for handsome. I know for a fact he looks amazing in a suit.

"Did he chop it down himself?" John asks. If it were John's tree, the answer would be yes. Knowing Kai, he bought the most expensive tree on the lot. I hope it fits in my living room.

Christmas at my beach cabin with my closest friends is my gift to myself this year. Even if our Christmas is a few days early so everyone could make it. We'd asked Ben and Jo to join us, but they're spending the holidays in Florida with her family. As Jo put it, it's the last chance to go to Disney World with sullen teens, and who wants to miss out on that fun. Selah's comments on the whole trip involved the words "sea of germs" and "hell portal."

"Baby, it's cold outside," she sing-says to the group. "I've done the strolling part of this evening, now how about some sipping?"

She's right about the cold. I tuck my plaid scarf tighter around my neck. Sitting on the bluff, Langley is exposed to the wind. A few flurries dance through the air.

"We have dinner plans." John drapes his arm around Diane. They stop walking, so we all stop.

"We do?" she asks

"I made reservations at Cafe Langley."

"You did?"

"I did." He smiles down at her.

"We have plans, too." Tom interrupts.

"Are you joining us?" Diane asks the group.

Tom and John exchange looks.

"No, um, our plans are separate. I've had enough festiveness for one evening." Tom gives Hailey a cautious look. He's normally so cocky and self-assured.

I don't know him well, but if I had to guess, he wants Hailey all to himself for the rest of the evening.

"Watch out for the mistletoe. The town is a minefield. Covered with the stuff." John points above our heads.

Gil rubs his hands together, a devilish glint in his eye. "I say we take full advantage of it. What say you, Maggie May?"

My old nickname always makes me swoon. I rise up on my tiptoes to kiss him. It's a soft, sweet kiss that ends too soon.

Gil scans the storefronts. "You owe me ten, no wait, twelve kisses."

I don't question his math. "Challenge accepted."

After saying goodbye and wishing us all merry Christmases, the two couples split off and walk in opposite directions down the crowded street.

Another surprise is waiting for Diane at the restaurant. I smile, knowing I did something really nice for John and his wife. After all, this season is about giving.

CHAPTER FIVE

DIANE

John isn't a reservation and fancy dinner kind of guy. Yet here we are at a white-cloth covered table at Cafe Langley, my favorite restaurant. Even more strange is they seated us at a table for four. It's packed in here tonight because of the event. I'm about to ask him what's going on when I hear my mother's voice.

Rather than turn toward her, I stare at my husband. "What did you do?"

He grins at me, but worry dances in his eyes. "I brought home to you, since you can't really travel for Christmas."

"You're my home, John Day. Our home is at the beach. Together."

He softly kisses my cheek, his beard tickling my skin. "I know, but I can't replace your parents."

"Hey sweetheart." My dad is standing next to the table now, wearing a Nordic sweater in a reindeer pattern. His bald head shines in the candlelight.

"Honey?" Mom asks, sounding worried. Her hair is shorter than the last time I saw her, but still a warm brown with highlights. Her face is thinner, too.

Tears spill down my cheeks as I stand up. "You're here."

I'm stunned stupid. "How?"

I hug both my parents as I cry. I'm not even sure why I'm crying.

Hormones? Probably.

Sentimental mush? Probably.

Realizing how much I've missed my mom? Definitely.

I'm now a blubbering mess in the middle of the restaurant. Not sobbing, but I do need to blow my nose soon or I'll get snot all over my mother's cashmere sweater.

"John called us and invited us to come out to visit you. He made all the arrangements and got his lovely friends Maggie and Gil to pick us up at the airport. She was there to get her friends from the city and brought two cars. Turns out we were all on the same flight. So everything worked out perfectly."

I gape at my husband. "You planned all this? To surprise me?"

His love shines in his eyes. Making me tear up even more, he hands me a bandana to blow my nose. He knows me so well. I blow my nose loudly, not caring I sound like an elephant, and wipe my eyes.

My mother hugs me again, wrapping her cashmere-covered arms around me from the side. "We're so happy to be here with you."

I nod, trying not to blubber again. Instead, I blow my nose once more. Exhaling a deep breath, I smile at the three people I love most in the world.

"You are all in so much trouble for keeping this a secret from me." My stern expression falters immediately. I'm too happy to fake it. "I love you so much."

John tucks me into his side and kisses the top of my head. "I love you."

He doesn't need to embellish those words. Those three are enough.

I stare up into his dark eyes. My stoic man who had closed himself off to love after loss. Even though the first time we met he yelled at me and accused me of being a burglar, there was something about him. I didn't know it then, but he'd captured my heart pretty much from that first day. Not that I was ready for him or a relationship either. For a while, he was my only friend on the island. Now he's my best friend and my everything.

I get teary again thinking about how much I love him. I inhale and exhale a deep breath.

"Let's sit." I take the lead and settle into my seat at the table. Despite eating ice cream not that long ago, I'm hungry again. I could totally eat a big bowl of pasta.

John's arm drapes across the back of my chair. His familiar heat is comforting. The feel of his fingers playing with the ends of my hair grounds me. The tears seem to have faded for now.

I'm still stunned he surprised me with my parents. My own gift for him feels inadequate with this grand gesture. I know after the baby comes, he'll need guy time. He'll fret and worry over both of us, to his own detriment. Mom and my grandmother have both agreed to come out to help. John's aunt is close and a couple of his cousins have volunteered to help us. It takes a village, or in this case an island, to care for a baby.

That's why I bought him and Tom a trip to go fishing in Alaska next summer. The trick will be getting him to go. Tom's going to help out with that part. John'll listen to him. At least I hope so.

"What are you smiling about?" John asks.

I give him a sly grin. "Payback."

He frowns. "Are you mad?"

"Not at all." I squeeze his thigh. "I just hate being outdone when it comes to gifts."

Dad chuckles and lifts up his menu, blocking his face and muffling his voice. "Son, you're never going to win. These women get competitive. You better watch out."

Mom sips her wine and nods. "Although, there aren't any losers in this game."

Mom's right. Trying to outdo each other with gifts is like trying to out-love each other. Nobody's a loser. Everyone wins. Tom and John go fishing for a week. I get a freezer full of salmon and halibut. Win-win.

CHAPTER SIX

TOM

Hailey and I drive home together. She's nervous and fidgety in the truck, changing the radio station around after a minute or two into each song. Something's up.

When she reaches for the glove box, I swat her hand away and swerve into the opposite lane.

"What do you need in there?" I give her one of my flirtiest smiles. "Condoms a plenty at home."

"Ha ha. Are you hiding something?" She reaches for the handle and pulls, only it doesn't budge. Because it's locked. Her eyebrow lifts in question.

"I think it's jammed." I point out her window. "Was that a coyote?"

There is no coyote. I need a distraction.

She turns her head to look out the back window. When she faces me again, she squints to study me, but doesn't say anything.

I need to make it home and get her inside, before her death stare makes me blow everything. She can be scary when she puts on that face.

We bump along the dirt road to my house. When we reach the clearing, a few fat snowflakes hit the windshield.

"Ooh, it's snowing." She jumps out of the cab as soon as I put it in park. Tilting her head back, she slowly spins with her arms out. Snowflakes land and melt on her coat and scarf, disappearing almost instantly. I lean against the warm hood of the truck, watching her enjoy the first snow of the season.

A certainty swells up within me. I didn't really have a plan for proposing other than asking my grandmother for one of the family rings. I was stunned when she gave me the one Pops proposed with. Over time she upgraded and changed styles, but this is the one he picked out all those years ago when money was tight and their future endless.

The ring is more of a diamond covered band than one of those rings with a big hunk of rock. It's far from flashy or a big statement. Hailey isn't that type of woman anyway. She doesn't even really wear jewelry. Something simple with a story behind it will be perfect. I hope.

What do I know about rings and women? What if she wants a new ring and a big diamond? My heart begins to race. I could seriously blow this whole thing with the wrong ring.

"It's always magical." She sighs and opens her eyes. "What? Why are you staring at me like that?"

I inhale, trying to stuff my rising panic back down. Blowing out a slow, long exhale, I try to give her a confident grin. I feel anything, but confident right now. My palms are damp with sweat. Blood races in my ears. I try to take another breath, but my lungs won't cooperate. Black spots dot my vision. *What is going on?*

"Tom?" Hailey rushes over to me. "You've gone pale. Are you okay?"

Her voice is far away even though she is only a few inches from my face. Her hands cup my head. I attempt to focus on her eyes, but they keep going all soft and blurry.

"You look like you're going to pass out." She gives my head a little shake.

I can't answer her. Instead, I slump against the truck, sliding down until I'm sitting against the front passenger tire.

"Tom." Her voice is all muffled and tinny. "Put your head between your knees."

I do as she suggests, tilting forward to rest my head on my knees. Cold air and snow prickle against my exposed skin covered in a thin layer of sweat. I'm hot, but I shiver at the sensation. I practice breathing like it's a new thing for me.

"I'll be right back." Her boots stomp on the gravel in the direction of the house.

I've blown the moment big time. At least I didn't have the ring out before I almost passed out from nerves like a virgin on prom night. Not that I would know. I wasn't a virgin at prom.

When the world stops spinning, I lift my head. Snow is sticking to the tarps and the pine trees across the yard. So much for just flurries tonight. I stare up at the falling flakes. They float and drift down on me. It's quiet and peaceful out here. I don't know where Hailey's gone to, but I think I can stand. I push off the ground. Things are still fuzzy, but the dizziness has passed.

Small yippy barks break the silence. It's not a coyote's high-pitched howl. It sounds like–

A tiny fur-ball comes careening around the front tire, barking at me. I'm sure he thinks he's fierce. Immediately he begins tugging on the leg of my jeans. The thing growls and tugs at the denim like he's going to take me down. It's like a chipmunk going after a bear.

I bend to pick him up, careful to avoid his mouth. He won't let go of my jeans, until I put my finger in the jaws of death to get him to release. His incredibly sharp teeth graze my skin a few times like tiny knives.

"Hey, fierce little–" I turn the pup over. "–Little dude.

What's up with the attack mode? You going to take me down?"

He squirms in my hands, wiggling himself around to chomp on my fingers or sleeve.

"Ouch! Now, you've got to stop that." I suck on my finger where he's made contact. At least there's no blood. "Where did you come from? Whose evil puppy are you?"

He's not wearing a collar or tags. We're close enough to my sister's house that he could have escaped from there, but he would've had to walk through the woods to get here. I doubt he'd be able to make it.

I tuck him under my arm like a football, so he can't bite me. I open the door and unlock the glove box to get the ring. The puppy tugs on my coat sleeve. I drop him and the ring box on the floor of the truck. He immediately goes after the box. I'm not worried he can swallow it because it's bigger than his jaw, but he's got it in his teeth.

I try to grab the box. He thinks it's a game, scampering around in the truck. I lean in further to get it, resting on my stomach across the seat to grab him before he gets himself wedged someplace I can't reach him.

"What are you doing?" Hailey's finally returned. "I went to get you some water, but then I got distracted because I lost something in the house. Why are you lying face down in the truck?"

"Got you!" I make a final grab for the puppy and wrap my hand around his belly. I shove back off the seat and onto my feet. Holding the tiny dog above my head in triumph, I forget he's holding the ring box in his teeth.

"Oh! You found Nameless." She sounds relieved. "What's that in his mouth?"

Oh, crap.

"Nameless?" I tuck him under my arm again and attempt to extract the cream velvet box before she can figure out what it is. Nameless growls and squirms, but unless I want to get bit again, he's not giving up his new toy.

"I, um, he's …" She stumbles over her words. Smiling she shouts, "Merry Christmas! I got you a puppy."

I stare at her in disbelief. "You got me a poodle puppy?"

Her smile is warm, but a little nervous. "I did. He's a Labradoodle."

"You got me a dog." I take a few steps closer. Now we're inches apart. "You got us a dog."

She nods, her expression soft and full of love. "I did. You can name him, though. That's why I've been calling him Nameless."

I kiss her because I don't know what to say. I kiss her because I love her.

Nameless uses my distraction to bite my arm again.

I jerk back from Hailey, nearly dropping the puppy. I fumble, but save him from falling.

The box drops onto the ground.

I'm pretty sure my hand is bleeding.

She bends down to pick up the box. The velvet is soaked in puppy saliva. So gross. She holds it between two fingers. "What's this?"

My breath goes shallow again. Her own expression holds an edge of panic.

This is one of those fork in the road life moments.

I can toss the puppy at her, hoping she'll drop the box to save him, and then I can stuff the box in my pocket, and deny everything.

Or I can man up, and do what I know I want.

I take the box and hand her the puppy. He stops squirming and settles into the crook of her arm. I swear he even gives me a smug look like he belongs there. If anyone is going to snuggle Hailey, it's going to be me. He's going to sleep on a dog bed. Downstairs.

My pulse races again, but I take a deep breath, calming myself.

I bend down on one knee, and look up at her. Her eyes are shining with tears. I say a silent prayer that they're happy tears before speaking.

"Hailey King, will you do me the honor of being my wife?" I open the box on the second try and present the ring to her.

She's nodding, but hasn't said yes. Snow swirls around and sticks to her hair, even her lashes have a few flakes that slowly melt into the tears now running down her face.

The ground is cold so I stand up still holding the ring and its box. "Is that a yes?"

She nods again before kissing me. The memory of the cold snow and her warm mouth will stay with me always. I don't need a verbal yes. Her kiss tells me she's mine.

I slip the ring onto her finger and enclose her in my arms.

She's my world.

My love.

My future.

The puppy bites my arm. Again.

I think about building him a heated doghouse as I carry them both inside the house.

OLAF'S CHRISTMAS CAROL

"It's the hap, happiest time—"

No.

No more.

The carolers have surrounded my front door again and are caterwauling loud enough to send the town's feline population into spontaneous heat. If I had a fire hose, I'd spray the crowd. The town should give me a medal for restoring peace and quiet.

Enough!

A man can only handle a certain amount of cheer before his brain begins to seep out his ears and his soul shrivels into a dried husk in the hollow shell of his chest.

No, not a roasted chestnut shell either.

Don't get me started on all the traditional garbage women force their families to eat because it's Christmas.

Fruitcake is a monstrous abomination of the words fruit and cake.

Mincemeat? In a pie? Stop it right now. No, I don't care if nuts and raisins are involved. You lost me at the word mincemeat. Not to mention raisins.

I had a grandmother who liked to set a plum pudding on fire after she dramatically turned off all the lights in the dining room on Christmas Eve. In my innocence, I was fascinated by lighting food on fire. That had to mean it would be amazing. Wrong. I never expected her to make us eat the flaming corpse of my shattered Christmas illusions.

Another painful right of passage from childhood is discovering your parents made you sit on a strange man's lap and took pictures for posterity.

Is there something about the Santa suit that smells like urine or do they only hire incontinent men for the part? I'm asking for a friend. It's been years since I've been close enough to smell the foul stench of lies and stale beer.

To make the worst month of the year worse, I have to deal with the annual Sip 'n Stroll taking over downtown Langley and clogging up the Dog House with merry revelers, aka sippers, who nurse a single beer and take up limited space for way too long.

Worse, the college kids who are junior alcoholics, return to the island and think the law of the great state of Washington doesn't apply to them or their half-pickled livers.

Hiring a bouncer to sit at the door and check IDs costs me money.

"Bah humbug," I mutter to myself as I pull a pitcher for a group of grown ups wearing green-striped onesie pajamas and Santa hats. Outside and in public for crying out loud.

I hope the good baby Jesus can't see the festival of the ridiculous his birthday has become.

"Olaf, did you just say—" John Day asks from the other side of the counter where he's waiting for his own pitcher. Thank the sweet Baby Jesus he's wearing normal pants. His dark eyes hold a concern I've finally cracked my nut.

"Bah humbug." I spit out the words, carefully enunciating my disdain. "And don't go calling me Scrooge. Ebenezer was a rich man. You see any bags of gold sitting around this place?"

"I think you're confusing the Dickens character with Scrooge McDuck, Old Man." Tom Donnely shares his unwanted opinion from the other side of John. I didn't see him come in. He's sporting one of those neon orange Carhatt beanies over his shaggy blond hair. The man always needs to be the center of attention. Guess dressing like a traffic cone works.

"You call me old again and you're banned for the rest of the year."

"That's only ten days. Might be worth it." The light to John's dark, Donnely strokes his blond beard in thought. "You going to have your tough bouncer throw me out, too?"

I follow the jerk of his head to the man outside the door. Carter Kelso, wearing a set of reindeer antlers, is set up on a stool outside. He brought his own flashlight to check for fake IDs. I have little faith in either Kelso offspring, but he eagerly volunteered for a few pitchers of beer and an agreement I'll recommend his goat business.

The boy is starting a goat business. I have no words for that nonsense.

At least it's better than last year when his younger brother stole one of my stools to take advantage of the mistletoe vandals hang all over town every year. Okay, the vandals are really the Ladies of Perpetual Annoyance or some other committee formed to better the town and bug honest business owners like myself. Bunch of miscreants with access to a suspicious amount of ribbon, if you ask me.

"Shouldn't you be home with your women instead of harassing me in my own establishment?"

John shrugs. "Diane's with Hailey down the street buying yarn or something. They keep talking about learning how to crochet."

"Knit," Tom interjects and gives his friend a smug smirk. "Something about tiny booties for the next baby."

"Or your baby." John teases back.

Tom stills his face and flattens his lips. "I expect I'll know that information before you."

"Don't tell me if you're working on making that happen. Try to keep it to yourself," I say.

Tom gives me a small salute. "Speaking of our better halves, they may be awhile. I saw them go into the tasting room before we came in here. "

"With the baby?" I ask.

John smiles. "Alene doesn't mind. She loves the lights. And being snuggled against Diane is her favorite place to be."

"Can't blame her." Tom dodges John's attempt to slap his shoulder. "I'm talking about the warm comfort of a mother's touch. Jeez."

No way in hell his original comment is innocent.

Ignoring Tom, John continues talking with a soft look in his eyes like he wants to walk to the end of the block and check on his women. "My aunt will pick her up and bring her home for the night."

Tom open palm successfully makes contact with his friend's shoulder. "Getting some action at the Saratoga tonight?"

"Aren't you banned from there?" I ask, already knowing the answer. During a holiday party for Donnely Boats last week, Tom and Hailey got caught having relations in one of the inn's rooms. What a man and woman do behind closed doors is nobody's business. Unless the door and the room don't belong to them. Tom tried to blame it on being newlyweds, but management didn't buy it.

The couple from Indiana who had reserved the room wrote a helluva review on Trip Advisor. Heard Tom framed a copy.

"O!" a familiar voice shouts from the double-saloon doors. Erik Kelso shoves his way through the crowd.

"The night gets better," I mumble and start a pint for him.

I blink twice when he sets his hoof on the counter.

"What the hell is wrong with you?" I eye the rest of his get up. I expect Tom Donnely to be a ham, but after all that bullshit earlier this year with Erik's naked tuckus, you'd think he'd keep a low profile.

Not dress himself up as the Christmas ass.

Erik glances over his shoulder and then down at his brown furry chest. "Nothing?"

With a shake of my head, I point out the obvious. "You're a grown man. Halloween was two months ago."

John and Tom chuckle into their pint glasses.

"Where's the Christmas spirit, O? No respect for Rudolf?"

The red dot on his nose makes more sense now.

"The sign says no shirt, no service. Don't make me amend that to ban hooves in here. Again."

John coughs as he sputters on his beer. "Again?"

"Someone put a cow in the backroom in the early twentieth century when this was a private club. You boys should learn your island history better."

"When are you going to stop calling us boys?" Tom asks, looking put out.

"Never. You'll always be younger than me and lacking good sense. You paying for those beers? Or you want a tab?"

"Start a tab," Erik says. "On me."

My eyes bugs out a little at his offer. I've never known a Kelso to be generous when it comes to money. If they could, they'd help out a friend without hesitation, but mostly by doing the physical labor. Most of the time growing up they didn't have twenty dollars in their wallets. Coffee business must be good.

"Oh for crying out loud," I say when I see Erik's wearing a fluffy deer tail on the back of his brown velvet costume. He catches me staring and shakes his backside for my benefit.

"The only onesie a grown man should wear is a Union Suit."

"With the trap door? Sexy, O!" Erik joins John and Tom at a table on the far side of the pool table.

I think about padding his bar tab for being a pain in my ass.

More people pile through the front door and fill the space around the stools. I'm grateful for hiring some kid as a bar back to help out during the holidays.

He's stranger than the Kelsos and named Falcon. Yes, that's really his name. I had to check his ID when I hired him.

And if he asks one more time if he can set up his drums in the corner for a drumming circle, I'm going to fire him.

Speaking of, where is that weirdo? We're running low on glasses. I scan the crowded room and spot his dreadlocked head next to Ashley Kingston's red curls.

For being smart enough to run a successful business, that girl has terrible taste in men.

I know her family and she's the perfect example of strict parenting inciting rebellion. For both her and her brother Jonah. He's got more holes in his head than God intended and she's got herself a bad reputation.

I'm about to throw something at Falcon's head to get his attention when Carter strides over and breaks up their conversation by stepping between the couple and turning his back on Falcon.

I can't hear Ashley's words, but from her tight expression I'm guessing she's not pleased.

This place has more drama than a soap opera. And I have a front row seat.

Lucky me.

Hold on. If Carter is pissing off Ashley, who's watching my door?

A monkey would do a better job at being a bouncer.

Falcon sets a tray of steaming hot glasses on the back bar with too much force, rattling the glass.

Perfect timing.

I put my hand on his shoulder like I'm offering him a promotion. "Get those organized and then go take over the door."

"Really?" His eyes light up.

I don't understand how this kid ticks. "Sure. Put on a jacket. It's cold out there."

"I never get cold." He bounces on his tip-toes and speeds off outside in his T-shirt and ripped jeans.

If he catches pneumonia, I'm going to put an ad out for a real trained monkey.

Dan keeps telling me I need to get more help in here and slow down.

At least he doesn't call me old to my face.

A breeze of fresh, but cold air blows through the open door. I see Falcon holding it open like a doorman. The thought he doesn't know what a bouncer does concerns me until I see a few familiar faces.

Maggie Marion and her group of friends stand near the door. I'm not too proud to admit I loved her mother from afar for years before her death. She won me over with her baked goods and class despite being older than me by more than a decade. I think a lot of men around here had crushes on her. Her daughter sold the bakery, but carries the same sparkle Ann did. Maggie's fella stands beside her along with another couple. A man holding a toddler is stuck between the swinging doors and the outside door.

I'm about to tell them this isn't a day care, when Diane walks in behind him carrying Alene.

The group of seven squeezes into an opening at the corner of the bar near the window. The little girl happily takes up residence on the bench in the window, patting the glass and smiling at the people outside.

Diane waves me over using Alene's chubby arm instead of her own hand.

"Kind of a late night for our little angel." My voice softens at the sight of Alene sitting on her mom's hip. Normally, kids aren't allowed in here in the evenings, but I guess I'll make an exception. At least she's not trying to charm her way past Falcon. Yet.

"She's started fussing." Diane gives me a weak smile while bouncing Alene."We're waiting on Helen to meet us here."

"Let me hold her." I extend my arms for Alene. She claps her mittened hands together and reaches for me.

"She's kind of going through a stranger-danger phase right now." Diane apologizes, but hands the pink bundle over the bar to me.

Alene attempts to tug my beard, but her fingers are trapped. Her forehead scrunches and her face darkens as she works herself up to a wail. I remove her mittens and set the world right.

Delighted, she tugs at my white whiskers.

"She probably thinks your the real Santa," Diane says softly. "You'd make the perfect one."

I stare into Alene's happy face.

Dammit if that little girl doesn't have us all wrapped around her fingers. Anything bad ever happens to her and it'd break all our hearts.

Yes, I have a heart. No, it's not three-sizes too small.

No way am I'm ever dressing up as Old Saint Nick.

"It's a Christmas miracle." Diane points to a quiet Alene, happily playing with my beard.

"Hello, Papa Silver Fox." The blond man with the toddler greets me with a friendly smile.

I lift an eyebrow at him.

"Quinn," Diane chides him. "Be nice to Olaf."

"I'm paying him a compliment! Silver foxes are all the rage. Hi, I'm Quinn." He extends his hand over the bar. I shift Alene and shake it. "The little one is Lizzy and the handsome man pretending to be a puppy with her is my husband, Ryan."

He says all of this as if I'll remember. "Nice to meet you."

The man and child in the window both give me friendly woofs.

Diane introduces me to the rest of her friends. I pretend I'm interested while smiling down at Alene.

"You should bring them to Sal's, Maggie." Diane gives her former landlord a knowing smile. The kind of looks women exchange that send a nervous tremor down the spines of men.

"We went there for lunch. Unfortunately the resident silver fox is on vacation this week," Maggie answers.

"Selah was heartbroken," Maggie's guy Gil says.

A shorter woman with dark hair pokes her head around his tall frame. "You know what helps with heartbreak? Beer. What do you have that's extra hoppy. Cause it's the hop, hoppiest time of the year."

After singing the last sentence, she grins at me as if she somehow knows how much I hate that song. I sense a kindred sister of sarcasm.

Reluctantly returning Alene to her mother, I recommend an IPA and fill the rest of their order. The tall blond one named Kai, who looks like an old Viking, slides a fancy black credit card on the bar, subtly letting me know he's paying for whatever they drink. I appreciate a man who doesn't waffle when it comes to taking care of the check.

John wraps his thick arms around both Diane and Alene before kissing their cheeks. "Helen's outside in the car."

Diane's smiles and then frowns. "You think she'll be okay? It's her first overnight without us."

He kisses his wife softly on the lips and tells her, "Without us? Or us without her? We can cancel. Or go home early."

She frowns again. "And give up the chance at a full night's sleep? Are you crazy?"

He grumbles about priorities before she kisses his cheek. "I'll walk her out and be right back."

John watches them go with love in his eyes and all over his face like he got smashed with a love pie right in the kisser.

I remember that feeling. Best one in the world.

Before the divorce. Before the kids grew up and moved away.

When I was a young man in the Navy, I fell in love with a teacher from Oak Harbor. She wasn't charmed by my stories from around the world or my good looks. To a young buck with an ego, I accepted her challenge, making it my mission to make her fall in love with me. I sent her pearls from Japan and fancy perfume from France. Before I got transferred from Everett, I made her a promise. If she married me, as soon as I finished in the Navy, we'd move back to the island and never leave again.

I kept my end of the promise.

She now lives on a golf course in Phoenix with a retired insole salesman. Our youngest son, Neil, calls him Dad, too. Neil's always been a little prick. Steve at least remembers to call me on my birthday.

I'm the one who never left. Born here, I'm going to die here. Not for a long time, God willing.

Here's the part of the story where the ghosts of Christmas past, present, and future show up, isn't it?

"Bah humbug," I grumble under my breath.

"Did you just say—" Diane asks as she returns childless.

"He's been muttering it all night." John slings an arm over her shoulder. "Shall we go take advantage of our hotel room?"

She grins and nods. "I made sure to avoid the Room of Unmentionable Things."

"I heard that! I highlighted that quote in the review!" Holding up his arm in triumph, Tom shouts from his table. How he heard her from across the room, I can't figure out. I can barely hear myself complain in my own head. Hailey nudges his shoulder and lowers his arm.

I watch the John and his wife say goodbye to their friends and dammit if my heart doesn't feel fuzzy and warm.

One thing people either get or don't get about this island is we're all family.

We have a bunch of crazy aunts in those ribbon-wielding gossipers, Sandy, Connie, and Sally. They meddle and gossip because they care.

The brotherhood of friends with John and Tom at the heart is as strong as blood. No longer boys, they've become honorable men.

For the most part. Maggie's circle is the only family she has now that her parents have passed. Knowing she is loved and cared for would make Ann happy again.

As the younger generation pairs off and starts their own broods, our family grows and expands to include the newcomers like Dan, his lady Roslyn, sweet Diane, and even the younger Kelso's girl, Cari. Despite our differences, Dan's become a true friend to me, pushing back the loneliness solitary life can bring.

Our family happily welcomes home the wayward sons and daughters like Hailey King. Hell, I'd greet my own boys with open arms and a smile if they came to visit.

Some may say we're stuck in the past here. Those people are the ones who don't understand the magic of life in a small town.

I feel a lump lodge in my throat and a burning behind my eyes.

Dammit.

"Bah humbug," I grumble to dispel the feelings filling up my crotchety old heart.

"Merry Christmas to you, too!" Tom shouts from the corner.

The Kelsos follow his lead and raise their voices. "Merry Christmas to us all."

Next thing I know, the whole crowd is echoing their words with glee.

"Merry Christmas, one and all," I softly say, catching Maggie's eye.

Louder, I shout. "Merry Christmas to all. Now go home. It's last call."

WINGMEN BABYPALOOZA

CHAPTER ONE

TOM

My life has turned out to be a live action version of *Lady and the Tramp*.

I should know. I've watched the cartoon version a million times recently with my pint-size Donnely family members. Seems a pregnant wife is the perfect excuse for my sisters to use me to babysit their spawn. For practice. Or so they say as they laugh their way out my front door every weekend.

The only practice I like when it comes to babies is the making kind. And as the saying goes, the only way to be the best is with lots and lots of practice.

Hey-o.

I made that joke in front of Hailey and three of our nephews.

Then had to explain I meant it like Little League practice. You know, choke up on the bat, keep your eye on the balls, don't forget to run the bases if you make a hit, and slide into home whenever you can because it feels awesome.

I think they bought it.

Anyway, getting back to *Lady and the Tramp*.

In case there's any doubt, I'm the tramp in this scenario.

Honestly, I've been called a lot worse than tramp by more than one woman.

I was the happy-go-lucky guy without a care in the world, minding my own life, and keeping my business to myself. Until one day, the lady, that's Hailey, batted her pretty eyes at me as she sashayed into my life. Or more accurately, kissed me in the hallway to the bathrooms at the Dog House. Yep. She definitely made the first move. Can't blame her—I'm irresistible. She stuck her tongue down my throat and begged me to sleep with her. When she asked me to come home with her, I didn't say no. That's the R rated version.

Next thing I know, I'm sharing my spaghetti, giving up my last meatball, and cleaning up my tramp ways. She may have made the first move, but the proposal was all me. Except for when her Christmas gift almost ate my grandmother's ring before I could pop the question. Nameless is lucky we kept him.

And here we are today.

Like the song says, first comes love, then comes marriage, then comes me shopping for a baby carriage.

"Why do they call them strollers now and not carriages?" I test the brake locks on an oversized baby transporter by trying to shove the contraption into a wall. Impressively, it doesn't budge.

Hailey casts a dirty look in my direction from where she's scanning a car seat cozy. It's not the actual car seat, but some fuzzy thing that looks like a sheepskin. For babies. That's going to be covered in bodily fluids in a nanosecond.

When I glance at the price, my eyeballs bug out. I could get a decent fishing rod for less.

While I'm wondering if you can hose off fur, Hailey sucks in a sharp breath. Panicked, I flip the stroller out of the way to get to her side.

"Are you okay?" Resting my hand on her belly, my heart races as I worry something's wrong with her. Or the baby.

Our baby.

Baby D is growing like a champ from the looks of Hailey's rounded belly. Seven months into this, and I'm amazed at the elasticity of her skin.

My wife's waddling around like a gorgeous, fat duck these days. I never thought a waddle could turn me on, but damn if seeing Hailey all curved out doesn't make me the horniest bastard ever. And we all know that's saying something.

Every time yet another person asks if she's having twins, she groans. I grin because the more she shows, the more beautiful she is.

"I'm fine. Heartburn or the baby is standing on some vital organ again." She rubs the top of her belly. Right below her full breasts. Of course my eyes lock on the area like magnets to steel.

For the first time ever, Hailey has cleavage. Spectacular is the word I like to use to describe her breasts. I love her body because it's her, but I'd be lying if I'm not enjoying every change and full curve.

I'm pretty sure babies in the womb can't stand, but if anyone could, it would be our baby. Baby Donnely would totally take home the gold for the in-utero Olympics. Not that it's a competition or anything. There's going to be some friendly comparison, especially when two of my buddies are expectant dads, too. Dan and John are going to be dads in December. Well, in John's case, Diane's having Baby Day numero dos.

Blame Valentine's Day or the Seahawks winning the Super Bowl. Or the late February ice storm that knocked out power for three days.

Olaf's been joking he's gonna need to add a changing table to the Dog House men's room with three of his regulars about to be dads.

"Are you sure?" Scanning her eyes, I rest my hand over

Hailey's. "You should probably sit down. Or drink some water. Put your feet up."

I don't mention her swollen ankles. Apparently, women pay attention to the circumference of their ankles and worry about something called "cankles."

If a guy's socks stay up and he can tie his boots, that's about as much thought as he ever gives to his ankles.

I shift my hand to her lower back and remove the scanner from her hand. "Why don't we call it a day? How much stuff does a baby need? Car seat, stroller, crib, changing table … some diapers and clothes. I bet most of that we can get from my sisters. Have you seen their houses? We could pilfer from them and they'd never even know anything was missing."

Not saying my sisters are hoarders, but they've got a lot of kid and baby shit. If I start now, I could take something every time we visit and fill the nursery with no one being the wiser.

"I don't want hand-me-downs for our first child. Leave that for the second." She meets my eyes and I see mischief in her green eyes. "Or third."

My gut clenches at the thought of sharing her with so many kids. "We'll see."

She allows me to guide her over to the furniture section. Flopping into an armchair, she pushes back and forth with her feet a few times before resting her legs on the matching ottoman.

"I like this one." She pats the navy plaid upholstered arms. "Reminds me of one of your shirts."

I glance down to make sure I don't match the chair. Nope. My shirt's brown and white plaid today. The price tag grabs my attention.

Blinking, I try to figure out why a baby chair costs so much. I could get a new leather recliner with the beer cooler built into the arm for the same price. You can't hose off a chair and there's no way this thing isn't going to be covered in baby mess.

"I'm sure there's a wooden rocker around the farm someplace. Probably the one Gramma used for all her kids. Keep it traditional." I frown at the thought of spending over a grand on a nursery chair.

"You have excellent taste." A petite blond saleswoman strolls up to us. "This is one of our most popular pieces of furniture. The Maserati of nursery chairs. Do you have any questions?"

I think she's overstating the luxury and aerodynamics a little. A family sedan like a Toyota Camry would be a better comparison. Comfortable, but not flashy. Oh, I have questions.

She's focused on Hailey, but I'm the one to respond. "Is it stain resistant and can you hose it off?"

The two women stare at each other for a few beats before Hailey laughs, shaking her head. "He's kidding."

"No, I'm not. These are important questions. I saw Alene projectile vomit last year clear across the room." I sit down in the twin to the chair Hailey's occupying. To my surprise, it reclines as well as rocks and swivels. I tilt back and settle my hands underneath my head. "Whoa. This is really comfortable."

Hailey smirks at me. "See?"

"Still think it's overpriced." I flinch and flick my attention at the saleslady. "Sorry."

"Think of it as an investment piece. Something you'll be able to use for many years."

"Not if it's covered in shi—stuff." We all know what I mean.

"Is there a washable slipcover option?" Hailey asks.

Great. A thousand plus dollar chair requires its own accessories.

This baby game is a racket.

An expensive one.

"Are you all done scanning the products for your wish

list?" The sales lady smiles at us and I see dollar signs flashing behind her thick eyelashes. Someone probably works on commission. "Or can I show you some more things? Do you have a crib selected yet? Bassinet? Binkies? Bouncing chair? Boppy? Bottle warmer? Breast pump?"

She's only listing products starting with *B* and has mentioned six things. I'm not sure what four of them are. I can figure out the breast pump. I saw them on the shelf and they remind me of a penis pump. Not that I've ever used one, or needed one, but the suction idea seems the same.

Something's wrong with me if I'm sitting here surrounded by pastels, baby ducks, and lambs galore and my mind has gone to erectile enhancement devices.

I need to stop her before she can rattle off more stuff we don't need and I lose my verbal filter all together.

"No." My voice is more stern than intended as I sit up straight. "We're all set."

Hailey sighs. "I think we have everything."

"I'll enter your scanner and give you the registry link to share. Now all you need to do is rest and wait for the presents to start rolling in." Saleslady smiles at Hailey and then gives me a wary, or maybe weary, look. "I'm sure you're anxious to get home for the Seahawks game."

My jaw's still hanging open as she walks to the registers at the front of the store. "Wait, did she just caveman me? Like I'm more concerned about the football game than the comfort of my wife and unborn child?"

Hailey adjusts in her chair while avoiding my eyes. "She's being considerate."

I lower my brow and frown. "You know your happiness means more to me than anything, right? If you want the chair, we'll get one. Hell, we'll get two. One for each of us. Or one for upstairs and one for down. But if we buy the chair, I want the giant grizzly bear in the corner."

Following to where I'm pointing at an oversized stuffed

animal, Hailey laughs, then appears on the verge of tears as her eyes water.

This is a new emotion for her. Lately, she's a combo meal of reactions. Happy, sad. Angry, laughing. Hungry and … everything.

"What are we going to do with a giant bear?" She wipes her eyes.

I lift my foot and place it on the same ottoman as hers. Tapping her shoe with my boot, I smile. "Oh, it's not for us. Alene will love it."

"Meaning you'll buy it to annoy your best friend?" She grins.

"It's a thoughtful gesture. We can bring it to their baby shower."

"Diane's not having one for the second baby." Hailey yawns.

"Why do they get to avoid the circus?" Well, that's not fair. I'm going to need to ask John how he gets out of stuff. I need him to Mr. Miyagi me on all the first-time dad tricks. He can be my personal Coach Taylor. Or Yoda. And I'll be the better looking and more charming protégé. The Good to his Ugly. I could go on, but Hailey interrupts me.

"Because they have most of this stuff already. The whole point of a shower is to set up a nursery." Yawning again, she rubs her belly.

"They don't have the bear." I stand and lean down to give Hailey a soft kiss. Her lips are still salty from the popcorn she ate earlier. "I'll be right back."

At the register, I smile at the saleslady, being my usual friendly and charming self. "Excuse me."

She blinks up at me and smiles. "Yes?"

I ignore the slight purr to her voice. Shopping for baby stuff with my wife is about as taken as a man can get. "I want to buy the plaid chair and a footstool."

"Want me to add it to the registry?" Dollar signs and a bigger commission dance in her eyes.

"No, we'll take it home today."

"I'll have to confirm with our warehouse. I'm not sure if we have one in stock." She types away on her keyboard.

I peer through the store to where Hailey naps in the big chair.

"Looks like we do have one in black and white buffalo check. Or red and black." Looking at me, she waits for me to choose one.

"Not the blue plaid?" I hesitate to go off the plan.

"No." Waiting, her fingers hover over the keys.

I have no idea what buffalo check is, but I don't want to have to come back here. "Black and white."

She nods and keeps typing.

"And I need the giant bear. We'll take that today, too." I pull out my wallet to pay. Cringing at the total, I sign away my name and kiss my new fishing rod good-bye.

Damn bear is expensive, but so worth it.

"Can you keep an eye on my wife while I load up the chair?" I tuck the receipt in my wallet before shoving it into my back pocket. "She's napping."

"Absolutely." She gives me a funny look before telling me how to collect the chair around back.

"Thanks." I salute her with two fingers. No idea why, but it feels right in the moment.

Once I have the chair strapped down and the plastic secured for the ride back to the island, I park near the entrance to get Hailey.

Curled up like a fat cat in the chair, she's softly snoring. I'm married to a sloth. I swear she sleeps more these days than she's awake.

I pick up the stuffed bear, which is almost as tall as I am, and march him toward her. Using the paw, I pet Hailey's head. Softly, I tell her, "Wake up, Sleeping Beauty."

Because I'm adorable, I expect my sweet, beautiful wife to wake up and smile, maybe even laugh at my charming antics.

Joke's on me when she opens her eyes, screams, and kicks the bear in the groin. Which is right over my own family jewels.

Thankfully, the stuffing provides enough padding I only grunt from the dulled impact. Until I lose my balance and fall on my ass, smothered by the bear landing on top of me.

Given my love of chainsaws and welding, I never thought I'd die by teddy bear. It's almost funny. My obituary will be hysterical. I can practically hear Pops laughing down at me from heaven.

Unfortunately, a woman screaming in a baby emporium draws the attention of every other customer in the store. The clatter of heels and lady sneakers running echoes like a herd of Shetland ponies racing toward us.

"Are you okay?" a female voice screeches from nearby.

Footsteps stop all around me. Instinct or self-preservation tells me to remain on the floor. I know Hailey's fine, but I'm certain this gaggle of ladies won't get my humor.

"I'm fine." Hailey's breathless. "I think I fell asleep and didn't know where I was when I woke up."

"Someone get her some water," an authoritative voice commands. I'm guessing she's a teacher or a judge. A single pair of feet scampers away from the group.

"Tom, quit hiding underneath the stuffed animal. You're like the witch crushed under the house. We can see your legs and shoes." A foot nudges my boot.

"I'm good right here." My voice is muffled, but I'm not giving up the safety of my bear cave.

Bright light from the fluorescents on the ceiling blind me as someone rolls the grizzly off of me. Blinking, I try to adjust to the burst of light, so I can make out Hailey standing over me. From this angle, I mostly see her big belly underneath her sweater.

"I didn't mean to scare you," I say softly. "Am I forgiven?"

"You're forgiven." She leans forward so I can see her face. Her lips twitch as she tries to keep her face serious.

"You can't go around scaring pregnant women, young man. Unless you're trying to induce early labor. Or make your wife pee herself. This must be your first baby," a woman scoffs at me from somewhere near my head.

I sneak a peek in her direction and am greeted with something I can never unsee.

Upside down camel toe in a pair of rainbow cat leggings.

To avoid a second gander, I execute a sideways crab-walk while getting on my feet. Yeah, I'm basically breakdancing in a baby store.

Hailey's biting the side of her thumb to keep her laughter contained. For her benefit, I do a pop and lock before I grab the bear and tuck him under my arm. "Breathe one word of this to anyone we know and I won't help you put on your shoes."

Her gasp is exaggerated and it sounds like she chokes on her laughter. "You're a heartless man, Tom Donnely."

"I have a reputation to protect." I sling my free arm over her shoulder and steer her toward the entrance. "If you swear your silence, I'll buy you an ice cream at Ivar's before we get on the ferry."

"And a clam chowder." Sliding her hand to my lower back, she slips a finger through one of the belt loops of my jeans. "No, cancel the chowder. Fried clams. So I can dip them in the ice cream."

I don't bother hiding my shudder or the loud gagging sound. "I might have to go up on deck while you defile two perfectly good foods that should never be joined in unholy matrimony."

"Totally fine with me. More deliciousness all to myself." She grins at me.

When we pull into the ferry waiting lot, I run through the

parked cars to place her order. Even though it's misting with a cold wind blowing off of the water, I order a swirl cone for myself. Because I deserve a reward for shopping.

Returning to the truck, the bear crammed into the back of the king cab makes me grin.

Makes the whole debacle worth it.

CHAPTER TWO

"You're not leaving that thing here." John jabs the grizzly in the belly. As soon as he answered the door, his mouth turned down into a frown. Now he's blocking me from entering his house. Not very hospitable at all.

From the other side of the doorway, I pop my head over the bear's shoulder. "Not sounding very grateful about our baby gift."

"We don't need a gift. You can come in, but the stuffed animal stays in the truck. Alene has enough toys." He's extra cranky sounding today. With his arms crossed and his feet spread, he fills the entire door, leaving me no room to shove the bear past him.

"Sounds like someone needs a hug." I outstretch the bear's arms and try to engulf John's torso. I manage to get one arm around him before he wiggles free. At least I've made it through the door. Baby steps.

"I'm serious." His voice lowers. "Alene sees this and you're in big trouble."

The happy chirps of his toddler daughter ring out above us, followed by the sound of little feet running down the hall.

Diane's footsteps chase Alene's before a loud rattling of the baby gate draws our attention to the stairs.

John shoves the bear at me and snarls, "Get out."

"Who's here?" Diane's voice carries downstairs.

"No one." John glares at me.

"Then why are you yelling?" There's an ominous click of metal on metal before Diane continues, "Hold Mommy's hand and the railing."

"Now." John shoves the bear.

"I can't. Screen's locked." I give him a shit-eating grin and bat my pretty blue eyes at him in innocence.

Instead of forcing me out, John's created a bear sandwich as he presses us both against the frame.

"Dadda, Dadda, Dadda," Alene repeats as she stomps down each step.

Resigned, John gives up. "Revenge will be mine."

I chuckle. "You'd make an excellent villain. The dark beard and sinister expression. I almost believe you're mad at me."

"What's that?" Diane asks from the base of the stairs.

"A bad idea," John mumbles.

"Hi." I lower my voice into a bear sounding growl. "I'm your new best friend."

The most ear-piercing scream I've ever heard echoes throughout the house. Miles away, I'm sure dogs begin howling at the high-pitched sound. Babe, the Days' yellow lab, rushes past me, somehow opens the door with his nose, and darts to freedom.

"Should I go wrangle Babe?" Already backing away, I jerk my thumb over my shoulder, nearly dropping the giant stuffed animal. I bobble the bear for a minute, causing it to lurch forward through the doorway again.

More screaming ensues.

"Right. I'll go get the dog." Feeling like a complete asshole for scaring a toddler, I readjust my hold on the bear and shove it in front of me. There's always Donnely family Christmas. I can gift the giant to one of the nephews. Pissing off my sisters is a holiday tradition.

"Tom," Diane calls out from behind me, "wait."

My steps pause on the path, and she catches up.

"Wow, it's even bigger up close." She touches the bear's fur.

I bite my tongue because even I'm over the "that's what she said" response.

"Walked into that one, didn't I?" She laughs and I release the hold on my own amusement. "It's really sweet you bought Alene a bear."

"Went over well." Mentally, I'm kicking myself while I shift the bear and try to tuck it under one arm. After struggling to get a grip on the middle, I sigh and set it on the ground, resigned. "I'm sorry if I traumatized her. It's over the top, and honestly, I got it because it reminded me of John."

Diane steps closer and studies the bear. "If it had a beard, I could totally see the resemblance. Maybe seeing the two of them side by side blew her seventeen-month-old mind. She's been having some major stranger danger lately."

"Better keep her away from the furry conventions," I say as a joke.

Diane lifts her dark eyebrow at me. Her coloring is similar to Hailey's but she's more petite and curvy where Hailey is tall and all legs. Legs and a giant belly.

"Not that I'd know when or where those take place, but come on, you know Seattle probably has one." *What am I talking about?* My mouth is speaking, but my brain is somewhere else.

Screaming Alene has turned me into a rambling teenage boy. My whole life I've never been awkward around women. Growing up with three sisters means girls were never mysteries to me. I knew too much too young.

So I *assumed* tiny size girls like Alene would be easy.

Yeah, the ass in that sentence is me.

"Okay then," Diane drawls out the words. "You want to try again?"

I'm totally confused. "Which part?"

"Giving Alene the bear."

"You don't want me to make it disappear?"

"He's cute." She picks up a big paw and waves it at me.

"John doesn't want it." The fun of annoying him has faded. Now I'm more than a little afraid of his revenge.

"He's being grumpy. Maybe focusing on hating the bear will distract him from worrying over me." Her hand rests on the lowest swell of her pregnant belly.

Now I'm worried, too. My focus stays on her hand when I ask, "Is something wrong?"

"My doctor's worried about my blood pressure. I feel fine, but once John heard I'm at the high range of normal, he's been fretting like a penguin sitting on a nest."

The image of John as a giant bird causes me to snort. "Maybe I should've bought a stuffed chicken."

"Don't poke him. He's not sleeping well. Neither of us are. Alene's the only one sleeping through the night. I swear, I get up to pee and he's up, making sure I'm fine." She rolls her eyes, exasperated.

I've seen the same expression on Hailey's face a lot recently.

"Are you two out here plotting something?" John's deep voice from the doorway makes me jump, like I'm guilty.

"Yes, your Christmas present," Diane replies with a straight face.

He grumbles about not needing anything. "Why are you standing out front with the bear?"

"I'm convincing Tom we want to keep it." Grinning, she waves the paw again.

"Why?" His voice says he thinks this is a terrible idea. Worst idea ever.

"Because he's adorable." Diane pets his arm with the paw.

"The bear or the man?" John eyes me with an arched eyebrow.

I jerk my chin back. "Both, of course."

"Alene's terrified of it," he grumbles.

"I think we can win her over," Diane says, voice full of confidence.

"How?" He crosses his arms.

"Dadda!" Alene shouts from inside.

"Where is she?" Diane asks. "She better not be in the dog crate again."

"That only happened a few times." John uncrosses his arms and rubs his beard. "She's in her high chair, eating some sort of puffed cereal."

I know of more than a few times when Alene could barely crawl she ended up in Babe's crate or curled up on his dog bed. Dog should be sainted. If that's possible.

"I say we bring it inside, set it on the floor, and let her explore at her own pace."

"And if she has nightmares or ends up with a fear of bears, Tom's responsible, right?"

"I'll start a therapy fund." I smirk at him.

Resigned, he sighs. "Okay, the thing can come inside, but if she starts screaming again, it's gone."

"You sound like Olaf," I say, poking the virtual bear while picking up the stuffed one.

"Put it on the floor by the couch." Diane ignores John's scowl as she leads the way back inside the house.

"Look, Alene, Tom's brought you a present."

Alene holds a fistful of pale orange puffs in her hand, and from the bulge in her cheeks, she's been practicing her squirrel impersonation.

"Fom," she mumbles with her mouth full.

"Hi, beautiful." I wave as I march the bear past her and into the living room.

After setting it down on the floor, I glance over at Alene. Wide-eyed, she absently chews on her mouthful of cereal.

I can't tell if she's enthralled or terrified, but she's not screaming or crying.

"I'm calling it a win," I declare.

"Hold off on that. Sometimes it takes her a while to warm up the engines again," John explains.

Still clenching her fistful of puffs, she warily eyes the newest arrival into her kingdom. Her forehead scrunches and her fist waves in the air as if she's silently commanding the bear to leave.

The three adults stand quietly in the living room, watching Alene like a group of explosive experts studying a bomb.

Cramming the crushed cereal into her mouth with force, she studies the bear with her dark eyes, and then us.

"Dadda?" she asks, sending crumbs flying.

"You want down?" John slowly approaches the high chair.

She lifts her arms in silent confirmation.

I hold my breath when he sets her on her feet.

"Dadda!" Alene waddles herself closer to the bear and gives it a big hug. Her chubby arms can barely close around its arm, but she squeezes as tight as she can.

"Wait, does she think the bear is daddy?" I choke out the question before laughing.

Happy as can be, Alene climbs into the bear's lap and pets it's furry face.

Diane joins me in laughter. "I'm sure she can tell the difference between a stuffed animal and her father. Ninety percent certain."

John stands next to her, arms crossed, and lips pressed together. Grumbling, "It doesn't even look like me."

"Oh, but it does. It totally does," I say, pleased with myself that my gift is a hit. "We can put one of your plaid shirts on him. Would probably fit."

"It's not staying," John grumbles.

"Honey, she loves it." Mirroring her daughter's actions, Diane scratches his beard.

"We don't have room. She has a million toys and the baby's going to have more stuff. We're becoming the old woman who lived in a shoe."

Diane glances around the room's jumble of toys and furniture. "I don't think we've reached that level yet, but we could use more space."

"You thinking of moving?" The thought never occurred to me. John's always lived on Sunlight Beach in his uncle's cabin. It's not huge, but it's not a tiny shack either. And it's right on the sand. One of the few non-mansions left.

"Never, but I want to expand the upstairs," Diane says.

"And I don't want to be one of those people who puts a huge house on a small lot," John argues.

By those people, he means summer people. Seattle people who "weekend" on the island in huge homes that sit empty for the majority of the year.

"How big are you talking?" I study the open concept kitchen, dining area and living room with a view over the bay.

"Not a mansion. Another bathroom. Maybe add a bedroom."

"Doesn't sound unreasonable," I agree with Diane.

"We have a baby coming." John states the obvious like we've forgotten.

"You wouldn't live here while there's construction. Move out. Hell, you could live in Ellie's place until summer while she's in Arizona." I offer a solution he hasn't asked for, but that's what we do. We fix things, including problems, whether we're asked to or not.

"See, John? There are options. Maybe not this winter, but next year could work? I'm not up for being sleepless and homeless." Diane mouths "no" while shaking her head.

"We'll see," John says, and I know he'll agree if she really wants this. He lives for her happiness. The old softy.

CHAPTER 3

On my way home from John's, I swing by Sal's Pizza in Freeland to pick up an order Hailey called in for dinner. When I walk in to the restaurant, I interrupt Roslyn and Dan in the middle of an intimate conversation.

"I'm fine. Doctor is worried about my 'advanced maternal age' because I'm over thirty-five. Jeez, like I don't know I'm facing down forty, you have to label me old on all my paperwork?" Roslyn's a force on a normal day when she's not pumped full of hormones. Her eyes flash with annoyance.

I swear the hairs on my arms prickle with the tension in the room.

"Love, your sugar levels are elevated," Dan says. He's her husband, the island pizza guru, possibly Batman, and a silver fox according to every woman I know, including my mother and Gramma Ellie.

Ros sticks her tongue out at him. "Still within the normal range."

Dan stares at her with his dark eyes and she glares right back, lost in a silent contest of their own. Giving up, he spins around to face the ledge separating the front counter from the open kitchen.

I'm picking up a pizza for my own pregnant wife. I don't have all night to let them battle for dominance.

"Is that my pizza on the counter?" I speak up and point to the box sitting under the heat lamp. Not that Dan can see me because he doesn't have an extra pair of eyes on the back of his head.

"No," he says, not glancing at me. "Yours is still in the oven."

"Okay, well, maybe I'll take a seat and let you two finish whatever it is you're doing." After saying hi, I slide around Roslyn and head toward the first booth.

"I'm fine," she whispers to me as I pass.

"All the pregnant ladies say the same thing," I say in the same hushed tone.

"Then why don't you men believe us?" She keeps her voice low and conspiratorial.

"Because *fine* is usually code for anything but. We've been trained to protect our balls when we hear women say *fine*," Dan responds loudly still with his back to us.

Roslyn's eyes narrow as she faces me. "Do you agree?"

My neck itches under her scrutiny. I'm damned either way. "You're kind of proving his point right now. Your eyes could shoot laser beams if you glare any stronger."

She blinks and shakes her head. "I didn't realize I was glaring."

Dan dips his chin and glances over his shoulder at me. "Tom, how're things going with you?"

"Good. Boat business is good. We're busy down at the yard. Hailey's finishing up a project by first week in December and we'll see what happens after that."

"If she's anything like Roslyn, I bet she's not planning on slowing down until the very last minute." Dan smiles at his wife. Even I can see the love in his eyes. The man's hopelessly in love when it comes to Roslyn. Guess when you found and then lost your love, you hold on tight if you get a second chance.

"My hearing is fine, too," Roslyn remarks, but there's no malice in her voice.

"You've never been sexier," Dan says softly. "Nor more beautiful. Never have I been more conscious of my heart living outside my body."

Roslyn sighs. "Damn you. You can't use your superpowers over me like that."

I swear she's blushing. When I first walked in, I felt like I'd interrupted an argument. Now, I'm the awkward third on their lovey-dovey date.

"Pizza done yet?" I ask, ready to get out of here so they can get on with it.

"You see a box on the counter?" Behind the counter, Dan flips his attention from Roslyn to me. "How about I give you some garlic knots while you wait?"

"If you insist." I'm not a fool to turn down free food from Dan.

"Are you taking maternity leave?" I ask, genuinely interested so I can use the information as leverage with Hailey.

"I run my own PR company and there's no way I can take six weeks of maternity leave. My clients will implode without me telling them what not to do." She sighs. "I know they'll be fine, but I'm not sure I can give up control."

"This is why your office is in the guest house," Dan says. "At least you don't have to commute off the island and management won't complain if you bring your baby to work every day."

"Is John as bad as Dan?" Roslyn asks, resigned but smiling. "I swear the three of you need your own support group. Maybe some drumming and marching around the fire pit like cavemen would help."

I ignore her jab. She's half right about us needing some guy time not involving baby talk. Or drum circles. I'll leave that to Falcon, the island's version of a human unicorn, or Jonah, because no one knows what he does in his off time.

"John's like papa bear but Diane's Goldilocks. Or some fairy tale with an overprotective bear-husband figure in it. I need to brush up on my nursery rhymes," I say as I try to remember the books I knew as a little kid.

"I don't think there are any with bear-husbands." Roslyn scrunches up her face. "Not that I can remember."

"Me neither. I think you're confusing your characters." Dan snaps open a brown bag before filling it with garlic knots from a tray under a heat lamp on the ledge separating the kitchen from the front counter. Holding one in his tongs, he gestures at me. "Speaking of being clueless, did you and Hailey sign up for the Baby 101 class in Coupeville?"

"Next Saturday morning. You?" I ask.

"Same. Guess we'll see you there." He folds over the top of the bag and then sets it on the pizza box. "Half Hot Hawaiian, hold the jalapeños, and half sausage. Still haven't gone over to the dark side of pineapple on pizza?"

"Never. No fruit shall ever destroy my pizza." I hand over my card to pay. "Can I place an order for garlic knots for class on Saturday?"

"You want me to bring snacks?" he asks

I shrug. "It's a four-hour class."

Laughing, he shakes his head. "I'd have to bring enough for everyone."

"You're right. Probably better to bring a couple of whole pies. Smart thinking." I'm mostly joking, but my stomach growls with real hunger.

"I'll surprise you," he says. "Flip the sign to closed on your way out. We're closing early tonight."

Catching the steamy look he gives Roslyn, I take it upon myself to turn off most of the lights when I get to the door.

Their laughter fades behind me as I eat a garlic knot on the way to my truck.

❄

Saturday morning greets us with cold, misty rain dripping off the cedar trees surrounding our house. Staring out the window next to the bed, I stretch and yawn.

"Can't we stay home and watch YouTube videos? You can learn everything from those videos," I whisper, trying to seduce her to my idea while spooning against her back. She's wrapped around her body pillow, that she charmingly named Momoa.

At first I thought she mispronounced the Disney cartoon, *Moana*. Of course my mind went to the cartoon given it's been on rotation lately during our *practice* babysitting. Then I realized she meant the beefcake actor. And despite my efforts to get her to rename it Tom, or Tom Cat, or hell, even TC, she's refused.

Here we are, me, the love of my life, and Momoa, warm and cozy in our bed early on a weekend morning. And I'm expected to get up, drive all the way up the island to Coupeville, and sit in a classroom full of expectant parents all day.

I thought registering for the shower was torture and that lasted only an hour. Maybe we can go over to town instead and test drive strollers around the mall. Sounds like a better plan to me, but I know Hailey will veto it without debate.

Snuggling closer, I slip a hand over Hailey's round belly and up to her full breasts. I have an idea to get out of class with distraction and delay.

"Mmm, sensitive." She stops my hand with hers.

Okay, I change my route and head south. Right when I reach her hip, she shifts away.

"Have to pee," she mumbles into Momoa.

Undeterred and sporting more than my standard morning wood, I give her ass a pat. "Go to the bathroom, but then come back to bed."

She shuffles to the edge of the mattress, shoving her body pillow behind her as she sits up. "Can't. I need to shower and we can't be late."

"I'm excellent at multi-tasking." I crawl over to her, sweep her hair off her shoulder, and kiss the soft skin of her neck. "Shower's big enough for both of us. I'll wash your fun bits and you can do mine."

When she twists to see my face, my eyebrow waggling earns me the laughter I seek.

"You're incorrigible," she says as she stands. Once vertical, she arches her back. "I swear I gained ten pounds while sleeping. Do I look bigger to you?"

It's difficult to tell in her loose pink and gray striped nightgown. Even after she supports her belly in her hands, I don't see a difference from yesterday.

"You look beautiful." I gently sweep my hands over her middle. Something ripples beneath my touch.

"Did you feel that?" she asks.

"The baby?" A familiar wave of emotion slams into me.

Hailey nods.

Blinking rapidly because I have too much water in my eyes, I stare at my hand. "Good morning, Sprout."

At the sound of my voice, a baby part presses against my palm.

"I think he just gave me a fist bump." Even to my own ears, my voice is full of awe.

"If that's true, she's standing on my bladder to do it." Hailey grimaces.

I feel another flutter, then the pressure disappears. "Maybe he's doing somersaults again. I mean, how could you not?"

"I wish he wouldn't use my organs as the springboard." She slips out of my reach and shuffles to the bathroom.

"I notice you switched to calling Sprout a he." Grinning, I crawl out of bed on my side. "Start the shower, I'll let Nameless out and make some coffee."

Her gaze settles on my flannel pajama bottoms and the tent from my erection. "Okay."

At the top of the stairs, the wood floor squeaks. Nameless lifts his head from his bed and blinks at me with sleepy eyes.

"Morning, dude," I say, climbing down the stairs.

His tail thumps in greeting before he stands and then stretches.

I sit on the bottom step and wait for him to bound over to me. More Doodle than Lab, he still resembles a mop more than a dog. At least his razor-sharp puppy teeth are gone.

Resting his front paws on my knees, he stands to lick my face. He's a sloppy kisser, all wiggles and tongue with zero control.

"Okay, that's enough. Let's go outside."

I let him out and he bounds off the deck toward the woods. While he does his business, I do mine. Once we're done, I dole out his kibble and head back upstairs as the coffee machine does its magic.

When I enter the bedroom, I head toward the sound of the shower in the adjoining bathroom. With a quick knock, I let Hailey know I'm back. We're not the kind of couple who has an open bathroom door policy, so I wait for her invitation.

"All clear," she shouts over the running water.

A cloud of warm steam greets me when I open the bathroom door. Quickly, I strip off my pants and T-shirt before joining her in the shower. Her hair sits on the top of her head in a soapy mess

"You started without me." I pout.

"I wanted to get a head start so we have time for sex." She grins at me with her eyes closed as she rinses the shampoo from her hair.

"Turn around," I tell her, grabbing the conditioner.

While I rub conditioner into her hair, she hums and leans against me. This puts her butt in line with my erection. She knows it, too, because she slowly grinds against my cock.

"It would seem I'm not the only one up for some action this morning." I drop my hands to her shoulders, slowly trailing them down her arms and softly brushing her breasts with my knuckles. "I love your body."

"I'm a whale."

"Whales don't have boobs, or curvy hips, or an ass that can make a man weep from pleasure. Or legs that are the stuff of many of my fantasies." I drop into a squat as I touch each body part. With a soft mouth, I kiss her hip, tasting both her skin and the water pouring down her body.

"What would whales do with legs?" she asks, bracing her hands on the shower wall.

I run my palms between her thighs, gently encouraging her to part her legs. Clearly, I'm not doing foreplay right if she's still thinking about whales. Less than gently, I bite her left butt cheek. Not hard enough to leave a mark, but enough she jumps in surprise. Soothing the same spot with a soft open mouth kiss, I replace the shock of pain with pleasure.

"Turn around again," I say, encouraging her with my hand on her hip.

"So bossy this morning," she says once she's facing me.

Her head is barely visible at this angle, my view mostly of her belly, but the amusement in her eyes is unmistakable.

"You can purse your lips all you want, but you can't deny you find me charming. In fact, you love me."

"More than I thought possible." She tangles her fingers in my wet hair.

I place a reverent kiss right below her navel, letting my mouth trace the dark line extending to the patch of curls. Dropping to my knees, I rest my hands on her thighs. I didn't really consider the logistics of going down on my very pregnant wife in the shower.

"Tom?" Hailey's voice is quiet, uncertain.

"I'm thinking."

"While staring at my bush?"

"Yes?" I rest on my heels so I can see her face. "I finally understand the purpose of those non-slip shower mats."

"We don't have to do anything." Her face crumples with disappointment but she tries to smile.

"Oh, I'm up for the challenge, just figuring out logistics." I kiss one thigh and then the other to buy myself some time. "Okay, step back and brace your hands on the wall."

She obeys, doubt still shadowing her eyes.

Sliding my hand down to her ankle, I cup her calf. "Lift and rest your thigh on my shoulder."

"Are you sure?" I hate the doubt in her voice.

"Why would I joke?" I kiss the inside of her knee.

Again, she follows my instructions.

"Perfect." I meet her eyes as my fingers open her for me.

I tease her with soft kisses from her knee to the top of her thigh. Nuzzling her with my nose, I exhale warm air across her tender skin.

"Tom," she pleads.

"Hmm?" I hum against her thigh. Water pelts my back and drips from my hair. With my tongue, I trace the path of a droplet as it runs down her thigh.

"It's not nice to be mean to a pregnant woman." She moans with a mix of pleasure and frustration.

"Hmm." My lips vibrate on her skin where her thigh ends and her ass begins. Unable to resist any longer, I sweep my tongue the length of her before swirling it around her clit. When she bucks her hips in response, I replace licking with sucking.

One of her hands rests on my head, her fingers knotting into my hair, encouraging me.

Slipping a finger inside of her, I curl my finger and locate the magic spot. She arches and grinds her hips closer to my mouth.

"More," she commands, her voice breathy and a little shaky.

I don't know if it's the increased blood flow because of the pregnancy or the hormones or another unsolved mystery of being a woman, but Hailey's more responsive than ever. Her fuse has shortened, and she goes from aroused to coming in record time these days. Not that I'm timing her. I have other things to focus on.

Another few strokes of my tongue and a steady thrust of my fingers, and Hailey's thighs begin to shake. With a moan, she clenches and flutters around my fingers as her body stiffens seconds before she explodes.

I soften the pressure and slow my rhythm, coaxing her orgasm out of her. When her standing leg sags, I support it with a hand to the back of her knee. Placing a final soft kiss on her curls, I rest back on my heels again.

A rosy flush covers her chest, which rises and falls with her shallow breaths. Her eyes are half closed and a blissful smile curls her lips.

"Beautiful." Standing, I pull her into my arms.

"I probably look like a wet rat."

"A beautiful, satiated, wet rodent." I kiss her lips. "Want me to wash your back now?"

Her warm hand wraps around my hard-on. "I have another idea."

Releasing my aching cock, she once again faces the wall, and wiggles her butt.

"Are you sure?" I stroke myself, seeking some relief at the same time I picture myself buried inside of her from behind. "Is this angle okay?"

She nods over her shoulder. "We need to have as much sex as possible so the six week wait won't seem as long."

If only sex worked that way where we could bank it for the dry spells.

I don't need to be asked twice. She's slick from her orgasm as I slide the tip along her entrance. Gripping her hips, I sink inside easily, and we both moan when I'm all the way in.

"This won't be slow and gentle." Already my balls tighten with pressure and I haven't even begun to thrust yet.

"Who said anything about gentle? I'm not made of eggshells." She grinds her ass against me.

"Damn, Idaho. What did I do to deserve you?" Sometimes I still slip and use her old nickname.

"Less talking, more hot shower sex." She folds her arms and rests her head on her forearms on the tile.

Angling her hips back, I change the angle slightly. With a groan, I slide out all the way to the tip before plunging back in her warmth in one quick thrust.

"Like that," she mumbles into her arm.

I repeat the movement again and again until the shower fills with the sounds of wet skin slapping against wet skin. My moans mix with her sighs.

If I could, I'd stay buried in her all morning. There's no place I'd rather be than totally consumed by Hailey. If only that were possible.

The point of no return speeds toward me.

"I'm close," she says, her voice needy.

I slip my hand around her hip and find her clit again as I try to hold off my orgasm.

With my thumb, I apply pressure to where she needs it as I keep thrusting into her.

"Oh, oh, oh," she chants as she clenches around me. "I'm, oh God, don't stop."

I focus on drawing out her pleasure even as my balls tighten.

Mentally, I give myself a trophy for holding off coming until she does.

The pressure releases as I come inside of her with one final thrust. I lean forward and rest my head against her back, kissing the skin along her spine.

"Are you okay?" I ask as soon as I can focus.

"Fabulous."

"We could spend the rest of the day doing that." I shift my hips to prove my point.

"Tom."

One syllable and I know my cause is lost.

Reluctantly, I slide out of her, and grab the body wash. "Fine. But I think we're going to be late. I'm happy to tell the baby coach why."

"You wouldn't." Her lips twitch as she tries to appear stern.

"We both know I would." I soap up her back and then gently and thoroughly wash her breasts.

"I think they're clean now."

"I'll be the judge of that." I slip my soap hands over her belly and between her thighs where she's still slick.

"Water's going tepid."

"We need a bigger water heater. Or one of the tankless kind. I'll get one installed." I'm serious even though it won't fix the issue today. "I can see if a plumber can come by while we're in Coupeville."

Hailey scoots by me to rinse off in the quickly cooling spray. "Ah, you finally admit you're going to baby class."

Damn it.

CHAPTER FOUR

I park next to Roslyn's giant Mercedes SUV tank in the hospital's parking lot. Knowing Dan will be suffering through this class with me gives me small comfort. I hope he brought the garlic knots.

"Ready?" Hailey asks.

With a tooth-filled grin, I give her two thumbs up.

She's not buying my fake enthusiasm. "Come on, it's going to be informative and maybe even fun."

Still doubting the fun part, I manage not to drag my feet as we cross the lot. I've never liked hospitals. Even when good things happen here, like my child being born. I still think of the horrible day Pops died. Passing through the main waiting room, I see the ghosts of my family sitting in the chairs, stuck between before and after.

Once again, we're here in a moment of before. Before Hailey goes into labor. Before our child is born. Before we go home as a family of three. This could be the last time we leave this hospital as a couple. Before we're parents.

The weight of change hits me like a softball to the chest. I rub the heaviness on my solar plexus.

"You okay?" Hailey asks. "You look a little pale."

"I'll be okay." I suck in some extra oxygen and focus on her face. Her still damp hair is twisted up in braids around her head and her face is clean of all makeup. Knowing this smart, funny, beautiful woman somehow loves me helps calm my nerves. "Thinking about Pops."

A line appears between her brows as she frowns. "I miss him, too."

I squeeze her hand. Two years ago when he passed, we weren't an official couple or an official anything. Feels strange to think of the time before Hailey was mine. "It's okay. I just hate hospitals, especially this one."

A woman in dark green scrubs and a name tag gives me a dirty look as she passes us in the corridor.

"Don't take it personally. I'm sure you're great." I flash her a toothy smile.

Hailey points at a hall to our left. "This way."

Pastels and baby animals decorate the walls of the new hallway. Obviously we've reached the maternity wing.

"No whales," I whisper to Hailey as we pass through the weird tribute to our mammal cousins.

"Wait, there's an orca and her baby." Hailey points to the far end of the hall where an ocean scene fills the wall.

"No narwhals? I see otters and dolphins. What about our horned friends of the north?" I pretend to study the mural.

"Quit stalling. We're here." She stops in front of an open door.

Following her inside, I scan the room for Dan and Roslyn. Set up in the back row, there's an open spot next to them. I don't recognize anyone else in the room. Which is kind of a relief given my single years on the island. I'm optimistic this day won't be as bad as I've imagined as we greet Dan and Ros, and sit down.

"What's all this stuff?" I poke the basket on the table in front of us.

"Educational supplies," Roslyn deadpans. As always, she's

polished and put together—not an auburn hair out of place and her outfit is all pale gray and soft. Dan looks like an old punk rocker in his faded Ramones T-shirt and sleeves of tattoos. If I were a betting man, I'd never have thought the local pizza guy would get a woman like Ros, but it turns out that Dan's anything but your average dough jockey.

"Did you bring the snacks?" I ask, eyeing both baskets of blankets, bottles, diapers, and baby dolls.

I'm not sure if we're allowed to rifle through the baskets before class starts, but I can't resist picking up our dark-haired doll.

"No, I didn't think you were serious." Dan leans back in his chair.

"I'm always serious about pizza." Holding our doll by the back of its head, I jab its plastic fist at Dan. I switch to a doll appropriate falsetto and say, "Unless it has fruit on it. Fruit on pizza is the devil's work. Satan made you do it."

"And now I'm going to have nightmares." Hailey removes the doll from my grip and returns it to the basket.

I'm still amused, so I tuck my hand underneath the doll's back and raise it into a sitting position. "No one puts baby in the basket."

This earns me a chuckle from Dan and a snort from Roslyn. And nothing from Hailey. Undeterred, I switch gears.

"Do you remember the dancing baby when we were kids?" I ask, completely amused by myself.

I'm in the middle of a decent version of the running man given the baby doesn't have bendable knees when our coach walks through the doorway.

"Ah, you must be Tom Donnely," a blond woman a little older than us says from the front of the room. "I've heard about you. I'm LuAnn and I'll be your instructor today. Think of me as Wikipedia for all of your questions about what to expect during labor."

Hailey groans while Roslyn doesn't hold back her laughter.

I'm a grown man in his thirties, but I still feel like a kid who got busted by the sub for clowning around.

At least I haven't slept with the baby coach.

I'd like to say class improves after my dancing doll icebreaker, but it turns out baby wrangling is tougher than it looks. Apparently, we had homework to read before class. The three other couples have all read it, leaving the four of us in the back row out of the loop during the discussion. Then we move on to the baskets and the practical stuff.

Swaddling isn't exactly like rolling a burrito, but it's close.

Diapers have fronts and backs.

And there's a lot more to quality burping than I was told in junior high when I thought being able to burp the alphabet should be an Olympic sport.

We take a short break, mostly for the pregnant women to pee. Exhausted, I slide down in my chair.

"You ready for all this?" I ask Dan, gesturing to the baskets.

"Probably not, but we won't know until we're in it. Like most things in life." He sounds resigned, but in a good way.

"Are you worried about messing up?" I allow myself to be serious for a moment.

"Of course. I think screwing up is inevitable. Perfect parents don't exist. No class or coaching will teach us what we'll learn by doing." He's not resigned, he's on another plane of acceptance. Calm, self-assured, and confident.

Then there's me. "I'm expecting it to be a shit show."

Dan chuckles. "Most definitely."

"How do you stay so calm?" I ask.

"Practice. We all deal with the unknown in our own ways. You process with humor. Roslyn makes a plan. Hailey focuses on the present. I focus inward. I think John does the same."

I shift in my seat to face him more fully, resting my elbow on the table. "Do you ever get scared? What if something happens to Hailey during labor? Or the baby?"

I'm not sure if it's nerves, or the soothing comfort of all the baby animals, but I'm bearing my soul to Dan like we're in a support group. I guess in some ways we are.

"Don't let your mind go there. We can't control everything."

"I hate that," I confess, my voice low. "I hate I can't always protect her from pain."

"This is where faith comes into play." He crosses his ankle over his knee. "Like the George Michael song, you have to have faith."

"You mean like church and praying?" I haven't been to a church in years outside of weddings and funerals. Our wedding was at a vineyard and the ceremony didn't include praying. At least not formally. Can't think of the last time I said a formal prayer other than a quick "oh shit, help me" in a moment of panic. I'm not even the kind of man who makes a bargain with God. Or the devil.

Dan's voice brings me out of my head. "If that works for you. Or trusting in some higher power, whatever you decide that might be. Have faith everything will work out for the best."

"And if it doesn't?" My heart clenches into a tight ball and stops beating for a second at the thought of losing Hailey or our baby.

"You deal with it. Somehow. You figure out a way to make it through the tough times." He meets my stare and I see wisdom in his dark eyes.

"Hey, what are you two talking about?" Hailey asks, slowly settling into her chair by bracing her hand on my shoulder.

"Pizza," Dan answers.

"Still? You're like a stray dog begging for scraps, Tom." Smiling, Hailey shakes her head.

"I can't help it. Now I'm really hungry. I didn't eat a proper breakfast." I slide my gaze to Hailey's face. From the way her cheeks heat, she remembers exactly what I ate this morning.

"I have cash if you want to raid the vending machines." Roslyn pulls out her wallet. "Get me a Twix and a bag of Sun Chips if you're going."

I wave away her money. "I've got it. Dan? Hailey? You want anything?"

"Surprise me. But no pork rinds or those awful orange crackers with the weird peanut butter. And no licorice. Or spicy," Hailey rattles off her don'ts. "Want me to write it down?"

"Not needed. I'll get you plain Lays and cookies."

"You know me so well." She gives me a soft smile. "But not shortbread. Oreos or the mini chocolate chip ones."

"I'll be back." I kiss my wife before leaving.

Meandering the familiar halls, I'm struck with another hospital memory. Of being here when Lori had Noah. Still on the down low, Hailey and I arrived together, but pretended we hadn't. We sat with my dad and ate snacks out of the vending machine that night, too. Seems like another lifetime now.

I locate the machine and slide in my debit card. Ten dollars and an armful of snacks later, I return to the classroom with my bounty.

I'm enjoying my Doritos right up until the instructor tells us we're going to watch a video depicting various birthing options.

When the lights go up, I'm still holding the half full bag of chips, my mouth refusing to close from what I just witnessed. I should've closed my eyes during the water birth, but I couldn't look away.

I wish I had. I'll never look at a kiddie pool the same way.

"Well, that was interesting." Looking a little rough for wear, Dan slaps his palms on his jeans and rubs his thighs.

Roslyn's skin is paler than normal.

Afraid of what I'll see, I haven't looked at Hailey. Instead,

I set my unfinished snack on the table and brush my hands over my face.

The couple in the front row animatedly chats with LuAnn while most of the room sits in stunned silence.

"So my options are to be sliced open like a haggis or be ripped open by trying to pass a pumpkin through a toilet paper tube." Hailey's voice wobbles like she's about to cry.

Slinging my arm around her shoulders, I kiss her temple. "You okay?"

Peeking at her from the corner of my eye, I know we're in trouble.

Her eyes are glassy and full of tears. "I don't think so."

Roslyn leans around me. "Hundreds of thousands of women give birth every day. We can do this."

Hailey shakes her head as tears spill from her wide eyes. "Why didn't Lori tell me this? She's my best friend. Talk about betrayal. Why the silence? There's some big conspiracy and secret keeping. No one discusses the pooping or the incontinence or the flapping vulva. It's all lies and happy diaper commercials."

We sit quietly as she melts down.

"I should've thought this out better. Instead I got swept up in the idea of having a baby, completely forgetting the part where the baby has to exit my body. Have you seen my belly? This kid is huge. I'm doomed. I'll probably never walk right again. Or be able to sneeze or laugh without wetting myself. I'll be buying Depends at Costco with all the little old ladies—"

I interrupt her. "Breathe."

She inhales a shaky breath.

"Now count to ten and slowly exhale for ten." While stroking her hair, I repeat the instructions I saw in the movie.

"Excellent, Tom," LuAnn says, walking over to us. "We're about to get on the floor and do some breathing exercises, but

I see you already know what you're doing. Why don't you come to the front and demonstrate?"

"Uh, sure." I change positions so I can stare at Hailey. "Are you okay?"

"We've made a terrible mistake." She wipes her cheeks.

"No, we haven't. Best decisions I've ever made have been about you. We'll get through this. Together."

She blinks and a couple more tears fall on her cheeks. I sweep them away with my thumbs. Part of me still wants to throw up after the video, but I know I have to be strong for Hailey.

"I love you," I tell her, then kiss her damp cheek.

"I know." She gives me a weak smile.

We all settle on the floor with cushions and yoga mats to make it more comfortable. If someone were to listen outside the door, they might confuse us with a sex therapy class with all the heavy breathing and grunting that takes place.

The focus and extra oxygen calm Hailey, and she recovers from her mini freak-out. Might be the breathing or the visualization exercises. Or the fact that the human mind has an amazing ability to block traumatizing memories.

No one speaks on the way out to our cars. Probably still in shock. I know I am. I'll never be able to look at vaginas and lasagna the same way again.

"You have Dorito dust on your face." Roslyn breaks the silence.

I rub my cheek. "Why didn't anyone tell me?"

"Kind of looked like tribal war paint during the breathing circle," Dan says.

"And that was okay, why?" I ask.

"Never said it was." He shrugs and laughs. At my expense.

"At least I'll never see those people again." I lift the tail of my shirt and rub it over my face.

"It's the island. Eventually, you run into everyone."

"Not if I never go into Langley again. Avoid the Dog

House. Only use Whidbey Joe's coffee huts. Quit my job. Stop shopping at Payless Foods. We can get all our food and toilet paper at Costco off island. Buying in bulk is better for the environment."

"All that effort to avoid a group of people who saw you with cheese dust on your face? Your naked ass is hanging all over the island." Roslyn reminds me of Erik's calendar.

"Fuck, I don't care about looking like a weirdo with my face covered in orange powder. We went through something today. We're veterans of the same battle. Seeing them might trigger PTSD." I'm almost serious. "We should have the baby at Harborview."

My friends and wife stare at me like I've gone full out Apocalypse Now Brando in the jungle.

"What?" I shrug, spinning my keys around my finger.

"PTSD? Really? How are you going to handle the actual birth?" Hailey asks.

"Because I love you. And loving you makes the most difficult moments bearable." It's the simplest and most honest explanation I can give. Leaning close, I give my wife, the love of my life, the mother of my children, a soft kiss on her mouth.

Beside us, I swear I hear Roslyn sigh.

"I love you, too," Hailey says against my lips.

"Okay, I can see why you keep him," Roslyn confesses.

"I'm irresistible?" I smile at my wife.

"You have your moments," Hailey admits.

CHAPTER FIVE

"Did you know elephants are pregnant for ninety-five weeks? Almost two years? And orcas carry their babies for seventeen months?" I read these fun facts off my phone as she gets dressed in her stretchy, black maternity leggings and a flowy white T-shirt top.

"Are you comparing me to a whale again?" Hailey's voice holds a warning I'm on thin ice.

I can't help it if she's wearing black and white. Like an orca. Thankfully, I've had enough coffee this morning to keep the coincidence to myself.

"No, I'm trying to make you feel better. You have six weeks to go. If you were a giraffe, you'd be preggo for four hundred days. Doesn't that make forty-two days seem short?"

Perfectly still like a statue, she stares at me blankly. Not even her mouth twitches. I can't tell if she's processing these cool, fun facts. Or plotting my death.

She's excellent at multi-tasking, so she's probably doing both.

"It's cold and raining out there. You'll probably want a sweater or something." I change the subject to the weather. "It's November and daylight savings ended last weekend, meaning it'll be dark by the time we get home from my parents' house this afternoon."

Today's the baby shower. The co-ed baby shower. Which I feel like is fundamentally wrong on many levels, but I've been promised lots of cake so I'm going to make the best of it. I mean, I was there for the conception and I'm going to be there for the birth and the growing up part. Yet I feel like this should be a day all about Hailey and the amazing job she's doing gestating a human inside of her body. That's all her. Can't think of a bigger reason to have a celebration than that. Plus, I'll be in the way and stealing attention.

Now, before someone labels me a sexist bastard for not wanting to ooh and ahh over baby gifts people bought us because we told them to, I don't like opening presents in front of everyone at Christmas either. Too many years of having to fake excitement over socks to change my opinion on this weird tradition.

I've been to plenty of these co-ed events to base my opinion on experience, not some lame he-man masculine separation of parental duties bullshit.

Then again, Hailey and I ran into each other at Lori and Nick's shower. In a big way, I owe my life to whoever decided men should attend baby parties. And my mother for black-mailing me with stuffing and bribing me with leftovers.

Clearly, I'm easily motivated by food.

PTSD or not, I'm here for everything this baby can bring. Good, bad, ugly, and smelly.

My mother is once again hosting the party. The Donnely farmhouse is bigger than our place, and Mom lives for these kind of events. She says the grandkids keep her young despite the streaks of gray in her brown hair.

We arrive early, but my sisters are already here, buzzing around like a busy swarm of bees, decorating and preparing food for the party.

"Dad in the family room?" I ask, sticking to the perimeter of the kitchen so I don't get in the way.

"I think he's out in the barn." Mom gives me a quick kiss on the cheek. Her familiar floral and vanilla scent tickles my nose. "You can go hide with him."

Relieved, I practically jog across the driveway.

Dad's got the radio on and is listening to the UW football pregame show while he rearranges a tool box on his workbench. Glancing around at the perfectly organized lawn equipment, I can tell he's been out here for a while already. I take after my dad in looks and some would say, personality. We both get our dimples and our charms from the Donnely side of the family.

"Tom, come to hide with your old man?" Grinning, he pats my shoulder.

"Why do men hide in garages and barns?" I gently slap his back in greeting.

"Because we're smart enough to know our limitations."

I nod in understanding.

"We'd only be in the way in the house right now," he continues. "Best to wait until the frenzy is finished and we can enjoy the spoils of all that cooking and baking."

"Do you ever feel guilty for not helping?" I lean against the bench, absently fiddling with a set of tin snips.

"Never. I do my part in other ways." He lines up his screwdrivers by type and size. "I try not to give too much advice, but now that Pops is gone, I guess I'm the old guy with the life wisdom to share."

Shifting my focus to my father's face, I study it closely. He's not old, but his hair has more white and gray than blond and it's getting thin on top. Lines and creases deepen the skin around his eyes and mouth. A few long hairs poke out from his eyebrows. I have no idea the last time I really examined his face, instead taking for granted he's always the same. Somewhere over the past couple of years, he's aged.

"You're starting to look more like Pops," I tell him.

"You think? Your mom keeps telling me to trim my eyebrow hairs and threatens to buzz my ears with clippers while I sleep if I don't keep the fuzz in check." He points to his earlobe. "I say it's just more of me to love."

He's sounding more like his dad, too. I wonder at what point I'll begin to mimic Ken Donnely. Maybe I already do.

"There are worse things to be compared to than Clifford Donnely," I reassure him.

"Truth in that." His smile is wistful and a little sad. "I miss him."

"Me too." I clear the thick emotion from my throat. "So what advice would you give me?"

"Are you asking because you're curious or are you being polite?" Dad sets down his tools.

"You said you're the old guy with wisdom to share."

He scratches his cheek and focuses on the ceiling. "Well, I suppose it's a little late for the sex talk."

We both snort.

"Right." He laughs. "I will say every kid is different. You'll never feel like you know what you're doing. Most parenting is winging it and trying to survive the day. At least with newborns. Then when you finally figure things out, you've got toddlers hell bent on testing every last one of your nerves. They'll seem easy when you get to teenager year and the rules change again. Buckle up and try to enjoy the ride."

"Winging it and wear a seatbelt? That's the wisdom? Reminds me of when you taught me how to drive."

"Pretty much." He nods with a smile. "Your mom can probably tell you about schedules and avoiding sugar and tiring them out, but the truth is, you have to learn on the job."

"Kind of like welding."

"Hopefully avoiding open flames and melting things. At least during the first years." He opens the door to his mini fridge under the workbench. "Want a beer?"

I accept the bottle of Alaskan Amber he hands me. After twisting off the cap, I clink the glass against his.

"Oh, and find a good hiding place. Garage, workshop. Preferably someplace just out of shouting range."

"I'm guessing you've reorganized your tools more times than needed over the years."

He sweeps the screwdrivers into a pile and dumps them back into the bottom of his toolbox. With a wink, he says, "I have no idea what you're talking about."

Eventually, Nick shows up. With his short brown hair and clean cut appearance, he's a good-looking guy. In his button down and khakis, he's definitely working on perfecting his dad look. I wonder if Lori buys his clothes and styling products for his hair. Dad hands him a beer.

"I was told I had ten minutes to bring you both inside so we can start the games," he apologizes as he sips his beer. "I set the timer on my phone so we have eight minutes before the second unit will arrive."

"Who's the second unit?"

"My mother," Dad says, his voice serious.

I laugh at the thought of him cowering from Gramma Ellie. "I guess you never grow out of being afraid of pissing off your mom."

He lifts his beer. "See? My wisdom is already rubbing off on you."

After finishing my bottle, I chuck it into the recycling bin. "What sort of games are we talking about?"

"If I remember from our shower, there's the classic Guess the Contents of a Diaper. Probably a round of guessing the circumference of the baby bump. And my personal favorite, betting on gender, weight, and birthday. My advice, if you're asking for it, is always guess chocolate and underestimate how big your wife's waist has gotten." Nick's advice is basic, but smart.

I tell him thanks and jerk my head toward the door.

"Ready?"

"Oh, and another thing. Practice your happy smile. Ooh and ahh when she opens the gifts, but don't overdo it. And don't ask what something is for or make jokes," Nick continues with his advice, his brow lined with worry.

"My happy smile?" I ask both men.

"Show us," Nick says.

I smile at them, showing lots of teeth.

"Not that. Maybe try nodding while you do it. Focus on how thrilled you are to be at the shower," Nick advises.

"I'm not." I lift my eyebrows and keep smiling.

"We can tell," Dad says.

"Shows that much?" I ask, feeling guilty I'm not more excited about today.

The two of them exchange a look.

"That bad?" I change my smile and widen my eyes.

Dad inhales through his teeth. "That's worse. Think about how much you love Hailey and how much you're going to love your kid. Keep your eyes on the long game. This is a marathon."

Nick's phone buzzes and he glances at the screen. "We've been summoned."

"Can't wait!" I pump my fist.

"This should be interesting," Dad mutters, giving his tools a longing look.

"Thanks for the vote of confidence." I shake out my arms and roll my shoulders. "You're both forgetting women love me. It's my pheromones and charming personality. I've got this."

Questions I think but am smart enough not to ask during the Opening of the Gifts:

Why ducks? They don't exactly have a reputation for being friendly.

What's up with all the hippo books? Those beasts are vicious assholes.

At what point did nipple cream become a topic for mixed company?

When did I start using phrases like "mixed company" and sounding like Gramma Ellie?

Who came up with this bizarre ritual in the first place?

Would it be rude to ask my mom to get me a slice of cake?

How many clothes does a baby need?

And why are we the proud owners of so many blankets?

So many blankets. And quilts and swaddling cloths and loops of cloth we can use to strap the baby to our bodies.

Good news. I know what a Boppy is now.

That mystery's been solved.

The thing's super comfortable. I sit through the remainder of the present unwrapping with the Boppy curled around my middle.

Hailey sags after opening the last of the gifts. A silver rattle —talk about a random gift and potential weapon. Her lids droop with exhaustion.

Gently touching her arm, I ask, "Tired?"

"I could nap. Who knew generosity could be so draining?" She widens her eyes to appear more awake, but then yawns, ruining the illusion.

I glance at the huge pile of gifts. "It's overwhelming. Why do we need so much stuff for a human who won't do more than eat, shit, and sleep for months? I doubt kids in the middle of the Gobi Desert have a Boppy."

She gives me a sleepy smile. "Do we need to buy another one for you?"

I pat the soft green fabric. "Maybe."

CHAPTER SIX

Thanksgiving is an exercise in controlled chaos. Two weeks after the shower and we all gather at my parents' house again. Hailey's parents join the Donnely clan, pushing our count over twenty people—not including the four foot and under crowd of pint-sized offspring.

Per tradition, the men folk watch football while the women get the meal ready. We're not crazy enough to try to offer assistance. It'd be like a little leaguer thinking he could pitch in the pros. Our jobs today include staying out of the way, praising the cooking, and eating seconds, even thirds to prove how thankful we are for family. Being a pro, Dad's wearing loose fleece lounge pants with an elastic waist.

Between sisters, mothers, grandmothers, daughters, and wives, the women in the kitchen represent every living generation of this family. More proof the Donnely men are not only *not* in charge, but vastly outnumbered.

I've learned an important life lesson today. Joking about being barefoot and pregnant in the kitchen isn't funny if your wife is all three of those things. At least not to the woman in question.

Thirty-six weeks pregnant, Hailey insists on supervising

from her seat at the kitchen table. I think she's in charge of rolling silverware in cloth napkins this year. Last time I checked on her from the safety of the hall, she had her socked feet propped on a chair and two baskets in front of her.

Okay, so she's not truly barefoot.

I dash into the hub of female power to grab a fresh bag of tortilla chips for the seven layer dip. Like in *Wonder Woman*, I'm Steven Trevor crashing into the Amazons' island. With a quick kiss to Hailey's forehead, I check in on my own wonder woman without hovering. "You having fun?"

"Sorting place settings is the most boring thing ever," she whispers. "I'm thinking about stealing a few sips of your mom's white zin when she's not looking."

I dip my chin and frown. "I'd prefer my daughter wait until at least college to develop a taste for pink wine."

At the word daughter, all hum of activity in the room ceases.

My eyes widen as I stare at Hailey. In a stage whisper even my grandmother can hear, I ask, "They heard me, didn't they?"

Hailey loudly sighs. "He's teasing you. We don't know. I swear."

My mom's exhale is loud enough to carry across the kitchen. "Thomas Clifford, it's not nice to tease."

"I'm an elderly woman," Gramma chides me before softening her tone. "I might not make it another month. You can tell me and I'll take it to my grave."

"Nice try." Giving my grandmother a disappointed shake of my head, I stand and then walk toward her. "You're in perfect health and will probably outlive us all. Plus, you're the first number at the top of the Donnely family phone tree, aka the grapevine. I love you, but you're completely untrustworthy."

"It's so old-fashioned not to find out." My middle sister Cara gives her unwanted opinion.

I stare up at the ceiling and exhale. "Didn't we go over this at the baby shower? We're not finding out. And, Gramma, don't try to get the info out of our doctor again while she's at the grocery store."

Gramma Ellie widens her eyes into an expression that mirrors my own attempts to appear innocent. I must get it from her. "Who told you? Was it one of those gossips? Sally?"

"Our obstetrician did, Mrs. Donnely. At our last appointment. Said you were very persistent," Hailey says, her voice soft.

Gramma huffs. "That's ridiculous. I was just making conversation in the cashier's line. As one does. People used to be more friendly around here." She busies herself with opening a can of fried onions and sprinkling them over the top of her green bean casserole.

I make eye contact with my mother, who shrugs as she sips her glass of wine. Sighing, I say, "I don't get what the big deal is."

"You won't tell us the gender. Or the name. You're ruining all the fun." Mom's disappointment's clear in her voice.

"Lori didn't find out either." I throw my youngest sister under the bus like we're seven and five again.

"Yeah, and I kind of wished we'd found out before Noah was born. Easier to plan things. Definitely for the next kiddo."

"Are you trying?" Amy asks, her voice full of excitement.

"You basically asked Lori if she's having lots of unprotected sex. In front of Mom, Gramma, and Mrs. King." I drop my jaw open in faux shock.

My mother-in-law pats my shoulder, her green eyes full of amusement. "Tom, I know how babies are made."

Jesus on a saltine. I glance at Hailey, who is silently shaking with silent laughter as she focuses on her task of bundling silverware inside napkins. The woman could get a job rolling cigars. She's very good with her hands.

I need to switch the channel in my head from Hailey's

manual dexterity back to the topic. "What's the big deal? You have other grandkids you can fawn over."

My oldest sister, Amy, snorts. "It's because you're the boy."

"That's not true," Mom argues. "You only become a parent once for the first time. This is special. And don't twist my words, Amy. I love each and every grandchild with my whole heart."

"Oh, please. Tom's always been your favorite." Lori takes a big sip of her own wine. I notice two empty bottles on the counter already.

"I don't have a favorite," Mom attempts to defend herself. After brushing her hands on her apron, she settles them on her hips, glaring at my sisters.

Amy and Cara refuse to look at me. We're close, but old family dynamics still exist. Lori's the baby, I'm the boy, and Amy has always been an adult. Cara's a classic middle child, lost between the bossy older sister and the obnoxious younger brother. She's great at making peace but even better at wisely picking her fights.

"I can't help it if I'm the most charming, smartest, and good looking of all." I'm safe to speak the truth because Hailey's the only one with access to knives at the moment.

Small objects pelt the side of my head and torso. Cara and Amy are throwing pecans at me.

"Ouch! I'm under attack." I dive behind Hailey, using her as a wall of defense.

"You're hiding behind your pregnant wife?" Amy scoffs. "Oh, Tom. You still haven't learned to stand up and defend yourself. When he was little, he'd always start crying and immediately run off to Mom or Gramma the second we picked on him."

"It's true." Nodding her head, Cara agrees.

"Keep talking about me like I'm not here and we'll have a repeat of the Great Mashed Potato War from two years ago."

Hailey ducks her head to smother her giggles.

"You wouldn't dare." Mom brandishes a spoon at me. "I can still see the spots on the wall."

"I knew better than to dare enter your lair." I eye a bowl of crab dip sitting on the counter. "I'll leave you to your lady party."

Stepping closer to the dip, I give my mom a quick kiss on the cheek. "Love you."

Before she realizes what I'm up to, I grab the dip and run out of the room.

"Share that with the rest of the guys!" Amy yells from the kitchen.

Like I'm going to eat an entire bowl of Gramma's famous crab dip by myself.

Okay, it's happened before, but only once.

Flopping on the couch next to Dad, I set the bowl on the coffee table. Among my own kind, I relax into the cushions.

Hailey's dad is in the recliner. Nick and Doug, two out of three of my brothers-in-law, are on the other side of the sectional. Sam, one of the nephews, is sprawled on the floor in front of Dad's giant TV.

"Where are the chips?" Nick asks.

I blow out a breath. "Shit. You're going to have to get them yourself. I can't go back in there. Maybe ever."

Nick and Dad laugh at me before Nick suggests, "Send Greg when he gets back from the bathroom."

Excellent. Brothers-in-law are safe from the hen pecking because of their lack of shared DNA.

A few minutes later, Greg steps into the room. Tall and working a dad bod, he's an all-around "good guy," who happens to resemble Seth Rogan's more handsome brother.

I stop him before he can sit down. "While you're up, can you grab the tortilla chips and maybe some more of those crackers in the kitchen?"

He gives me a sidelong look. "You were supposed to get them. Did you get yourself kicked out of the kitchen again?"

Everyone but me thinks this is hysterical.

"No, but for the future peace of familial relations, it's probably best I stay right here for now." I slide down until the back of my neck rests on the top of the cushions.

Greg shrugs and ambles into the den of lionesses. He returns a minute later, carrying chips, crackers, and a tray of cocktail weenies stabbed through their middles with toothpicks.

I try not to take it personally, but reflexively cross my legs anyway.

"What happened in there?" Dad asks quietly.

"Why is it always my fault?"

"Baby stuff getting to you?" he asks, picking up a tiny hot dog and twirling it around.

"Busybodies are pressuring us to find out if the baby is a boy or a girl." I eye the wee sausage and decide it's the most appropriate snack for everyone's obsession today.

"I don't really understand it. Sure, I wanted a son, but I was happy when each of my kids were born healthy." Dad happily munches on the new snack.

"Is that true or just something you say?" I hand him another weenie and the bowl of bbq dipping sauce.

"You'll find out soon enough how quickly your life can change. We never thought you'd settle down, then Hailey blew up your world. If you think you feel love now, wait until you hold your child." I swear his eyes get a little misty as he speaks.

We sit quietly as halftime finishes and the game starts again. Lost in my head, I barely pay attention to the plays and couldn't tell you any details of the game other than who's playing.

My two-year-old ginger nephew, Noah, comes tearing into the room like a shopper into Walmart's Black Friday sale. Takes me a few seconds to realize he's butt-naked from the waist down.

"Hey, little dude." I trap him with my legs as he tries to round the coffee table.

Lightly squeezing, I immobilize him. Tiny man has some serious finger strength as he grabs at my jeans and attempts to free himself. I grimace when he manages to pull on my leg hair through the fabric, but I don't release him. When his face turns the same color as his hair, I know he's going to blow.

"Hey," I speak slowly. "Where are you going?"

He pauses in his attempt to free himself and says, "Fuck."

Pretty sure there isn't a place in the scrapbook for Baby's First Curse Word.

Dad snorts beside me while Nick coughs and sputters on his beer.

"You teach him that?" Dad asks as Noah repeats himself.

"He's saying truck," Nick answers with a sigh.

"Sure he is. Do you want your truck?" I ask my pantsless nephew.

"Fuck," Noah says in his little voice. "Fuck!"

"Noah Donnely Crawford!" Lori shouts from the door. She's standing there with a fresh diaper in one hand and tiny pants in the other. "Diaper and pants first, then you can play with your truck. Tr-uck."

"Fuck?" Noah repeats.

"Tr," Lori stresses the *t* and *r*.

"Fuck?" Noah asks.

I can't take much more without full out laughing.

"If you think this is so funny, one of you can finish changing him." Lori hands Nick the pants and diaper.

He tosses them to me. "Tom needs the practice."

"Seriously? Everyone acts like putting a diaper on is super difficult. We spent an hour on diapering and swaddling at Baby 101."

"Then you should be a master. I'll time you." Nick pulls out his phone.

"Asshole," I mutter under my breath.

"Asso," Noah echoes. "Asso."

"Wonderful," Lori says from behind us. "At least put his diaper on before he pees all over you."

My legs spring open, allowing Noah to escape. On the loose again, he stalls as he tries to scramble over my dad's feet, giving me the chance to scoop him up.

"No," he pleads as he struggles in my arms. "Noo."

"Listen, we do this fast and you get your truck sooner." I use my no nonsense allowed voice.

Nick softly snorts. "Never bargain with a toddler."

Parenting advice from a guy whose kid swears like a pantsless trucker? Give me a break.

"I've got this." Holding Noah under one arm, I grab the diaper and his pants with my free hand.

"Ten bucks, someone ends up covered in piss." Dad's serious.

"I'll take that bet and double it if he hits the ceiling, an eye, or more than one of us," Greg says, then adds, "It's happened before."

"In the eye?" I'm both disgusted and impressed.

Noah wiggles around like Gramma's Jell-O salad.

"Work with me, dude." I stand him up and brace him against my chest with my right forearm while I try to open up the diaper and align it with his bottom. "Okay. Let's do this."

With ninja skills I never knew I possessed, I open, peel, bend, flip, slip, slide, and contort my arms as I diaper the human version of a water weenie. At one point, I have Noah flipped over my shoulder and at another he's face up on my lap. There's laughter and even a few tears. Mainly from me. Victory is one adjustment and a sticky tab away when I feel a foreign warmth spreading across my chest.

No, it's not the satisfaction of proving Nick wrong. Or an overwhelming love for another human. I wish.

"Dammit." I manage to get the flap closed to stem the stream. "Noah, we had money in the bank."

Dad, Nick, Greg, Lori, and even Noah laugh.

"Sure. I see how this works. You and Grandpa were in cahoots the entire time, weren't you?" I hold him away from me and my wet shirt.

"You can borrow one of my shirts," Dad offers, taking Noah from me. He addresses the smiling toddler, "Your uncle did the same thing to me. More than once. About time he was on the other side of things."

I swear Noah gives my dad a tiny fist bump.

"You're all assholes," I tell the group as I stand.

"Assos," Noah says, clapping his hands.

"You're welcome." I glare at Lori and Nick.

I pull off my shirt as soon as I'm in the hallway, passing the kitchen.

"Hey there, hot stuff," Hailey purrs as I pass. "What happened to your shirt?"

Her eyes are focused on my abs. Can't blame the familiar expression of lust on her face. Pregnancy definitely makes Hailey horny. Her eyes have a glazed look and her mouth twists like it does when she's having dirty thoughts.

"I'm covered in urine," I warn her.

In a flash, her face goes from "let's sneak up to your old room, put on the Backstreet Boys, and make out like teenagers" to disgust.

"Ew." Her mouth purses like she's sucked on a lemon. Or her formerly hot husband is covered in piss.

"Apparently, I got off lucky. Nick got it in the eye once."

Her mouth drops open.

"Yeah. I'm going to take a quick shower and borrow one of Dad's shirts."

Ten minutes later, clean and urine free, I bound down the stairs in a *#1 DAD* baseball style T-shirt. It's tight and I wonder if it's from the eighties when we were little.

"I plan to keep this one," I announce when I reclaim my seat on the couch.

"That's not how it works. You need to earn that title," Dad chides me with a laugh.

"I don't think anyone takes proclamations on clothing or mugs seriously. You think Al down at the boatyard is really the number one boss? Or anyone would ever vote for him? Yet he has a *#1 BOSS* mug."

"Who's ready to eat?" Mom asks, skimming over me while she addresses the room. "Why are you wearing that shirt?"

"Got pissed on," Dad and I say at the same time.

Shaking her head, Mom scans the room. "Okay. Better it happened before we're all seated. Ellie, would like to say the blessing this year?"

I'm not sure if she thinks I peed on myself or not, but I don't bother to clarify as we all take our seats for the family feast.

CHAPTER SEVEN

"Weather's forecasted for a helluva wind storm this week. Maybe bring some ice with it." I rub my hands together before cupping them and blowing warm air over the frozen skin. The sky is heavy with dark clouds, dimming the afternoon light and making it feel much later than two o'clock.

"Can smell the snow in the air." Olaf sniffs loudly. In his red plaid shirt and matching hat with ear flaps, he's the world's crankiest elf. Or the dwarf named Grumpy.

"You know you're not a real snowman, right?" I press my luck in poking him. I'm still not banned from the Dog House, despite many threats over all these years, but I like to test the limit. Especially after Hailey and I got ourselves kicked out of the Inn after last year's Donnely Boats' holiday party.

I stand by my statement that if you have a party at a hotel with bedrooms and you don't want shenanigans to occur in said rooms, keep the doors locked. Newlyweds is apparently enough of an excuse to avoid charges, but not enough to keep us out of the police log. I've got the incident report framed and hanging over the toilet in the downstairs bathroom.

No shame in loving my wife.

"Damn cartoon," Olaf grumbles. "One of those ribbon and wreath ladies offered to have some high school art kid come paint my windows with Disney characters."

"What did you tell her?"

"This is a tavern, not a daycare. People don't care if the place is festive as long as I don't run out of beer."

I almost mention that we're out here in the cold hanging up pine garlands around his tavern's windows and doors. The annual holiday stroll is tonight and O's reluctantly agreed to do his own decorations to avoid too much "fancy bullshit" from the official event committee.

Up on a ladder, I'm doing the lifting and hanging while he grumbles from his spot on the sidewalk. After his heart attack last year, he's not allowed to over exert himself.

"Speaking of daycare, you know you can't bring your babies in here when you come to play pool? Not even if you have them strapped to you like a bomb." He scowls as he unfurls more garland to hand to me.

I snort and don't bother to cover it. "Bomb?"

"Ticking-time bombs. Any second they can explode with ear piercing sounds or projectile body fluids."

Shaking my head and still laughing, I hang the last of the swag on this window and lean back. "How's it look?"

"Festive," he spits out the word like an unwanted lemon seed.

"Then I think we're done out here. My hands and balls are about to freeze off. I believe you mentioned earlier about rewarding me with a beer if I helped you."

"Bullshit. You volunteered. Or Dan forced you to come down here because he thinks I'm old and feeble." He holds the ladder as I step down. "Fine. Put your gear in the truck and meet me inside. Don't leave anything laying around or someone will pretend to trip on it just to sue me."

He mutters about the downfall of society as he opens the door and steps inside.

I stroll to the middle of the crosswalk and examine our handiwork. The old red-painted clapboard exterior with its white trim does look festive with the long boughs of evergreen framing the front windows and doorway. Multi-colored lights twinkle in the gloomy afternoon light. Glancing to my right up the street, I see the colorful buildings and storefronts of Langley similarly decorated. The charm is nearly unbearable. Downtown has been transformed from quaint to holiday quaint.

Next year, we'll have a kid to bring to these events. Standing in the middle of the road, I'm struck by how much life's changed and how it feels like everything's speeding up.

A car honks at me and I wave my hand over my shoulder to tell them to go around. Can't they see I'm having a moment?

Brushing my hand over my scruffy beard, I stare up at the Dog House as my past flashes before my eyes. Three years ago, Hailey and I kissed for the first time here. Two years ago, I proposed to Hailey the night of the annual Sip n' Stroll.

Our history is tied to this old building and these familiar streets.

A loud rapping on glass snaps me out of my memories. Olaf's mouthing something as he slams his fist against the window.

When I step through the door, he gives me a disapproving shake of his head. "One minute you were complaining about the cold and the next you're standing in the middle of the busy street with your mouth hanging open. It's a bunch of dead branches. Don't let it go to your head."

As I slide onto a stool at the bar, I chuckle despite his intended insult. "Got lost in some old memories. You invite me in here for my free beer?"

"Beer's free, but I still expect a tip." He picks up a pint glass from the shelf behind the bar. "IPA?"

"Sure." I watch as he pulls the handle and angles the glass to get the perfect head.

Finishing the pour, he sets the pint in front of me on the bar. Under his breath, he mumbles, "Thanks for your help."

It's the nicest thing he's ever said to me and I'm stunned speechless for a beat. "Um, you're welcome."

He busies himself with wiping down the already clean wooden bar top. "How's Hailey doing?"

"Good. I think. Tired and complains about her back. And ankles. Has to pee every ten minutes. Eating weird foods together. Like clams and ice cream. Which might explain the farting when she sleeps, which is a lot."

"Whoa, I didn't ask for all the details." He flicks the white towel to his shoulder and holds up his hands, palms facing me. "Best advice is to keep some mystery between a man and a woman."

I sip my beer to keep from laughing at the horror in his eyes. "Times have changed since you were a new dad."

"You mean other than the whole world going to shit?" He barks out a snort. "Back then, when people had more sense, the men smoked in the waiting room until someone announced our name over the speaker. By the time I first saw my sons, they were squeaky clean and safely stored in their plastic baby tray in the nursery. Much more civilized."

I can't imagine any of that scenario. "You could smoke in the hospital?"

"Sure. In those days, you smoked anywhere you wanted." He nods, proud about this fact.

"Doesn't seem healthy." I frown into my glass.

"Eh, we lived. So did our kids." He dismisses my concern with a shrug.

Honest wisdom from Olaf. "I don't know how my mom did it with the four of us."

"Nowadays everyone's afraid of germs and getting dirty. Best advice I can give you is to let the kid eat dirt."

"Gotcha." I'm not sure Hailey would agree, but I nod anyway.

"That's enough baby talk for me. You about finished?" Olaf slaps his hand on the bar and points at my pint glass, which is two-thirds full.

"Why are you rushing me out? Gotta change into your Santa costume for the kiddies?" I chuckle at the thought.

"If Diane and her little angel Alene can't convince me to play that jolly bastard, it's time to let the joke die." He pets his scraggly white beard.

"Then maybe lose the beard from Thanksgiving to New Year's. I remember a group of toddlers waddling after you down the street last year during the holiday parade like a pack of unemployed elves."

Olaf scowls and opens his mouth. "Keep it up and I'll ban you. Don't need some punkass half-grown kid—"

In my jacket pocket, my phone plays the opening notes to "As Long as You Love Me." I lift my finger to pause his tirade. "Hold that insult. It's Hailey."

Months ago I assigned Hailey a new ringtone and made her promise to call, not text if it's an emergency. Cheesy as hell, but the inside joke never gets old. Her name appears in the text window and I exhale with relief.

Where are you?

I quickly type out my reply.

At the Dog. Helping Olaf get in the holiday spirit.

After hitting send, I add another short message.

Everything okay? Need anything?

The bouncing dots appear and then disappear before reappearing.

I stare at my phone, waiting for her response.

"You know, you can use those things to actually speak to people," Olaf mumbles from the other side of the bar.

Ignoring Scrooge, I read Hailey's text.

Oh, can you bring me a slice of garlic clam pizza from Village?

You'll be here in two hours for the Sip n' Stroll. Can you wait until then?

Her response is instant.

NO.

I smile at her all caps reply.

Swallowing a third of my beer, I push the glass closer to Olaf. "Gotta go."

"Hailey's not in labor, is she?" Genuine concern furrows his brow.

"No, she's not due for another two weeks. She's craving a slice of pizza."

"Babies don't care about calendars. They come when they're ready. Some are impatient and others are stubborn."

"Thanks for the wisdom." I tug on my Carhartt jacket. "And the beer."

I pull out my wallet, and he shakes his head.

"On the house."

"You're welcome," I respond to his unspoken thank you. "See you in a couple of hours."

Outside, the wind's kicked up to a half-hearted howl. Against the bitter bite of the damp air, I flip the collar on my jacket before digging my hands into my pockets. The walk to the pizzeria is only one long, cold block.

It's too early for holiday strollers, but the sidewalks are an obstacle course of holiday decorations. I accidentally, and not at all on purpose, kick a kissing ball of mistletoe.

"Oops. Sorry 'bout that." I pick the ball up from the gutter and replace it on the pile.

"No problem …" an unfamiliar female voice says from above me on a ladder. "Wait, aren't you Tom Donnely?"

My feet freeze in place. This usually doesn't end well. I peer up at the woman looming over me. Her face is unfamiliar, and that's all I have to go on because she's wearing a big fuzzy beanie and a padded down coat.

I've been with Hailey for three years and the memories of the women who came before her are fuzzy. Still, I can usually remember a face, if not a name. I know my reputation would say otherwise, but the list isn't that long.

Lifting my eyebrows in happy surprise and giving her a friendly, but cautious smile, I greet her. "Hey?"

I don't mean for it to come out as a question, but my voice lifts like I'm going through puberty again. Yeah, it even cracks at the end.

"I'm June." She waves at me.

So I wave back while wracking my brain for a woman named June I've slept with. Nothing. Maybe she goes by a nickname.

"Hey." I repeat myself because I don't really have anything else to say.

"You have no idea who I am, do you?" She laughs and steps down from the ladder. I step closer to hold it steady for her. Always the gentleman.

"You're June." I give her my standard deflection answer. Damn, small town on a small island.

"I work at Diane's Pilates studio, as well as here." She points at the knitting shop we're standing in front of. "I'm new to the island."

Still doesn't ring a bell, but I exhale with relief she's never seen me naked.

"I recognized you from the Naked Whidbey calendar."

Cancel the last part. Sometimes I forget everyone's seen the glory of my bare ass thanks to Erik Kelso's antics.

Yeah, I volunteered for the calendar, because there's no way I'd ever let those Kelso brothers outdo me.

"Right, of course." My neck heats. I'm not shy, but I'm a married man and about to become a dad. The idea of being an anonymous piece of fantasy man meat doesn't sit right.

"I have something for Hailey. Can I give it to you? I thought I'd see her tonight, but it's kind of big to be toting around the streets of Langley." She's already walking inside the store.

Now that I'm sure she's not hitting on me, I follow her. "I've never been in here before. Yarn, huh?"

The walls are filled with cubbies stuffed with a rainbow of yarn. The whole place smells like wool.

She removes her beanie. Warm brown hair spills around her shoulders. Her eyes are hazel and crinkle up in the corners when she smiles at me. Pretty in an objective way. "You should take up knitting. There are a couple of men on the island who knit. You could form your own circle."

Men forming circles doesn't sound like anything I want to be a part of.

"I'm better with wood." I swallow awkwardly over the double-entendre. "And chainsaws."

Nothing sexual about chainsaws. Unless you have a *Friday the Thirteenth* fetish.

June hoists a large, brown paper bag from behind the counter. "It's more bulky than heavy."

I eye it warily. "What is it?"

"A blanket for the baby. I know you had a shower and probably have a million things already, but we still wanted to make something. Our knitting group tries to make a blanket for every new island baby."

They're lucky we're not having a population explosion.

"Uh, thanks." Great. Another blanket. I pick up the bag with one hand under the thin handle and the heavy weight surprises me. Barely avoiding dropping it, I give her a half-smile. "Did you knit it with iron?"

She doesn't laugh. "Of course not. Local alpaca."

And my sense of humor fails to hit its mark. "Probably softer for the baby. And smarter since they won't get stuck to any large magnets."

June blinks at me with a lost smile on her face.

I tell her thanks again and back out of the shop with a wave.

My phone vibrates with a new text.

Starving. What's your ETA?

Lately, Hailey goes from a little peckish to hangry in a flash. Her text is a warning I'm wise not to ignore.

I text her back.

On my way. Need anything else?

I pick up my pace the rest of the way to the pizzeria. The delicious smell of garlic and fresh dough greet me when I pull open the door.

"Ahh, Tom. Wondered when you were going to show up. Hailey called a few minutes ago. She ordered you a meatball sub." Joe gives me a sympathetic frown as he sets a large pizza box and a bag on the counter. "Said something about promising not to tell Dan she's cheating on him."

Handing over some cash, I ignore his lifted eyebrow and smirk. "We're equal opportunity pizza eaters. Happy to keep you both in business. You know, spread around the love."

Joe chuckles and focuses his attention on counting out my change. I notice he's pierced his eyebrow. It's a nice complement to the large gauges stretching his earlobes. *Probably going to regret those when he's older.* Great, now I'm channeling my dead grandfather.

"What am I missing?" I scrunch up my brow and pretend to laugh along with him.

"Eh, old gossip. You know." He winks at me.

The problem is I don't know, but I don't have time to figure out which rumor he's talking about.

"Gotta get the pizza home while it's hot." Tucking the handle of the baby blanket bag in the crook of my arm, I pick up the pizza box with both hands and balance the bag with my sandwich on top.

"You give me hope, man." He holds out his fist for me to

hit it.

"Well, you keep up the good work." I stick out my elbow not holding a bag and tap his balled hand.

Avoiding the booby-trapped sidewalks with all their holiday decorations, instead I walk down the street. Thinking the entire way back to the truck, I try to untangle Joe's comments and wink. He's a strange one. Reminds me a little bit of Jonah Kingston, Erik Kelso's business partner and brother of Ashley, Carter Kelso's true love and my old …

I trip over my own feet and tip forward, almost dropping the pizza box.

Once I steady myself, I glance over my shoulder at the pizzeria.

Wait a damn minute.

I'm a father to be, dutifully fetching food for my pregnant wife, and the hired help has the giant *cohones* to bring up my past? And insinuate we're swingers.

For the record, no one is sharing any wives in my circle of friends.

No way.

A guy gets dragged to a *party* one time, leaves by himself once he figures out what sort of *party* it was, and years later, he has to deal with a knowing wink-wink while picking up a clam pie.

Okay, clam pie sounds way dirty.

Grumbling like Olaf, I open up the truck and slide the food across to the passenger side before I start the engine. Lived my whole life on this island, going to the same places, and knowing the same people. Always loved it. Now this town feels too small for both my past and my future to coexist.

Rolling down my window as I blast the heater, I duck my head out the opening and yell to anyone who can hear, "People change, you know!"

A few pedestrians turn their heads in the direction of the truck, but I'm already pulling away.

CHAPTER EIGHT

"I was downtown a couple of hours ago. Do I really need to go back? You can't sip and you can barely stroll. I'm not sure this is a good idea." Currently sprawled on our couch in the living room, I'm rubbing Hailey's feet through her fuzzy socks.

Because I'm a loving husband. And I'm hoping it will lull her into a long nap after her two slices of pizza, handful of mozzarella sticks, and three large bites of the meatball sandwich she supposedly ordered for me. Okay, she ate half the sandwich, but only asked for "a bite or two." I have no one to blame but myself.

"It's tradition." Hailey yawns and covers it with her arm.

"You should take a nap."

"No, I'm not even tired. I don't want to miss the holiday decorations." Her eyes droop and her blinking slows.

"The decorations will be there tomorrow. And the next day. You know some of those shopkeepers will leave that shit up until after New Year's."

"It's our last chance to go as a couple before the baby." She pushes out her chin in defiance. So stubborn.

"Eh. Everyone says the holidays are more magical when you have kids."

She narrows her green eyes at me. "Did John cancel?"

"Haven't heard from him. I don't need a wingman."

"Are you sure? Remember the carolers two years ago?"

"Bunch of busybodies. I do remember one of the Kelsos trapping you under some mistletoe." I scowl at the memory.

Hailey shifts and switches her feet in my lap. "You can't still be upset with Erik for that."

"Not that. Why'd he have to get famous for being naked and stupid?"

"Are you jealous? You know your month in the calendar is my favorite."

"Better be." I squeeze her arch and she moans. "Hey, speaking of the calendar, I forgot June gave me something for the baby. I left the bag in the truck."

"June?" She wrinkles her forehead. "The yarn lady? What does she have to do with the calendar?"

"I ran into her outside the shop and she knew me, but I didn't know her. She brought up the calendar." I shrug and twist my head to avoid Hailey's stare.

"Usually that makes you preen and brag." She presses her foot against the middle of my chest. "What's wrong?"

The woman's stubborn.

"Nothing."

"Thomas Clifford, look at me." Her toes dig into my pec.

"Ouch. You have viciously strong monkey feet." Sitting up, I rub the tender spot.

"Another thing you love about me. Maybe our baby will have monkey feet, too."

I lean my head back on the arm of the couch and stare up at the ceiling.

"Or not. He'll probably have your feet with the hairy toes." She tries to tickle my side with her feet.

Instead of finding her charming and flirting back, I'm feeling grumpy.

When she sits up, I release my hold on her. Lying still, I let her shuffle to get her feet on the floor and stand. "Seriously, you're in a weird mood. I promise I won't make you wear a reindeer onesie or the elf ears."

"Never going to happen."

She scrambles over me, ungracefully swinging one leg over mine and wedging it between mine and the couch back. "I'm going to sit on you and not let you up until you tell me why you've switched from being Tigger to acting like Eeyore."

"Here's a tip, straddling me isn't punishment." Sliding my hands over the baby bump up to her full breasts, I gently squeeze them while staring into her eyes. In case she misses my point, I tilt my hips, rolling my semi against her leggings.

Hailey's eyes close before she responds by grinding against me. "You're trying to distract me with sex."

I widen my eyes to appear innocent. "I'm not the straddling party here."

"I wasn't thinking about sex when I sat on you. More like an elephant sitting on a mouse."

"Are you saying I'm small?" I remind her of how not small I am by rolling my hips again. "And stop saying you're huge. You're beautiful. Supple, ample, lush all come to mind, not an elephant."

She softly moans and the sound goes straight to my dick, which happily swells at the thought of being inside of her. I'd rather fuck my wife on the couch than face nosy neighbors in downtown Langley.

I know I've won when she presses my hands against her breasts, encouraging me to cup them. Wanting to kiss her, I sit up and lean closer. It's awkward, but she tilts forward and manages to sweep her lips over mine. The belly makes it impossible to get close enough to fully make out. Hailey sighs, defeated, and then sits up straight.

Before she can attempt to slide off of me, I grip her hips. “Oh no you don’t.”

“I’m too huge for sex.”

“The important parts still line up. And there’s always doggie style.” I wiggle my eyebrows.

“I need one of those signs across my ass that says ‘wide load.’” Exasperated, she shakes her head. “Some things can’t be unseen.”

“Saw it and loved it in the shower last month.” I remind her of our shower sex. “If I can continue going about my daily business after watching birthing videos, I think it’s proof we can all recover from sudden trauma. My body still responds to yours the same way as always.” I remind her of how much I love her body with another arch of my hips, accidentally sliding against the exit only backdoor.

Her eyes bug out to the point I see white all around her irises. “No way. I’m not trying anal. And not on the couch. No, uh uh. I could never sit here again.”

I about choke on my tongue. “Who said anything about anal?”

“You just knocked on the backdoor.” She creates space between our bodies like I’m going to magically lose my sweats and just plow through her maternity leggings like a ramming rod.

“Accident. I swear.” I pull her against me again.

Her lip trembles and her eyes fill with tears.

Oh shit.

“Hey, I swear. It was the angle. You know I’d never push you to do anything you didn’t want to do. Or make you do something that doesn’t give you pleasure, too.” I mean the words and stress the point by petting her thighs in soothing circles.

“I know.” Her voice wobbles and we’re about seven point two seconds from full hormonal meltdown. “It’s not that.”

"What is it, sweetheart?" I brush the escaped tears from her cheeks and smile up at her.

"I'm going to be a mom. I'll have a kid."

"The two are usually a package deal."

"I want to be a good mom. Like my mom. Or yours. Or Ellie. They're all amazing mothers." More tears fall from her eyes.

"True. And you will be." I attempt to reassure her.

"I don't know how to be a mom," she wails. "Now it's a done deal, and I've never had anal sex. Or gone to Paris. Or been to a sex club. Or had a fetish. Or visited the Alamo."

My brow lowers and my eyes feel like I'm watching a tennis match as I try to process her list of nevers.

"Hold on, what are you even talking about?" I attempt to slide my legs out from between hers so I can sit up more. Because, like my fading erection, the moment of opportunity has passed. We sped past the off ramp to sexy times and have arrived in the middle of downtown crazy town. "What do those things have to do with each other?"

"I don't know!" She's full out crying now. "I should've traveled more. Or experimented more."

"With fetishes?" I'm so lost. A strand of her dark hair sticks to her wet cheek. "Why can't we go to the Alamo with kids? Family road trips are as American as apple pie and hamburgers. You, me, the kid, and the open road. We can get a camper. Or a sidecar for a motorcycle." When I see the horror in her eyes, I backtrack. "Okay, not sidecar."

"We need to sell the motorcycles."

Now she's talking complete nonsense. "Why? It's not like we're going to take the kid on the bike."

"Marijuana is legal and I haven't even eaten the special cookies. Now if I do, I'll be the mom that the other mommies whisper about at the PTA meetings." Her voice quivers again. "We need to be responsible adults."

Forget tennis, this conversation is a championship ping-pong tournament with Chinese Olympians. I can't keep up, so I go for humor to add some levity to the crazy. "I've been called the other A word a lot in my life, but I think I'm more insulted now."

"Adorable?" she asks.

"Asshole."

"That too."

"By you. More than once."

"Also true," she agrees. "Because you were."

"Past tense?"

"For the most part, yes."

"Hmm," I hum against her warm, smooth skin.

"Tom?" Her voice is breathy, encouraging me.

"Mmm?" I open my mouth to place a soft kiss on the inside of her wrist.

"Unf."

"You had a question?" Lifting my eyes, I meet hers before kissing the same spot again.

She exhales slowly through her mouth. Kind of like we learned at baby class. "I forgot it."

"I love you."

"I know," she whispers.

"You better. I never want you to doubt it."

"I don't. Not ever." Her green eyes fill with more tears. "I'm so lucky you're my husband."

"I'm the lucky one."

"Can we have sex now?" she whispers.

"No holiday stroll?" I don't hide my joy at the idea of skipping the whole event.

"We can do both."

She looks so happy, I can't deny her.

We slowly peel off each other's clothes, dropping them to the floor. Even with a fire in the wood stove, the air chills our skin until I pull the throw over us. She straddles me again, and I let her take charge as I stare up at her in wonder.

"How did I get so lucky," I say, holding her hands and bringing them to my mouth. Softly, I press open mouth kisses to her wrists.

"Because you're getting laid?" Rolling her hips, she smiles down at me.

"No, because I have you as my wife." I release her hands and pinch her butt. "To have and to hold as long as we both shall live."

Lifting up, she lets me slip out of her all the way to the tip before she slides down to the base. Swallowed up by her wet velvet warmth, I thrust up into her, seeking more.

"What happened to honor and obey?" she asks with a smirk.

"Honor always, but we left out the obey from our vows for a reason. Nameless is the only one around here who should obey anyone." We're having sex and chatting. I need to up my game if she can still think in complete sentences.

"Less talking, more moaning." I gently cup her breasts, enjoying the feeling of their fullness. She encourages me by pressing her palms over my hands, and I squeeze. With my thumb and forefinger, I not so gently pinch her nipple. When her eyelids flutter closed and her full lips part, I lower one hand to where we're joined.

This earns me the moan I've been seeking. I live for making her happy. Giving her pleasure is easy. Almost as easy as loving her. She's my world and I can't imagine loving her more than I already do. But every time I think that, I'm proven wrong. When I fell in love with her, when I proposed, when she walked down the aisle in her simple white dress, when we saw the two pink lines on the pregnancy test, when she let me feel the baby kick for the first time, I thought my heart would explode with love for her because how could I love her more? Yet I do.

"I'm so close," she murmurs as she increases her pace,

grinding her hips against mine and rubbing her clit on my pelvic bone.

This is my favorite moment. Watching and feeling her come apart because of me.

"I love you," I say, trying not to come until she peaks.

"I know. So much." She shatters above me, rocking her hips and pressing my hand over her heart.

The love in her eyes, the thump of her heart under my palm break my hold on my own orgasm.

She slumps over me, resting her forehead against mine. "I'm going to miss this."

"We don't have to become those parents who never have sex." Lowering my voice and drawing soothing circles on her back, I reassure her.

"I meant over the sex draught post-partum." My hair muffles her voice until she lifts her head. "We need to have all the sex in the next two weeks."

"I say we ditch the Sip n' Stroll and spend the rest of the night naked. We have leftover pizza and there's ice cream in the freezer—at least four different kinds."

"Three. I finished the mint chip while waiting for the pizza." She lifts her head, biting her lip.

Pressing my thumb against her mouth, I free her lip. "Then we better get more."

"We can stop on the way home from Langley." She shifts off of me and I immediately feel the cold air replace her warmth. "First we need to shower."

I lift my eyebrows and curl my mouth into a wolfish grin. "Round two?"

"We'll be late." She laughs, trying to bend over to pick up her sweater.

"Leave them." Standing, I scoop up our discarded clothes. "No one will notice if we're late. And if they ask, we tell them the truth. Especially if Connie or Sandy are doing the asking."

"No. No way. Those women have vivid imaginations. I

don't need them picturing me naked, too." She dips her chin to make her meaning clear.

"Fine." I follow her up the stairs. With a pinch to her heart-shaped ass, I tease her, "Strangers at the hospital will see you in all your glory."

She stops abruptly and I bump into her back.

"Sweetheart?" I tap her shoulder.

"Is it too late to buy a kiddie pool?" she asks, her voice quiet.

"Yes. It's the middle of December."

"Home birth?"

"The nurses at Whidbey General have seen more vaginas than …"

Me.

"Than Leonard DiCaprio?" She gives me an out from the hole I was about to dig myself.

"Yes, that guy." I kiss the skin in the middle of her back.

Glancing over her shoulder, she reaches behind her for my hand. I entwine my fingers with hers before we continue up the stairs.

At the top, she turns and wraps her arms around me. Or as far as her belly will allow.

"Tom, your past doesn't matter to me as long as I'm your present."

"And my future." I place a soft kiss on one corner of her mouth. "And my forever." I kiss the other corner. Beneath my lips, I feel her smile curl and spread.

"Deal." She inhales sharply and frowns. "That was weird."

My eyes seek hers as my hands immediately go to her belly. "What's wrong?"

"Mmm." She breathes in through her nose. "Not sure. Probably nothing. Just a weird pinchy feeling. Maybe your giant penis bruised my cervix."

"I appreciate the compliment, but we've had a lot of sex

over the years, and you've never had pain after intercourse before."

"It was probably the angle. No big deal."

I eye her as we shower, watching for a sign she's feeling pain.

"Could it be Braxton Hicks contractions?" I ask as we dry off.

She furrows her brow as she considers the possibility. "I don't think so."

"Tell me if it comes back. We'll drive up to the hospital in Coupeville."

"I don't want to spend the evening at the ER for nothing. We'll miss all the fun." She walks out of the bathroom naked.

I'd still rather spend the night in bed with her, but I follow behind her to get dressed.

CHAPTER NINE

Against my better judgment about good life choices, we return to Langley for the holiday stroll.

After parking, we meet up with John and Diane in her Pilates studio.

"You're late," John says. His dark eyes take in my wet hair and I swear he knows exactly why we're late.

Ignoring him, I give Diane a half hug. Her baby beach ball is even bigger than Hailey's.

"Are you still teaching?" I ask her.

John scowls, which makes me laugh. It probably makes me a bad friend to take joy from his discomfort, but I can't help it. This is the role I play. I'm the court jester to his brooding prince.

"I'll take Mr. Grumpy's face as a yes," I say to Diane.

"Doctor says it could help speed things up. My due date was two days ago and nothing's happening down there yet. The baby's dropped, but I'm barely dilated. If I don't go into labor soon, they'll induce next week."

From the birthing class I know all too much about what she means. I'm thinking Olaf's right about keeping some things a mystery. Like mucus plugs, blood, and poop.

While Hailey and Diane share details about their last doctors' appointments, John and I stand in comfortable silence. Once again I'm reminded of the joy of being around my best friend, who never needs to fill a gap in conversation with words. I have a feeling quiet is going to be in short supply soon.

"Ready?" Hailey asks us, snapping me out of my thoughts.

"As ever," I answer her. "Where's Alene? Isn't this whole night for the kiddies?"

"She's with my aunt. Doing the hand-off on the corner." John helps Diane with her blanket wrap. Like Hailey, there's no way she could button anything over the belly. Honestly, it's impressive how big they've gotten. Like Violet Beauregard in *Charlie and the Chocolate Factory*. Only not blue. Or a couple of those middle-aged men with the giant guts and skinny legs. Only sexy. And less hairy. For the most part.

Last week I shaved Hailey's legs for her. I figured it would be the same as shaving my face, but it wasn't. Like most things with women, it was more complicated. However, toilet paper is good for leg cuts, too. Another life lesson learned.

Bodies are weird. Over the last few months, I know I've put on a few pounds. I run a hand down my own abs, thankful they're still there. No dad bod for me yet. Sneaking a glance at John, I try to tell if he's growing a man gut, but his thick red and black plaid jacket makes it hard to tell what's him and what's artificial padding.

Dan's older than us and doesn't have a dad bod. This gives me hope that it's not an automatic given.

"What are you thinking about?" Hailey tucks her gloved hand in mine.

"Dad bods."

"Is that why you're eyeing your best friend like he's smuggling something under his coat?" Her voice is quiet, and filled with amusement.

"A lot of men gain weight with pregnancy." I scratch the

back of my head, embarrassed to admit I'm thinking about my own body while she's the one growing a human.

"You're still hot." She releases my hand and pinches my ass. I notice she doesn't try to lie about my weight gain.

"And you're legally obligated to think so." Recapturing her fingers, I entwine them with mine.

"I know." She arches up, silently asking me to lean over so she can give me a kiss.

Instead of giving her my cheek, I turn at the last second and capture her lips. Halting our steps, I envelop her in my arms and deepen the kiss, slipping my tongue between her parted lips. She softly moans, wrapping her arms around my neck. The baby means I can't crush her to me like I want, but we still manage to earn a "get a room" from some random on the other side of the street.

"If you two end up in the police report again this year for public shenanigans, I'm disowning you." John laughs at us.

Giving Hailey one more quick, soft peck, I release her. Laughing, I ask, "Shenanigans?"

"There are kids around." John shrugs.

"For the record, in case anyone was wondering, we didn't actually consummate at the Inn last year. Imagine what a great story that'd be if we conceived that night?" Holding up my palm, I wait for a high five from my wife.

Hailey groans and hides her face behind her red gloves.

"Come on, I'm teasing." I peel her fingers away, grinning when she opens her eyes again. "Love you."

She shakes her head. "I know."

A crowd of people block the sidewalk ahead of us, watching something in the street.

"Oh, no. Is it the carolers?" My voice is full of dread.

"I don't hear any singing." Hailey lifts up on her toes to see over the crowd.

"Do I hear tambourines?" Diane asks.

I listen more closely, tempted to shush the people in front

of us. "Is it Santa?" I ask, forcing enthusiasm into the question. "Is he here?"

"You sound like Will Farrell in *Elf*," John says with less excitement.

"Let's not get carried away with the insults," I tell him.

"It's Olaf!" Diane and Hailey exclaim simultaneously.

"What's he doing out here? Who's watching the bar?" Curious, I force my way to the front of the group.

I'm greeted with a sight so strange and amazing, my jaw drops in awe.

Not one Olaf, not our favorite cranky bartender, but a group of Olafs. Grown-ups in snowman onesies stroll down the middle of the street, bumbling into each other and acting like idiots in an impromptu parade.

"Is that Carter?" John points to the middle of the group where a tall blond guy does a little jig.

"I think the other blond Olaf kissing the shorter Olaf is Erik, so that's probably Cari." Diane draws our attention to the couple kissing. I recognize Cari's dark hair poking out from her hood.

"Get a room. This is a family event," I yell, and they jump apart, much to my amusement.

"They're definitely getting banned this year." John's composure breaks as he cracks up in a big belly laugh.

The Olafs wave and toss candy to the kids in the crowd as they pass us.

A flash of red hair catches my eye. Ashley Kingston and I have a long history. Not as long as she and Carter, though. Their happiness shines as bright as their new wedding bands in the holiday lights. Guess she's a Kelso now. Our chapter is over, and I'm happy for them. We all deserve happiness.

Spotting us, Erik comes bounding over, waving his fake stick arms and grinning like a fool. "Happy Holidays!"

He executes a slow spin, showing off his onesie. "You like it?"

"You better stay away from the Dog tonight," John warns.

"Eh, Olaf's going to get a kick out of it. It's in homage to him." Erik even sounds like he believes his own bullshit.

"We're totally getting banned," Cari says as she joins our little group. "YOLO and all that. Plus, these things are super cozy."

"I can't believe how warm they are," Ashley echoes her. "Hi, Tom. Hi, Hailey."

We all say hello. No reason not to be friendly. The island's a small place with a long memory, but we don't have to get stuck being the people we once were. Plus, it's the holidays.

"Feel how soft this is," Cari encourages Hailey to pet her fuzzy arm.

Great. The last thing I need is my wife dressing up as a snowman. Or a pregnant snow woman. We can leave the costumes for Halloween.

"You already have your kangaroo onesie," I remind her.

"It doesn't fit anymore. I can't believe how big I got in the past six weeks." Her hand rests on her belly.

"You're huge," Erik blurts out. "Both of you."

"Smooth, bro. Real smooth," Carter chides him.

"Sorry. I swear you've gotten bigger since last time I saw you," Erik explains. Or tries to.

"Yeah, that happens when you're growing a baby. It's the miracle of life," John adds, sarcastically.

He's on fire tonight and I mentally high five him.

"Or an alien parasite that will gnaw its way out of your abdomen." Erik doesn't know when to stop.

Ashley groans. "Okay, Halloween's over. No one needs the visual. I'm just getting over the stomach flu."

Everyone takes a step away from her.

Now that I study her more closely, Ashley's skin does have a slightly green cast to it. It's a festive combination with her red hair.

"Ha ha. I'm not contagious. If I were, Carter would be sick, too."

He gives her a sympathetic half-smile. "Still think you got a bad taco from that random truck in Seattle."

"It was worth it." She pulls her hood off and fluffs her hair. Sweat dampens her hairline. "Jonah goes there all the time and he's always been fine."

"I miss tacos," Diane says with a resigned sigh. "Can't do spicy food with this baby."

"Me too," Hailey agrees. "The acid reflux ruins all my fun."

I think back to today's snack and afternoon sex with a chuckle.

"Okay, maybe not all my fun. Did I see the donut truck was going to be here?" She glances around the street. "Anyone else want some?"

"None for me." Ashley frowns and then sticks out her tongue. "I'm sticking with ginger ale and crackers tonight."

"Maybe you should go home," Diane says, concerned.

"I can rally. Worth it to see Olaf's face." Ashley gives us a thumb's up.

"Let's do this." Erik waves his brown stick arms over his head as he jogs away. His brother joins him while Cari and Ashley trail behind.

"I'm not walking in with them," John tells me. "They can sink their own ship, but I'm not going down with them."

"Aye aye, Captain, my Captain," I tell him with a snappy salute. Apparently, I salute people all the time now.

We slow our pace, letting the merry band of assholes get a substantial lead on us.

"Ashley looks like she's going to puke again," Diane says what I've been thinking.

"How long does food poisoning usually last?" I ask.

"We need to avoid her. Not being a bitch. I mean if she's

potentially sick. No way can any of us get sick right now. I puked enough the first trimester." Hailey's eyes widen.

Diane's expression mirrors my wife. "She could be ..."

Both women turn to face the retreating Olafs, like they can tell if another woman is pregnant by looking at her. Maybe they can. Maybe there's a special hormone or pheromone they can smell the rest of us can't.

"Guess we'll find out eventually," Hailey says after a moment of studying Ashley's back.

"Shall we? It's cold and now that Hailey mentioned donuts, I'm hungry." Diane rubs her rounded belly. "Baby Boy agrees."

Unlike us, the Days know they're having a boy this time. I imagine a tiny lumberjack living in a tiny log cabin in the middle of her abdomen. Like one of those sugar eggs with an oval cut out of the side where you can peer in and see a miniature world.

"Has a baby ever been born with a beard?" I ask no one in particular. "Because I have to be honest, I'm picturing a smaller version of John in there."

John casts me a dirty look, but Diane laughs.

"Apparently you're not the only one. All the baby gifts have been either plaid or wood themed," she says, tucking her arm through his. "Including a tiny felted wool axe."

We stroll down the sidewalk with the two of them ahead of us.

"I thought they weren't doing a shower. Why weren't we invited?" Yes, I'm hurt I wasn't dragged to another baby shower. But this is John, my wingman for life.

Hailey whispers back, "People still send gifts. Even without an official shower."

I pause my steps. "Hold on. We're going to be getting *more* stuff? What else can we possibly need? We have enough blankets and quilts for the biggest fort ever."

She laughs. At me, not with me. "Our friends and family want to celebrate our baby. It's a good thing."

Suddenly her laughter stops and her smile turns into a grimace. "Uff," she groans.

I press my hand over her belly. "You sure you're okay?"

"Probably." She doesn't sound confident in her answer. "I think the baby just punched a kidney. Or dented a rib."

Rubbing circles over her bump, I lean closer. "Listen, little ninja, Mom's going to get you a donut and then sit down for the rest of the night. Think you can hold off on the martial arts for a bit?"

Standing up, I catch the amusement in her eyes. "What?"

"You're adorable." She arches her neck, inviting me to kiss her.

"Don't tell anyone I'm sweet. I'll never hear the end of it at work." I give her a soft peck.

"You're lucky I can be easily bribed with donuts," she says, smiling against my mouth.

"And you're lucky I'm happily bribed with sex. Win-win for everyone." After another quick kiss, I take her hand in mine.

"My husband is insatiable."

"When it comes to you? Always. I'll shout it from the rooftops like Santa." I point to the festive lights on the Dog House.

"Not necessary." She pulls our joined hands closer to her.

"How about in the middle of First Street?" I ask as we cross the intersection.

"You're crazy."

"And yet you love me. I think that makes you crazy, too." I kiss her again, middle of the street, not caring who sees us because I want the world to see what real love looks like.

"We're all mad here." Her warm breath caresses my face when she laughs.

"Wouldn't have it any other way. Now let's find you some

donuts." I spot the donut truck parked kitty-corner to the Dog House. White lights stretch from the roof to an umbrella stand, creating a cheerful landing strip to guide us to the truck.

"Ooh." Diane changes directions ahead of us, making a straight line for the truck. Too big to run, she and Hailey speed waddle to the front of the line.

CHAPTER TEN

Two bags of mini donuts along with large cups of cocoa purchased and partially consumed, we stroll toward the bar. We pause near the small park because carolers in hideous holiday sweaters block the door.

"Any sign of the Olafs?" Diane asks, biting into a cinnamon sugar covered donut.

"Maybe they're already inside?" Hailey's mouth is full and her words come out in a jumble.

The chorus is mid fa-la when they abruptly stop singing.

"Uh oh," Hailey whispers between bites.

Carolers scatter as a mass of white tumbles out the Dog's front door.

"Enough! You're all banned for the rest of the year," Olaf shouts, not amused.

"That's only seventeen days," Erik says, sounding disappointed.

"Shut up. You want longer?" Carter grumbles and shoves his brother into the street.

"I swear they want to get banned for life. Last year was the Rudolf onesie and then the grumpy old man costume for

Halloween." I'm both impressed and scared for them. Even I know when to draw the line.

Once Olaf's stormed back inside, we approach the Kelsos. Carter's rolled down the top of his onesie and tied the arms around his waist. He's got to be cold in only a white T-shirt.

"You still look like a snowman," John tells him. "Only now you're half melted."

He makes a good point. "You shouldn't antagonize Olaf. He has a heart condition. You want him to blow an artery over your antics?"

I'm about to start yelling about staying off of Olaf's lawn. John rests his hand on my shoulder. "I think you made your point. I don't think anyone is trying to murder Olaf with laughter."

"No one wants him dead," Erik says, serious for the moment. "Dan's taken over managing the business for him so Olaf can focus on being cranky."

"Where is Dan?" Hailey asks, and I don't like the eagerness in her voice when she says his name. I'm well aware all the women on the island have a crush on him.

"He's in Seattle with Roslyn," Erik replies. "Some fancy party. He was grumbling about wearing his tux."

"Batman," Carter and I say at the same time.

"Where's Ashley?" Cari spins around. "Why didn't she get kicked out with the rest of us?"

"I think she's in the bathroom," Carter answers, his brows drawn together with worry. "She's been in there a while."

Cari and Diane meet eyes. "Uh oh. We'll go check on her."

Hailey joins them, leaving the guys standing on the sidewalk surrounded by confused carolers, the sippers, and the strollers.

A woman with two pint-size mini humans approaches and asks if her daughters can get their picture taken with Carter and Erik.

Even ridiculous, the two of them are magnets for selfies.

Erik agrees, but asks the pics don't end up online or social media. The mom looks confused, but agrees. She must not be from around here.

After they get their pictures, the group wanders away singing about building snowmen.

"You two should take it on the road," I suggest.

"We could dress up the goats. People love goats in pajamas and costumes." Carter takes me seriously. The man is obsessed with goats.

"We could have onesie day at the coffee house. I bet Jonah would be into it," Erik muses out loud.

"Where is the dark one?" I ask.

"He said he had an event over in town tonight. I don't think holiday festivities are his thing," Erik explains.

"Anyone know what his thing is?" John asks. "Just curious. He's always kept to himself."

"He likes live music. Obsessed with good coffee. And tattoos. And his old VW Bus." Carter lists random things like he's reading off Jonah's dating profile.

That's it. Four things we know about Jonah.

"He also doesn't mind standing around in a coffee hut all day." Erik doesn't add much to the knowledge pool.

"He's always been quiet," John comments, which coming from a guy who doesn't talk a lot himself is saying something.

A sharp blast of icy wind shakes the boughs around the windows and jostles the decorative bells.

"Why are we standing around outside? We're not banned." I jerk my thumb toward the door. "I'm going inside for a beer."

John agrees and we head inside.

There's no sign of our wives, Ashley, or Cari near the front of the bar. We order beers and find a spot near the wall to stand.

"How long until we send a search party into the women's room?" John asks, then swallows a third of his pint.

"They're fine." I sip my own beer and watch Olaf yell at more customers who start singing "Do You Want to Build a Snowman?" near the door.

"No blocking the exit," Olaf shouts from his spot behind the bar. In that position, I can imagine him hiding behind a wall of snow, lobbing snowballs at his enemies. Maybe next year I'll bring him a supply of real snow to toss at anyone who pisses him off. Knowing him, he'd probably complain about the snow melting on the wood floor.

"Hey." Hailey slides next to me.

"Hey yourself. Everything okay with Ashley?" I sling my arm over her shoulders.

Diane makes a small gagging noise. "She barfed again."

"We've all been there," I confess, vaguely recalling a night right after I turned twenty-one. "I upchucked off the back deck."

Ashley appears at her side in leggings and a long sleeve T-shirt wearing Diane's sweater, her onesie balled up in her arms. "Ugh. This might be worse than when I threw up on the ferry."

"I've never prayed at the porcelain throne here," John brags.

"Me neither." Diane grins up at him. "Then again, I didn't grow up here."

"We'll make you a plaque," I tell them. "Are you okay, Ashley?"

"I feel better, but think I'll call it a night. Where's my dear husband?" She scans the crowd.

I point to the front door. "Out in the cold with the rest of the exiled snow people."

Cari joins our group. "Oh no. For how long?"

"Only two weeks." John laughs.

"Erik will be disappointed, yet relieved it's not for longer,"

Cari says, with a disapproving shake of her dark hair. "He's a magnet for trouble."

"Olaf must be feeling generous with the holiday spirit." Ashley gives us a weak smile. "And on that note, I'm going to go home. If I don't see you before, Merry Christmas."

"Hopefully we'll have this baby before then," Diane says as they hug. "You're on the phone tree list, right?"

Ashley nods. "Roslyn's too."

Hailey fidgets next to me. We're way past her having any reason to be jealous over Ashley. Our mutual history is ancient. But the two women are never going to be best friends. Still, Hailey rubs Ashley's shoulder and gives her a friendly smile. "Hope you feel better."

"You too. Get off your feet and drink some water." Ashley squeezes Hailey's hand. "And with that, this girl is going home."

She and Cari weave their way through the crowd around the pool table.

My eyes go to Hailey. "Are you okay?"

"My back's bothering me and I'm feeling a little crampy."

"Are we sure Ashley's not contagious?"

"I hope not." Hailey's hands drop down to support her belly. "There's been enough vomiting tonight."

"And enough talk about it, too." John finishes his beer before setting it on the ledge behind us. "We need to collect Alene from my aunt. They're at the gingerbread house display down the street."

Diane's eyes widen. "I completely forgot about our daughter. I'm a horrible mom."

"Blame the Kelso brothers and their shenanigans," Hailey offers. "That's what Tom does."

I nod. "Always makes me feel better."

John pulls his phone from his jacket pocket. With a couple of taps, he opens up a picture of Alene happily smiling, face streaked with red, green, and white icing. "She's fine."

"We should go give your aunt a break." Diane wraps her blanket scarf around herself.

"You're going to freeze out there." John pulls off his jacket and cocoons her inside it. Even pregnant and about to deliver a baby, the coat swallows her up. Because John's a giant.

Beside me, Hailey sighs.

"I can give you my jacket if you want," I whisper to her. "Anything for you."

She sighs again. Or exhales with force. I can't tell the difference.

"Hailey?" I step away from her to get a better look at her.

Carolers open the front door and begin entering the bar as they sing and play their tambourines.

"Christmas, Christmas," the women in their festive holiday sweaters sing. The carolers in the front jam themselves between the exterior door and the swinging bar doors like cows in a chute.

"No!" Olaf shouts.

The soloist drowns out his voice as she sings the first words, "The snow's—"

"Leave! You're trespassing!" Olaf waves his white bar towel in a circle around his head. "Out!"

Only they can't exit because they're shoved together in the narrow space, blocked by the ones behind them, all belting out the joy of the season at the top of their voices.

"I just peed myself," Hailey shout-whispers in my ear over the carolers' singing.

CHAPTER ELEVEN

Add peeing herself to the list of things I never expected to hear my wife tell me in public. Especially not at the Sip n' Stroll. Or standing in the middle of the Dog House.

Or anywhere.

"Better here than in the fancy baby store on a thousand-dollar chair," I shout back, figuring that will make her feel better.

Or not.

Her eyes are wide, and I take her expression as embarrassment.

"At least you didn't puke." I lean close to reassure her and speak directly next to her ear. "Don't worry. Olaf's had far worse on this floor. He's got a bucket of industrial cleaner in the back. He's distracted enough I can probably grab the mop and take care of it before he notices. In fact, steal that empty barstool and chat him up while I clean up."

Frowning, she presses her hand against her belly.

"Oh, right. You probably don't want to sit in pee pants."

Her brows crease together and she continues to sweep her hand low over the baby.

"Sweetheart, it's not a big deal. I'm sure it's happened to

other pregnant women, too. Want me to find Diane? Maybe she has some spare maternity leggings at the studio." Reassuring her, I pat her shoulder, slowly turning her in the direction of the stool with my other hand.

"Tom," Hailey says my name so quietly I barely hear her

"You're right. We should go home. How many times can we listen to Sally take a solo on this song before we want to jump off the bluff? And you're completely sober. I'm an asshole. We should've left after your jumbo cup of cocoa. No wonder you peed."

"Tom." She repeats my name, but this time with a serious tone. "Stop."

I lift my hand off of her shoulder so she can face me.

The carolers finally finish "Baby Come Home" and the crowd politely claps while Olaf tries to herd them out of the bar.

"If you want to stay, you all have to buy something to drink. Cash only," he bellows at them as he tries to get through the crowd.

"I think my water broke," Hailey shouts at the same time the room quiets. Her words echo around the bar like we're in an empty cavern.

"Your water broke?" I yell into the silent void because maybe the two guys at the urinals in the men's room didn't hear her the first time.

Embarrassed color heats her skin while she nods. "I think so."

Two young bucks in elf onesies take giant steps away from our general area like she might blow again.

It's too late to avoid the splash zone. Not that there's much to see. Not like in the movies. Given the lighting in here, I can't see anything on the floor. But I'm not about to put my face down there to take a closer look.

"Tom?" Hailey's voice is far away and muffled.

Olaf's grumbling and stomping around, madder than

normal. He rings the large brass bell at the end of the bar he normally reserves for last call or closing time. "I'm only going to say this once, so everyone listen up. I need you caterwauling miscreants to zip it, and back the hell up. Clear the damn door! There hasn't been a baby born in this bar in over fifty years. That's not going to change tonight. We've got a woman in labor. I need all you numskulls to clear a path to the door."

While he's rambling on, I'm staring at the floor. Someone snaps their fingers in front of my face.

"He's frozen," a woman's voice comments and a few people snicker at the movie pun.

"Carry him out if you need to, but you better get to the hospital." Olaf's familiar snarl breaks through the fog.

"Your water broke?" I ask for confirmation.

Hailey nods. "We should go."

"To the hospital?"

"I think we can go home and call our OB," she corrects me. "I don't think I'm having contractions."

"You're not due for another two weeks." I'm not ready. I thought I was prepared, but I'm not. Panic and flashbacks from the birthing videos release a cold sweat down my back. "Are you sure it wasn't pee?"

"I went while we were all in the bathroom."

"There's a storm coming in. We should go to Coupeville." I don't want to delay and get stuck.

"We'll probably be sent home," Hailey says, with a grimace. "Oh. Uff."

Her face crumples and she grips my arm tighter.

"Contraction?" I stare at her stomach as if I can see through her body.

"Maybe?" She exhales through her mouth.

Resolved, I straighten my back. "That's it. We're going to Coupeville."

"We don't have my bag or the things for the baby with us."

Hailey stalls. "Just because my water broke doesn't mean I'm having the baby tonight."

"We're going to the hospital. Storm's kicking up and I don't want to recreate some sort of pioneer home birth with boiled water and shredded bed sheets. Someone can swing by the house and get everything. Text your mom on the way to Coupeville."

Hailey nods and exhales again. "That was definitely a contraction."

She's in labor. Something clicks inside my brain. "How bad's the pain? Should you sit down?"

"No sitting. No babies born in this bar. I'll call nine-one-one if I have to." Olaf's shooing people out the door. Even though he's slowly clearing us a path, he tells us to go through the side door.

Outside the wind howls through the trees as it blows up from the water behind us. Temperature's dropped and a fine mist of sleet is falling. The kind that turns to ice if it gets cold enough.

"Nope. We're going back inside. You can sit down and I'll go get the truck." I pause to breathe. "First, we need John and Diane. They've been through this. You shouldn't be alone."

"Tom," Hailey touches my arm, "I'll be fine. I'm sure I have hours and hours of labor to go. Get the truck and I'll text Diane."

Lifting my eyebrows in doubt, I study her face. "Are you sure?"

"Fine. But if I do have the baby here, we're naming him Olaf. Go." She leans up to kiss my cheek.

I'm halfway down the deck when I catch she called the baby a boy. Grinning, I spin around and yell, "No way our son's going to be named after a snowman!"

She grins as she goes back inside the bar.

As I cross the street, I spot John and Diane in front of the

Clyde. Alene sits on his shoulders, banging out a drumbeat on his head. I reroute to tell them the news.

Diane's eyes grow big and she's already crossing the street before I can finish giving them the details.

"Go get your truck," John reminds me of my mission. "We'll go to your house and bring your stuff to the hospital."

With a quick thanks, I jog through the alley and cut through the parking lot to shave off a minute of my trip to the studio.

My lungs burn from the frigid air by the time I reach my rig. Inside, I crank up the heat to warm things up for Hailey.

A paper-thin layer of ice coats my windshield. The wiper blades scratch over it as more tiny pellets hit the surface.

Damn ice. Better we're going now than later tonight. We might not make it up the island if the wind keeps up. With one main road, a few downed trees can cut us off pretty quick. There's always the ferry, but if the storm gets bad enough, they'll stop the runs early tonight.

Honking my horn, I send people scampering out of the way. I pull to a stop in front of the Dog House, not caring I'm going the wrong way on the street. Until I get Hailey to the hospital, I can't waste another second. She says we have hours, but that's how those stories on the news about babies born in the back of cabs always start.

Flanking Hailey, Diane and John escort her out the door. I jump out and run around to her side.

"I think she's having a real contraction," Diane explains while Hailey pants beside her.

"Hold up." Hailey lifts her hand and bends forward, breathing heavy.

I freeze and watch her, helpless to do anything.

"You should start timing them," John tells me. "They're going to ask when you arrive at the hospital."

"Right, right." I scramble for my phone and drop it on the

wet asphalt. I cringe before picking it up and exhale when I see the screen isn't cracked. "Timer."

My fingers feel too fat to punch in my code or open the timer.

"Here." Hailey holds out her hand. "I'll handle the phone while you drive."

"Contraction over?" I rub her back as I help her around the truck to get in.

"For now."

Diane leans around me. "Breathe through the pain. Don't hold your breath. We'll be right behind you."

The two of them hug for a second before Diane steps back. Hailey nods, her eyes watery.

"Okay, this truck is going to baby town and I need everyone to get the fuck out of our way," I tell the crowd of holiday strollers.

Sally's in the middle of her solo on "Do They Know it's Christmas Time?" and messes up her words.

Her head spins around to face me as the lights on her yeti sweater blink and flash blue, casting her face in an eerie light. "Baby?"

Shit.

"Gotta go." I climb into the truck and put it in gear.

"Guess we won't need to worry about making an announcement," I tell Hailey. Glancing in the rearview mirror, I see Sally pull out her phone and start tapping the screen.

"Saves us the effort." Hailey types on her own phone and I can hear ringing as she switches to speaker phone. "Hi, Mom. The baby's coming."

CHAPTER TWELVE

Hailey has several more contractions on the drive to Coupeville. Despite my urge to speed, I follow the posted limits, even slowing further when we hit water on the road and possible black ice. The last thing I want is to end up in a ditch because of impatience.

Beside me, Hailey breathes through another contraction. There's nothing I can do for her other than to hold her hand and match my breath to hers. When her grip loosens, I know the pain has passed.

"How long was that one?" she asks.

I glance at my phone in its holder on the dashboard. "Thirty seconds."

"Longest thirty seconds ever," she mutters. Staring at her own phone and its separate timer, she says, "Closer to eight in between that time."

"That escalated quickly," I joke with her. Because if I lose my humor, it will allow the creeping panic to take over. My role is to be strong, to support her through this process.

She half laughs, lacing her fingers through mine.

Tiny ice pellets fling themselves against the roof and windows of the truck, pinging off the metal and glass like miniature BBs. The windshield wipers create a soothing rhythm against the sound of tires on the wet road. Clouds block out any moonlight on the dark two lane road. My brights highlight the falling drops and downed branches from the wind.

"Helluva night," I say to fill the silence.

Hailey pats her belly. "You better not be teasing us, little one. We could be home in bed, eating ice cream, cuddling with Nameless, and watching Netflix."

"You realize our entire lives are about to change, right?" So much for being cool about what's about to happen.

Her laughter fills the cab before ending with a snort. "Yes, I'm aware. This winter will be all of the above, plus breast-feeding and diaper changes."

"I'm not sure I'm into wearing a diaper. I think we can pause whatever we're watching long enough for bathroom breaks."

"Stop, I might actually pee if I laugh more." A crease forms between her brows. "I think I'm having another contraction."

"How long has it been?" I reset the timer on my phone as I roll to a stop at the one traffic light in Coupeville.

"Seven minutes and ten seconds." The words come out in a rush as she breathes through the pain.

"We're almost there." I take the right turn and another right to pull into the hospital lot. Parking in front of the doors, I jump out and rush inside, leaving the truck running and Hailey waiting in the cab.

"My wife's in labor," I shout as soon as the sliding doors open.

"Where is she?" an older woman with gray hair asks from the desk.

"In the truck." I gesture in the general direction of the door.

"First baby?" she asks, peering over her glasses at me with her judging eyes.

"Yes. I'll, uh, go get my wife."

"Use a wheelchair," she calls after me.

Weird, but I locate one near the door and push it outside.

Hailey opens the door and stares at the chair.

"Required transportation for my lady," I use a falsetto voice while making a sweeping bow.

She raises her eyebrows, but doesn't question the wheelchair or my weird voice.

Once inside, a nurse takes over my driving duties and tells me to check in at the desk while she wheels Hailey away.

I fill out the paperwork as quickly as possible and hand the clipboard back to the woman in the yellow cardigan and glasses.

"Have a seat and someone will be with you," she tells me without looking up.

"I'm having a baby, I mean, my wife is in labor. Can't I just go back to her room? I, uh, don't want to miss anything and she shouldn't be alone. We have breathing exercises and I have the timer on my phone. For the contractions. We've been timing them since they started." I hurriedly stumble over my words and overshare.

"Sir, have a seat. I promise, you won't miss the good stuff." She points a red painted nail at the ER waiting area. Only a few people occupy the uncomfortable chairs.

"Thanks, I'll stand."

"You do you," she says and picks up her phone again.

Dismissed, I pace toward the closed doors where Hailey disappeared.

"Sir, don't think about sneaking in there. Trust me. Everything will be fine." Cardigan in charge catches me.

"Do you tell everyone that? Because it's not always true. My grandfather died here a couple of years ago. Not everything was fine then. Bad things happen in the hospital. So excuse me if I'm worried about my wife who is about to have another human exit her body." Now I'm a combo meal of emotions. "I'll be over there."

I walk to the far side of the waiting room and lean against the wall. *Elf* is playing on the TV angled on the wall in the corner, but the volume is too low to hear. So that's pointless.

Pacing is better.

Making a long loop from the waiting room, I pace past the desk toward the forbidden doors, past the exit and halfway down the hall but not far enough away I'm out of earshot should someone call my name.

"Tom?" a familiar voice says from behind me.

John and Diane stand a few feet behind me near the cardigan wearing gatekeeper.

"Hey." Relieved they're here, I pace closer to them.

"Where's Hailey? Everything okay?" Diane asks, peering around me to the waiting area.

"They took her back an hour ago and won't let me see her." I glare at the gatekeeper.

"Sir, you've been here ten minutes. Fifteen tops. You're probably going to be here a while, so I would encourage you to dig deep and find some patience."

My brows lower as I glower at the top of her head because she's already looking down at her phone again.

Diane intervenes. "Can you tell me the OB on call tonight?"

"Dr. Price," she replies without glancing up at us.

"Wonderful," Diane says. "We'll be over here."

"Can I get anyone a cup of mediocre coffee from the café? It's only seven thirty, they should still be open," John offers. "Something to do while we wait?"

"Donnely," a nurse calls my name. "Donnely?"

"Over here." I wave at her.

"Come with me."

"We'll be here. Let us know when you're settled in a

room." Diane gives my arm an encouraging squeeze.

Stoic as ever, John nods and pats my shoulder. "She's going to be fine."

Coming from him, the words don't feel hollow. He knows what it's like to suddenly lose someone he loves.

I follow the nurse through the doors and down a hall lined with curtained rooms. She's talking about vital signs and fetal monitors, but I'm only half listening. Instead, I hear the beep of various machines and the squeak of her rubber soled clogs on the clean floor.

"Here she is." Pulling back one of the curtains like she's revealing a prize on a game show, the nurse reveals Hailey propped up in a hospital bed.

"Hi, stranger," she happily greets me. "What took you so long? Trouble finding parking?"

"Shit. The truck's still parked at the curb. Do I have time to move it?" I ask the nurse.

She chuckles and winks at Hailey. "Plenty."

When I return, Hailey's by herself, eating ice chips.

"Where's the nurse? Shouldn't the nurse be in here?"

Hailey laughs. "We're going to be here a while. If it wasn't for the storm and the chance we couldn't make it back, they'd send us home."

"So we're staying?" I eye the world's most uncomfortable chair next to the bed.

"Don't worry, we're moving to the maternity ward and a birthing suite. It's a bigger room with a cot for you," the nurse tells us.

"Sweet." Leaning over the rail, I give her a kiss. "Sexy nightgown by the way."

"I'll ask if I can bring one home." She pets the ugly cotton fabric.

"Are we ready to do this?" I ask.

"No and yes." Her hand finds mine. "I'm ready not to be a tiny human's punching bag but I'm scared of the pain."

Her eyes hold fear and worry. There's nothing I want more than to erase both, but I'm sure she sees the same behind my eyes.

"We're going to get through this. Together." Bending over, I lower my face close to hers so our noses almost touch. All I can see is her face, her beautiful evergreen eyes framed by dark lashes, and the fullness of her bottom lip. She's my whole world. "I love you and I can't wait to meet Tom Junior."

We've discussed names and have a running list of favorites, but junior isn't in the serious running.

"Nice try." Her smile fades as a contraction begins.

The nurse reappears and checks the monitors.

"Everything looks normal. We'll be moving you upstairs in a couple of minutes." Her monotone is probably meant to be reassuring.

Once we're in the private room, I text John and Diane our new location. Even with their company, time crawls as we wait for Hailey's labor to progress.

Hours go by and her contractions stall around four minutes apart.

"You two should go home," I tell John after he yawns for the tenth time.

"Can't. Big cedar is down on Bayview and we're cut off. No way to get down to the beach until they clear it."

"Figures it would be the one stretch of the island with no drive around options."

"Tell me about it. Did you hear the ferry shut down an hour ago because of the waves? Dan texted me on their way back from Seattle. They caught the last boat. Left early because Ros wasn't feeling well."

"Let's hope she doesn't have the same flu as Ashley," Diane says with a shudder. "Oh, that was weird."

"What?" John asks, shifting in his chair to face her.

Diane's hand rests just below her navel. "Not sure."

"Do you need the nurse?" Hailey's finger hovers over the

call button.

"No, I'm okay. I think. Mind if I use the bathroom?"

John and I meet eyes when she excuses herself.

He shrugs and stretches out his long legs in front of him. "She's been having back pain all day, but says it doesn't feel the same as Alene's labor. And to quit fussing over her."

"She is past her due date," Hailey reminds us.

Diane returns a few minutes later and stands in the doorway to the hall.

"Everything okay?" John asks.

"Uh, I just lost my mucus plug," she says with a cringe.

Add that to the list of things I didn't expect to hear tonight. At least she didn't lose it at the Dog House. Olaf might've exploded from information overload.

"Are you in labor?" Hailey asks, hope in her voice.

"I think so. I'm waiting for the nurse." Diane's eyes meet John's. "You better call your aunt and let her know she might have Alene longer than we thought."

John stands up and stretches. "I'll be right back."

After they both disappear, Hailey turns to me. "Isn't this exciting? Our babies are not only going to grow up together, but might share the same birthday? We can have co-parties."

"Great." I fake mirroring her enthusiasm.

Shortly after, John texts me that Diane's getting admitted. He pops his head in our door and tells us they're set up in the room next door. When the nurse gives Hailey the go ahead to get out of bed and walk to help her labor progress, her first stop is Diane's room.

As the minutes crawl closer to midnight, Diane's labor speeds up much quicker than Hailey's. From our room, we can hear the sounds and moans of her actively pushing shortly after eleven.

Disappointment creases Hailey's brow. "Why aren't I pushing? I've been in labor longer."

"Honey, it's only been a few hours. This is their second

baby. From what I read, labor with the second child is typically quicker."

She blinks away the tears stuck to her lashes. "You read the baby books?"

I nod. "Of course I did. I read the e-books on my phone during lunch so the assholes at work wouldn't have shit to tease me about."

"I love you," she says over the loud grunting and moaning through the wall behind her bed.

"I know." I softly kiss her forehead, then her temple and each cheek before pressing my lips against hers.

The sounds of labor go quiet and a high-pitched scream announces the arrival of the new baby.

"Will you go check on them?" Hailey asks.

"Uh, I'm really terrified of walking in and seeing Diane's vagina," I answer truthfully. "So how about we wait until John comes back?"

My confession makes her laugh.

About half an hour later, John knocks on our door.

"Congratulations," Hailey says with a tired smile. "How are Mom and baby?"

His eyes go soft and unfocused for a second before a happy grin reveals his teeth. "They're great. Mack is healthy and Diane's a champ."

"That was fast," I say, envious their wait is over while Hailey's contractions have stalled completely. At this rate, they might give her Pitocin, and if that doesn't work, a C-section because her water already broke.

"We barely had time for the epidural before he was ready to come out."

"I love the name." Hailey's voice breaks with emotion.

"His full name is Malcom John Day. For Diane's father. Mack for short."

"I can't wait to meet him," she says through her tears.

"Diane's resting and trying to get him to nurse, but maybe

if you're up and walking around later you can come for a visit."

"I'd love that." A big fat tear rolls down her face.

"Sweetheart, our baby is going to be here soon. There's no going back now." I try to comfort her, but I'm not sure my words make a difference. Men are supposed to be strong and tough, but going through labor with my wife only reinforces my belief that women are far stronger and fearless than us.

"You're doing great," John reassures her with his calm voice. "It'll all be over before you know it."

Easy for him to say. I don't think they've even been at the hospital four hours and they're done with the hard part.

After he leaves, I carefully crawl into bed with Hailey and wrap my arms around her the best I can with the tubes and monitor wires attached to her.

"Let's get some rest while we can." I yawn into her hair.

She snuggles into my arms on her side, fighting her own yawn as she mumbles, "I'm going to be pregnant forever."

If I could take her place, I would. If I could wave a magic wand and speed up the process, I'd wear wizard robes for the rest of my life. I hate the helpless feeling of not being in control and not being able to fix this for her.

I dim the light above the bed and pull the blanket over us as we drift off to sleep.

Voices in the hall wake me up. I have no idea how long I've been asleep. The room is still dark and outside the sky is as inky as it was before. It could be a half hour later or early morning.

Hailey's still softly snoring. Easing myself off the too small for two bed, I tuck the blanket around her before tiptoeing to the open door. A quick glance at the clock tells me it's two fifteen.

I'm not expecting to see Ros and Dan. She's in a wheelchair being pushed down the hall by a tired nurse while he walks beside them.

CHAPTER THIRTEEN

"I have a birth plan. We toured Harborview's labor and delivery wing. This isn't how we planned it." Roslyn's near tears. Her normally neat hair is in a messy bun and she's wearing green plaid pajama pants and a pink sweater. Like she woke up and got halfway dressed.

Dan soothes her. "Nothing is how we planned and our lives have turned out better than I ever imagined. We have to give up control and have faith that this is how it's meant to be. Dr. Price and her team are excellent."

Roslyn begins to cry. "I wanted our daughter to be born in Seattle. Like me."

"We can forge her birth certificate," he tells her and I believe him.

"How?" she whispers.

An exhausted John appears next to me and mumbles, "Batman."

"Pizza mafia," I say, quietly, bringing up our old joke about Dan's mysterious life outside of Sal's Pizza.

The new arrivals haven't noticed us yet.

"It's the weirdest slumber party I've ever been to," John voices what I'm thinking.

"None of them had the same due date. Was it something in the donuts?"

"Maybe, but Roslyn didn't have any." He foils my conspiracy theory with reality.

Dan lifts his head and stares at us with his mouth open. "Hey, what are you two doing here?"

"Having babies. All the cool kids are doing it tonight apparently. At least the Days," I answer with an edge of snark.

Roslyn's eyes widen. "Did Diane have the baby? Hailey, too?"

"Yes and no. Mack Baby Day is here, but Baby Donnely is being stubborn," I say.

"Imagine a stubborn Donnely," Roslyn replies with a smirk.

I fill them in on the highlights of the evening. The fake Olafs getting kicked out by the real one, Hailey's water breaking by the pool table, the mad rush to get here in the storm, and now the waiting.

Dan nods and frowns in the appropriate places. "That's why we're here. Roslyn wasn't feeling great at the party so we headed home. Caught the last boat and wished we drove around. I've never been on the ferry when waves crashed over the sides."

"I thought I was going to puke," Roslyn says. "When we got back to the house, I still was feeling nauseated and crampy. Dan decided to call our OB and he told us to come to the hospital in spite of the storm. It's icy and miserable out there."

"Maybe you have the stomach flu like Ashley. She yakked in the ladies' room at the Dog." I forgot to mention that detail in my recap.

"I hope not." Roslyn frowns. "I'm confident it's Braxton Hicks contractions. But Dan wouldn't listen."

He gives her a loving smile. "Better to be here than stuck at home if it's not a false alarm. The doctor agreed."

"Hmmph," Roslyn responds.

"Tom?" Hailey's sleepy voice calls to me from her room.

"Gotta go."

"We'll be down the hall." Dan points to the door two down from where we're standing.

I enter the room to the sound of beeping from the baby monitor. Before I reach Hailey, Betty the nurse rushes past me.

"Is everything okay?" I stand at the foot of the bed, touching Hailey's foot just to make contact with her. Her face crumples in pain.

"Contractions have resumed," the nurse states the obvious in her monotone.

"It woke me up," Hailey says through gritted teeth.

"On a scale of one to ten?" Betty studies the monitor's lines and numbers.

"Eleven." The word comes out on an exhale once the contraction ends. "Much worse than the earlier ones."

"I'm going to check to see if you've dilated more." Betty snaps on a pair of purple latex gloves.

I step out of the way as Betty has Hailey open her legs underneath the sheet.

"Looks like we're having a baby this morning," Betty tells us while removing her gloves. Her tone lacks the excitement this statement should require.

A wave of emotion crashes into me as salty tears prick at my eyes. "We are?"

"Kid's going to come out one way or another." She gives me a comforting pat to my forearm. "I'll get Dr. Price."

Seeking out Hailey's hand, I gently sit on the side of the bed near her head. With our fingers entwined, I raise our hands to my mouth. I kiss the side of her thumb and meet her eyes. "Ready?"

"No," she says, her chin wobbling.

"You could try crossing your legs," I tease.

"Should've thought of that thirty-eight weeks ago." She grimaces.

"Another one?" It's soon. I didn't time this one, but it's only been a couple of minutes. If that.

She nods and grips my hand with impressive strength. Like her, I breathe through the pain as each contraction comes and goes.

Dr. Price arrives and greets us with her typical warm smile. In spite of it being four in the morning, she's bright eyed and friendly.

"I think we're ready for an epidural," she says after her exam. "If you want one."

Hailey nods her head vigorously.

A short man in a rumpled white coat helps Hailey roll to her side and then sticks a needle into my wife's spine like it's no big deal.

What follows is a blur.

There's more snapping purple gloves, more equipment being wheeled into the room, and more nurses. Betty is back along with a nurse named Jenny for the baby. Soon, or hours later, I've lost track of time, Hailey shifts to the end of the bed to begin pushing.

For some reason, I focus on the Santa oven mitts Betty slips over the cold metal of the stirrups. They're weirdly festive and out of place for the seriousness of the moment.

Hailey's parents arrive. I don't remember calling them, but someone must've. I'm grateful they're here as backup. Hailey cries when her mom hugs her. Her dad excuses himself shortly after they arrive.

"He doesn't do well with blood," her mom explains.

Mrs. King flanks Hailey on the other side of the bed when things get serious. I try to focus on Hailey and this moment, committing everything to memory as she pushes.

The helpless feeling returns. I hold her hand, brace her back, murmur words of encouragement, but this is all her. Her strength, her ability to endure the pain amaze me. There's no way I could do this.

"Want to see the head crowning?" Dr. Price asks from where she's sitting between my wife's legs.

I do and I don't. The desire to witness the very second I become a dad wins out. I nod, unable to speak because a thousand emotions jam my throat.

I blink and try to comprehend the impossibility of this moment. There's blood and fluids and Hailey groaning, almost screaming. And the doctor speaking, encouraging me to hold Hailey's thighs. I breathe and blink and try not to cry. Or pass out.

"One more push," Dr. Price commands. "Give me one good push."

Lifting my gaze to Hailey's face, I feel tears streak down my face. We're not alone, but when our eyes lock, the rest of the room disappears. I whisper, "I love you."

"I know." She closes her eyes and her body clenches as she pushes.

"Here we go," someone says as I focus on Hailey. "The baby's almost out."

And in that moment of love, in our bubble, our baby is born.

"It's a boy," Dr. Price says.

Gawking at the tiny, white-goo and blood covered, howling human she's holding, I try to absorb her words.

"A boy," Mrs. King whispers, emotion thickening her voice. She's holding up her phone, recording this moment. I'm grateful because it never occurred to me to pull out my phone.

Tears run down my cheeks into my beard. "Shit, look how big his balls are."

Yes, these are the first words I say as a father.

Hailey laughs, soft and exhausted, but it turns into a guffaw that ends in a snort.

"They're really huge." I meet her eyes, moving closer so I can kiss her. "He's definitely a Donnely."

"Want to cut the cord, Daddy?" Dr. Price asks as our baby squawks and squirms at the rudeness of being born.

Awed, I nod and make the snip between the clamps.

The nurse lays him on Hailey's chest. "Meet your son."

And now we're all crying. Well, not Betty, but she does crack a smile.

A few moments later, she tells us she needs to measure and weigh him.

My son continues to announce his arrival with impressive wails as he's weighed, measured, foot and finger printed, and given his tiny baby ID bracelet matching Hailey's.

"Want to hold your son?" Betty asks, stepping to my side with a tiny burrito in her arms. At least he's no longer screaming.

"Are you sure that's a good idea?" I imagine my arms losing their ability to follow my brain and the baby dropping to the ground or being flung across the room.

"He's sturdier than you think. Come sit down." She gets me set up in the chair next to the bed and shows me how to position myself before placing him in my arms.

"You're a natural," she encourages me.

I feel wooden and anything but comfortable, but I put on a brave face.

Once the rest of the delivery is over and all messy evidence is cleaned up, Mr. King returns, my parents following behind him.

"Congrats, Dad," my own father tells me as he peers down at my son.

More tears fall and I don't try to hide them. The moment is surreal.

"Thanks."

The room turns into a lovefest with the "I love yous" bouncing from person to person. Hailey holds our son, looking more beautiful than ever.

John shows up and we hug. Another first.

"Congratulations," he says. "Do you have a name picked out?"

Hailey clears her throat. "Shaw Clifford Donnely."

The log jam of emotion bursts in my throat. This is real.

Dad takes a shaky inhale. "Your grandfather would be proud of you."

Mom's full out crying on Mrs. King's shoulder. "This is the best first anniversary gift ever."

Oh shit. Amid all the baby prep, I completely forgot our first wedding anniversary. Sneaking a peek at Hailey, her surprised expression, all wide eyes and parted lips, tells me she forgot too.

"Paper is the first year, right? Does a birth certificate count?" she gives me an apologetic smile.

"Best gift ever. And we don't need to build a new house to store it." With a kiss to the crown of Hailey's head, I say thank you.

"Let's give the new parents and baby some quiet time to rest. They've been up most of the night." Betty herds our family out of the room.

Hailey holds Shaw in her arms and I curl around her on the bed.

"You amaze me. I thought I loved you with everything I could, but I was wrong."

Sighing, she twists her head so she can see my face.

I place my hand on Shaw's tiny back where he's snuggled against her chest. "I love you more. You've never been more beautiful than in this moment, holding our son."

Her hair is a mess, her eyes are bloodshot with exhaustion, and dark circles hollow out her face above her cheekbones, but I speak the truth.

"I love you, even when you lie." She softly laughs, her focus on Shaw. "We have a baby."

I rest my hand over hers on his back. "I suppose it's too soon to talk about having more."

Hailey blows out a breath through her mouth. "Way too soon."

Later in the morning, Hailey's sitting up in bed, inhaling a piece of coffee cake and I'm drinking a quadruple latte from Whidbey Joe's when Dan makes an appearance.

"Hey, I hear congratulations are needed." Shaking my hand, he grins at both Hailey and me.

"This is Shaw." Hailey proudly points at her exposed breast where our boy is nursing like a champ.

Yep, he's a Donnely.

"He's perfect," Dan says, his voice full of awe. Not even commenting on seeing Hailey's boob, Dan jabs his finger at my cup. "You have coffee?"

He sounds jealous.

"Erik brought a whole tray." I point at the windowsill. "There's a macchiato and another latte, if you want to claim them."

"How's Roslyn?" Hailey asks, sprinkling crumbs on her robe.

"She's sleeping. False alarm last night, but with the weather, we stayed over. Room was already paid for."

Like money's a concern for them.

"I'm sorry," I tell him because I am.

"Thanks." He sips from the large paper cup. "We'll induce if nothing happens by Christmas."

"Is this where the party is?" Carter pokes his head through the door.

"What are you doing here?" I ask, accepting his half body hug.

"Right now, visiting all the babies." Waving, he tries to peer at Shaw. Or check out Hailey's boob.

"Aren't the roads a mess?" I ask, feeling like we've been here for weeks. So long that I'm sure we live here now.

"Not too bad. Sun's supposed to come out this afternoon and warm up the ice."

"You didn't have to come all the way up here to see us. Baby's not going anywhere." I'm touched by the fact he showed up, but it's unexpected. We're not close.

"Ashley woke up sick again, so I told her enough is enough. She's waiting on some tests in the ER." His brows pull together. "Might not be food poisoning."

His phone chirps with a text notification. Glancing at it, his brows relax. "Jonah's on his way. Said he got stuck over in town last night but he's driving around."

"Is it serious?" Hailey says, shifting the baby to her other breast.

Hopping up, I cover her exposed nipple. I mean, this is a natural mothering moment, but I don't need every guy I know getting a gander.

She scoffs at me. "No one cares."

"I do." I kiss her cheek and Shaw's cap covered head.

"Tests results are in," Carter says. "I'll be back as soon as we know something."

"Wear a hazmat suit. Don't come back if you're contagious," I advise him. "Or at all."

I say that part after he's left.

Dan eyes Hailey's coffee cake. "Are there more pastries? I'm starved."

"You should always travel with garlic knots. I've told you this more than once." I hand him the bag of baked goods. "Bring some to Roslyn, too."

After he leaves, the morning is a revolving circus of family and friends visiting. The women sniff Shaw's head like witches inhaling bits of his soul while the men stand around and feel awkward. At least I do.

Roslyn and Dan stop by on their way out, but don't linger. Not that I can blame them.

Diane and Mack visit for a while with John hovering over both. Our babies don't share a birthdate, but close enough. I imagine our sons growing up together, being best friends and wingmen.

Jonah shows up after our families leave. He brings a fresh round of coffees and more food. His white shirt and black jeans are rumpled and overall, he looks worse for wear. His dark hair is a rat's nest on top of his head and it looks like someone drew a lightning bolt on his forehead with a sharpie.

"Rough night?" I point to my own forehead.

Embarrassment colors his cheeks. "Uh, yeah. Mind if I use the bathroom?"

"Not at all," Hailey replies.

"Any word about Ashley?" I ask him when he returns with a clean face.

He rubs his lips together like he isn't supposed to share.

"Think we were right?" Hailey asks Diane.

"Right about what?" My focus shifts between the two women.

"Not food poisoning?" Diane's eyes go wide and then she smiles. "I'd put money on it."

"Ugh, if I get the two exits, no waiting from them, I'm going to be pissed." I glower and cross my arms. Damn Kelsos.

"You can't catch what she has," Hailey says with a smile.

"Huh?" I turn to John and Jonah. "I'm lost."

"No idea. Is it serious?" he asks Jonah.

"Life changing," Diane proclaims with a knowing nod of her head.

"Sounds serious," I say, worried.

"She's pregnant," Hailey bursts out.

"Act surprised when they tell you. I wasn't supposed to say

anything." Jonah stares at us. "You guessed it, so I didn't break my promise."

"Sheesh, what's in the water around here?" John mumbles.

"Stork better get his own wingmen." I grin down at Hailey.

"Still too soon," she whispers before laughing.

CHAPTER FOURTEEN

"I have a birth plan. We toured Harborview's labor and delivery wing. This isn't how we planned it." Roslyn's near tears. Her normally neat hair is in a messy bun and she's wearing green plaid pajama pants and a pink sweater. Like she woke up and got halfway dressed.

Dan soothes her. "Nothing is how we planned and our lives have turned out better than I ever imagined. We have to give up control and have faith that this is how it's meant to be. Dr. Price and her team are excellent."

Roslyn begins to cry. "I wanted our daughter to be born in Seattle. Like me."

"We can forge her birth certificate," he tells her and I believe him.

"How?" she whispers.

An exhausted John appears next to me and mumbles, "Batman."

"Pizza mafia," I say, quietly, bringing up our old joke about Dan's mysterious life outside of Sal's Pizza.

The new arrivals haven't noticed us yet.

"It's the weirdest slumber party I've ever been to," John voices what I'm thinking.

"None of them had the same due date. Was it something in the donuts?"

"Maybe, but Roslyn didn't have any." He foils my conspiracy theory with reality.

Dan lifts his head and stares at us with his mouth open. "Hey, what are you two doing here?"

"Having babies. All the cool kids are doing it tonight apparently. At least the Days," I answer with an edge of snark.

Roslyn's eyes widen. "Did Diane have the baby? Hailey, too?"

"Yes and no. Mack Baby Day is here, but Baby Donnely is being stubborn," I say.

"Imagine a stubborn Donnely," Roslyn replies with a smirk.

I fill them in on the highlights of the evening. The fake Olafs getting kicked out by the real one, Hailey's water breaking by the pool table, the mad rush to get here in the storm, and now the waiting.

Dan nods and frowns in the appropriate places. "That's why we're here. Roslyn wasn't feeling great at the party so we headed home. Caught the last boat and wished we drove around. I've never been on the ferry when waves crashed over the sides."

"I thought I was going to puke," Roslyn says. "When we got back to the house, I still was feeling nauseated and crampy. Dan decided to call our OB and he told us to come to the hospital in spite of the storm. It's icy and miserable out there."

"Maybe you have the stomach flu like Ashley. She yakked in the ladies' room at the Dog." I forgot to mention that detail in my recap.

"I hope not." Roslyn frowns. "I'm confident it's Braxton Hicks contractions. But Dan wouldn't listen."

He gives her a loving smile. "Better to be here than stuck at home if it's not a false alarm. The doctor agreed."

"Hmmph," Roslyn responds.

"Tom?" Hailey's sleepy voice calls to me from her room.

"Gotta go."

"We'll be down the hall." Dan points to the door two down from where we're standing.

I enter the room to the sound of beeping from the baby monitor. Before I reach Hailey, Betty the nurse rushes past me.

"Is everything okay?" I stand at the foot of the bed, touching Hailey's foot just to make contact with her. Her face crumples in pain.

"Contractions have resumed," the nurse states the obvious in her monotone.

"It woke me up," Hailey says through gritted teeth.

"On a scale of one to ten?" Betty studies the monitor's lines and numbers.

"Eleven." The word comes out on an exhale once the contraction ends. "Much worse than the earlier ones."

"I'm going to check to see if you've dilated more." Betty snaps on a pair of purple latex gloves.

I step out of the way as Betty has Hailey open her legs underneath the sheet.

"Looks like we're having a baby this morning," Betty tells us while removing her gloves. Her tone lacks the excitement this statement should require.

A wave of emotion crashes into me as salty tears prick at my eyes. "We are?"

"Kid's going to come out one way or another." She gives me a comforting pat to my forearm. "I'll get Dr. Price."

Seeking out Hailey's hand, I gently sit on the side of the bed near her head. With our fingers entwined, I raise our hands to my mouth. I kiss the side of her thumb and meet her eyes. "Ready?"

"No," she says, her chin wobbling.

"You could try crossing your legs," I tease.

"Should've thought of that thirty-eight weeks ago." She grimaces.

"Another one?" It's soon. I didn't time this one, but it's only been a couple of minutes. If that.

She nods and grips my hand with impressive strength. Like her, I breathe through the pain as each contraction comes and goes.

Dr. Price arrives and greets us with her typical warm smile. In spite of it being four in the morning, she's bright eyed and friendly.

"I think we're ready for an epidural," she says after her exam. "If you want one."

Hailey nods her head vigorously.

A short man in a rumpled white coat helps Hailey roll to her side and then sticks a needle into my wife's spine like it's no big deal.

What follows is a blur.

There's more snapping purple gloves, more equipment being wheeled into the room, and more nurses. Betty is back along with a nurse named Jenny for the baby. Soon, or hours later, I've lost track of time, Hailey shifts to the end of the bed to begin pushing.

For some reason, I focus on the Santa oven mitts Betty slips over the cold metal of the stirrups. They're weirdly festive and out of place for the seriousness of the moment.

Hailey's parents arrive. I don't remember calling them, but someone must've. I'm grateful they're here as backup. Hailey cries when her mom hugs her. Her dad excuses himself shortly after they arrive.

"He doesn't do well with blood," her mom explains.

Mrs. King flanks Hailey on the other side of the bed when things get serious. I try to focus on Hailey and this moment, committing everything to memory as she pushes.

The helpless feeling returns. I hold her hand, brace her back, murmur words of encouragement, but this is all her. Her strength, her ability to endure the pain amaze me. There's no way I could do this.

"Want to see the head crowning?" Dr. Price asks from where she's sitting between my wife's legs.

I do and I don't. The desire to witness the very second I become a dad wins out. I nod, unable to speak because a thousand emotions jam my throat.

I blink and try to comprehend the impossibility of this moment. There's blood and fluids and Hailey groaning, almost screaming. And the doctor speaking, encouraging me to hold Hailey's thighs. I breathe and blink and try not to cry. Or pass out.

"One more push," Dr. Price commands. "Give me one good push."

Lifting my gaze to Hailey's face, I feel tears streak down my face. We're not alone, but when our eyes lock, the rest of the room disappears. I whisper, "I love you."

"I know." She closes her eyes and her body clenches as she pushes.

"Here we go," someone says as I focus on Hailey. "The baby's almost out."

And in that moment of love, in our bubble, our baby is born.

"It's a boy," Dr. Price says.

Gawking at the tiny, white-goo and blood covered, howling human she's holding, I try to absorb her words.

"A boy," Mrs. King whispers, emotion thickening her voice. She's holding up her phone, recording this moment. I'm grateful because it never occurred to me to pull out my phone.

Tears run down my cheeks into my beard. "Shit, look how big his balls are."

Yes, these are the first words I say as a father.

Hailey laughs, soft and exhausted, but it turns into a guffaw that ends in a snort.

"They're really huge." I meet her eyes, moving closer so I can kiss her. "He's definitely a Donnely."

"Want to cut the cord, Daddy?" Dr. Price asks as our baby squawks and squirms at the rudeness of being born.

Awed, I nod and make the snip between the clamps.

The nurse lays him on Hailey's chest. "Meet your son."

And now we're all crying. Well, not Betty, but she does crack a smile.

A few moments later, she tells us she needs to measure and weigh him.

My son continues to announce his arrival with impressive wails as he's weighed, measured, foot and finger printed, and given his tiny baby ID bracelet matching Hailey's.

"Want to hold your son?" Betty asks, stepping to my side with a tiny burrito in her arms. At least he's no longer screaming.

"Are you sure that's a good idea?" I imagine my arms losing their ability to follow my brain and the baby dropping to the ground or being flung across the room.

"He's sturdier than you think. Come sit down." She gets me set up in the chair next to the bed and shows me how to position myself before placing him in my arms.

"You're a natural," she encourages me.

I feel wooden and anything but comfortable, but I put on a brave face.

Once the rest of the delivery is over and all messy evidence is cleaned up, Mr. King returns, my parents following behind him.

"Congrats, Dad," my own father tells me as he peers down at my son.

More tears fall and I don't try to hide them. The moment is surreal.

"Thanks."

The room turns into a lovefest with the "I love yous" bouncing from person to person. Hailey holds our son, looking more beautiful than ever.

John shows up and we hug. Another first.

"Congratulations," he says. "Do you have a name picked out?"

Hailey clears her throat. "Shaw Clifford Donnely."

The log jam of emotion bursts in my throat. This is real.

Dad takes a shaky inhale. "Your grandfather would be proud of you."

Mom's full out crying on Mrs. King's shoulder. "This is the best first anniversary gift ever."

Oh shit. Amid all the baby prep, I completely forgot our first wedding anniversary. Sneaking a peek at Hailey, her surprised expression, all wide eyes and parted lips, tells me she forgot too.

"Paper is the first year, right? Does a birth certificate count?" she gives me an apologetic smile.

"Best gift ever. And we don't need to build a new house to store it." With a kiss to the crown of Hailey's head, I say thank you.

"Let's give the new parents and baby some quiet time to rest. They've been up most of the night." Betty herds our family out of the room.

Hailey holds Shaw in her arms and I curl around her on the bed.

"You amaze me. I thought I loved you with everything I could, but I was wrong."

Sighing, she twists her head so she can see my face.

I place my hand on Shaw's tiny back where he's snuggled against her chest. "I love you more. You've never been more beautiful than in this moment, holding our son."

Her hair is a mess, her eyes are bloodshot with exhaustion, and dark circles hollow out her face above her cheekbones, but I speak the truth.

"I love you, even when you lie." She softly laughs, her focus on Shaw. "We have a baby."

I rest my hand over hers on his back. "I suppose it's too soon to talk about having more."

Hailey blows out a breath through her mouth. "Way too soon."

Later in the morning, Hailey's sitting up in bed, inhaling a piece of coffee cake and I'm drinking a quadruple latte from Whidbey Joe's when Dan makes an appearance.

"Hey, I hear congratulations are needed." Shaking my hand, he grins at both Hailey and me.

"This is Shaw." Hailey proudly points at her exposed breast where our boy is nursing like a champ.

Yep, he's a Donnely.

"He's perfect," Dan says, his voice full of awe. Not even commenting on seeing Hailey's boob, Dan jabs his finger at my cup. "You have coffee?"

He sounds jealous.

"Erik brought a whole tray." I point at the windowsill. "There's a macchiato and another latte, if you want to claim them."

"How's Roslyn?" Hailey asks, sprinkling crumbs on her robe.

"She's sleeping. False alarm last night, but with the weather, we stayed over. Room was already paid for."

Like money's a concern for them.

"I'm sorry," I tell him because I am.

"Thanks." He sips from the large paper cup. "We'll induce if nothing happens by Christmas."

"Is this where the party is?" Carter pokes his head through the door.

"What are you doing here?" I ask, accepting his half body hug.

"Right now, visiting all the babies." Waving, he tries to peer at Shaw. Or check out Hailey's boob.

"Aren't the roads a mess?" I ask, feeling like we've been here for weeks. So long that I'm sure we live here now.

"Not too bad. Sun's supposed to come out this afternoon and warm up the ice."

"You didn't have to come all the way up here to see us. Baby's not going anywhere." I'm touched by the fact he showed up, but it's unexpected. We're not close.

"Ashley woke up sick again, so I told her enough is enough. She's waiting on some tests in the ER." His brows pull together. "Might not be food poisoning."

His phone chirps with a text notification. Glancing at it, his brows relax. "Jonah's on his way. Said he got stuck over in town last night but he's driving around."

"Is it serious?" Hailey says, shifting the baby to her other breast.

Hopping up, I cover her exposed nipple. I mean, this is a natural mothering moment, but I don't need every guy I know getting a gander.

She scoffs at me. "No one cares."

"I do." I kiss her cheek and Shaw's cap covered head.

"Tests results are in," Carter says. "I'll be back as soon as we know something."

"Wear a hazmat suit. Don't come back if you're contagious," I advise him. "Or at all."

I say that part after he's left.

Dan eyes Hailey's coffee cake. "Are there more pastries? I'm starved."

"You should always travel with garlic knots. I've told you this more than once." I hand him the bag of baked goods. "Bring some to Roslyn, too."

After he leaves, the morning is a revolving circus of family and friends visiting. The women sniff Shaw's head like witches inhaling bits of his soul while the men stand around and feel awkward. At least I do.

Roslyn and Dan stop by on their way out, but don't linger. Not that I can blame them.

Diane and Mack visit for a while with John hovering over both. Our babies don't share a birthdate, but close enough. I imagine our sons growing up together, being best friends and wingmen.

Jonah shows up after our families leave. He brings a fresh round of coffees and more food. His white shirt and black jeans are rumpled and overall, he looks worse for wear. His dark hair is a rat's nest on top of his head and it looks like someone drew a lightning bolt on his forehead with a sharpie.

"Rough night?" I point to my own forehead.

Embarrassment colors his cheeks. "Uh, yeah. Mind if I use the bathroom?"

"Not at all," Hailey replies.

"Any word about Ashley?" I ask him when he returns with a clean face.

He rubs his lips together like he isn't supposed to share.

"Think we were right?" Hailey asks Diane.

"Right about what?" My focus shifts between the two women.

"Not food poisoning?" Diane's eyes go wide and then she smiles. "I'd put money on it."

"Ugh, if I get the two exits, no waiting from them, I'm going to be pissed." I glower and cross my arms. Damn Kelsos.

"You can't catch what she has," Hailey says with a smile.

"Huh?" I turn to John and Jonah. "I'm lost."

"No idea. Is it serious?" he asks Jonah.

"Life changing," Diane proclaims with a knowing nod of her head.

"Sounds serious," I say, worried.

"She's pregnant," Hailey bursts out.

"Act surprised when they tell you. I wasn't supposed to say

anything." Jonah stares at us. "You guessed it, so I didn't break my promise."

"Sheesh, what's in the water around here?" John mumbles.

"Stork better get his own wingmen." I grin down at Hailey.

"Still too soon," she whispers before laughing.

EPILOGUE

THE NIGHT BEFORE CHRISTMAS

White lights on the Christmas tree illuminate our living room in a warm glow. It's Christmas Eve and barely a creature is stirring. Even Nameless is snoring on his bed in front of the wood stove.

Sitting in the most comfortable baby chair ever with a Boppy propped under my arms, I glance around the room, finally understanding the Grinch's point-of-view. My heart must have grown in physical size to accommodate the emotion I feel for my wife and child.

Hailey holds Shaw nestled against her chest, only the top of his head visible outside his baby burrito wrap. Next to her on the couch, Mack sleeps in Diane's arms after nursing. In my old recliner, Alene snuggles on John's lap, listening while he reads her *The Night Before Christmas*. Every now and then, her head dips forward and she jerks it back as her lids droop with sleep. I don't know how she's still awake.

Ros and Dan are curled up together on the other couch. Their daughter was born three days after the babypalooza. Ginger haired Ione sleeps on Dan's chest, swaddled and snug. I'm pretty sure Ros is asleep.

I blink away the tired burn in my own eyes. Neither Hailey nor I have slept more than a few hours at a stretch the past ten days. I can't imagine John and Diane have gotten much more than us, given they have a toddler and a newborn.

The logs snap and pop, the room warm from the fire as snow lightly falls outside. White flakes cling to the boughs of the cedar trees and grass. Some random Christmas music softly plays through the speakers as people recover from the big feast.

Shaw's only nine days old, but whenever he sees Alene, he stops crying. And he cries a lot. But when she's close by, he's content. I'm not sure if he can even focus his eyes yet.

Then again, he *is* a Donnely. With his pale blond fuzz and a single dimple, he already takes after his father. Handsomest baby around.

John's not amused and has declared more than once my son will never be allowed to date his daughter.

We'll see about that.

That's a long way off. We have years of these kids growing up together. Another generation of island boys chasing girls and making fools of themselves.

I hope they end up even half as happy as I am now. A few years ago if you told me I'd be married and a dad, I would've laughed my ass off and then called you crazy.

Stranger things have happened, but in my life, nothing has been better than falling in love with Hailey. Loving her has made me a better man, someone worthy of loving her and Shaw. The tomcat has been domesticated and I've never been happier. If I could, I'd probably purr with contentment.

Yeah, I'm that much of a mush ball.

It's probably the lack of sleep.

Let's go with that.

John reads the last line of the poem, "Happy Christmas to all, and to all a good night."

"Peace on earth, goodwill to man," I respond, the words holding more meaning now as we hold the future in our arms.

Wouldn't change a thing in my life.

Except another little combo of Hailey and me. Or two. Twins.

It's always good to have goals for the new year.

A DAN & ROSLYN BONUS SCENE

DAN

"Are you sure we're doing the right thing? We hardly know that woman. She could be a baby smuggler." Roslyn peered in the tiny side mirror of the convertible. "We should go back. Park here and we'll return on foot. Keep the element of surprise. Maybe cut through the olive grove. Or better, the grape vines will provide better coverages. We'll sneak through the vineyard. That's the best idea."

Fighting my grin, I shifted the vintage Alfa Romeo Spider into third gear.

"Why aren't you slowing down?" She glanced over her shoulder at the billowing cloud of dust behind us before staring at me. "What are you doing? We need to go back and make sure our daughter is okay."

The rising screech in her voice told me she was making herself panic.

"Love, she's fine." I ignored her glower, downshifting to take a tight curve. Ahead the road narrowed into a single lane under an arched bridge. No one was coming from the other direction, so I sped up, swiftly gliding through the underpass. "Maria Cristina is a nonna. She has five children and seventeen grandchildren of her own. If anyone is capable of watching Ione for two days, it's her. Our daughter will be doted upon and spoiled, fed pastine and fresh burrata like a tiny queen. We'll be lucky if her first word isn't Nonna."

Roslyn's gasp was soft and barely audible over the car's engine, but the horrified expression on her face confirmed I've gone too far. Her chin wobbled and two fat tears rolled down her cheek.

She brushed her fingertips beneath her oversized sunglasses. "You … you don't think that will happen, do you? She's probably a genius and will start speaking early. What if we miss it?"

I lifted my hand from the knob of the gearshift and gave her thigh a squeeze. "We won't miss it. She's six months old. Months away from talking. I promise."

"You can't keep that promise." Pushing her glasses to the crown of her head, she swiped at her eyes. "This was a mistake. You should go to Venice on your own. I'll stay at the house with Maria Cristina and Ione. Maybe she'll teach me how to make pasta or harvest chicory. Or hunt for non-deadly mushrooms."

The road we were on was too narrow to pull over and I was forced to keep driving while my wife softly cried in the passenger seat. Tall umbrella pines lined this stretch of the Appian Way. I was grateful to the Romans for their civil engineering, but wish they had the foresight to make wider roads. A few hundred yards ahead, I spotted a small gas station and pulled into their lot.

"Are we going back?" Ros eyed me hopefully.

"Is that what you really want? Or would you rather FaceTime Maria Cristina and reassure yourself Ione is okay, then continue our trip to Venice and be wined, dined, and thoroughly seduced by your loving husband?" I tucked a wild strand of her auburn hair behind her ear, dragging my finger over the sensitive skin there and then down the soft expanse of her neck to her shoulder. Her white sundress had thin straps and already the strong Italian sun heated her skin, leaving it slightly pink.

With a sigh, she leaned into my touch. "Am I being ridiculous?"

There was no right response to that question. Instead of answering it, I leaned across the small gap between us and kissed her softly. "We can go back if that's what you really want. Venice isn't going anywhere."

"It's sinking. Rising sea levels mean eventually it will disappear." She blinked away the tears lingering on her lashes. Taking a deep inhale, she held it for a few seconds before slowly blowing out the air. "I'm okay. We can go. Maria Cristina is more than capable."

"Want to call her?" I pointed at my phone on the dash where it's showing our current location on the map.

"No, that's a lose-lose situation." She flipped down the sun visor and checked her face.

"How so?" I asked, placing a soft kiss on the warm skin of her shoulder.

"If Ione is inconsolable, my heart will crack into a thousand pieces and we'll have to go back immediately. And if she's fine, then my heart will break because she doesn't even miss me." She faced me, her lips trembling again. "I don't want to spend our entire weekend crying."

"Oh, sweetheart." With my index finger, I turned her chin toward me so I could brush my lips against hers. "You will never be replaced as Ione's mother. How is this different than when the nanny cares for her while you work?"

"For one thing, I'm normally in the guest house across the driveway. I can't run from Venice back to Lazio if something happens."

"I can't promise nothing will happen, but between Maria Cristina, Luca, and Teresa, they'll take good care of her. Back on the island, we've let Tom and Hailey babysit her."

Her lips twitched with a smile. "I trust Hailey."

"What about my cousins?" Maria Cristina's mother was my grandfather Sal's sister. This made her my second cousin, or first cousin once removed. Something like that. Didn't matter, family was family. Especially here in Italy. We've been embraced with love and fed until bursting by people I've only met a few times in my life.

"I trust them more than Tom. Or the Kelsos." Roslyn removed her sunglasses and picked up her enormous sun hat from the floor by her feet. "I'm better. We can go."

"Promise?" I asked, softly, my fingers tracing the small eyelets in the fabric covering her thigh.

She nodded. "I love Maria Cristina. Remember when she made me special pasta for pregnant women when we were here last summer? I know Ione will be fine."

"Are you sure?" I had to triple check.

"Yes, take me to Venice and ravish me. We can spend all day making love in the hotel and order room service."

"We could do that in Rome and save ourselves the drive." I offered, half serious. "We could back to Antico Forno Roscioli. Or that pizzeria on the road behind the Vatican."

She peered at me from beneath the oversized brim of her hat. "We already spent a week in Rome. Does this have anything to do with those shiny pizza tools you were eyeing at the ferramenta in Genzano?"

I gave her a shy grin. "Busted. I can't help it. They're so beautiful. Handcrafted. The quality of the pizza peels is better than anything we can get at home. Jeff and Coop back at Sal's will be over the moon. Did you see the olive wood handles? Bellisima!"

I touched my fingers to my thumb, kissed them, and then released them into a single jazz hand. Roslyn laughed and rolled her eyes. "Everything in Italy is bellisima to you. Before we arrived here, I thought you only used that word for me." She pushed her full bottom lip into pout.

"There are many beautiful things in the world, but only

one tesoro mio." While staring into her eyes, I lifted her hand and placed soft kisses on the inside of her wrist.

"Dial it down, Romeo." She laughed, but her pupils were dilated and her pulse fluttered beneath my lips.

With a final kiss, I released her. "Too much, tesoro mio?"

Her eyes fluttered closed. "You know what that expression does to me."

"Then I should call you tesoro mio every day." I snuck a quick peck to her lips. "Shall we go?"

She replaced her sunglasses gave me a cheeky smile. "Andiamo, mi amore!"

I melted whenever she called me her love. She was right about the Italian making the little terms of affection ten times more powerful.

Once we were on the straightaway and I didn't have to shift as often, I reached for her hand, entwining our fingers together. We drove that way in silence for a while, enjoying the sun and scenery.

"I have an idea," she said above the wind. "You could buy the guys the David aprons with the magnifying glass over the penis. Those seemed to be a popular near the Pantheon. They'd be much easier to pack and they'll fit in our checked bags." Her teasing me was a good sign we were past the mini-freakout.

"First, I'll ship the new pizza equipment home. Second, why in the name of all that is good and holy in the world, would I want my kitchen crew to look like they're naked? That was the worst idea since whoever decided to make those aprons." My scowl was exaggerated to emphasize my disgust. I released her hand to downshift because of a slow truck ahead of us.

Her grin turned into full giggles. There was nothing in the world more beautiful than Roslyn full of joy. Apologies to Michelangelo and his fellow masters.

With a knowing arch to her eyebrow, she rested her hand

high on my thigh. "The only person I ever want to see naked in the kitchen is you."

"Too bad you're not the only one. I still have second thoughts about the Naked Whidbey calendar." I grimaced. "At least me and my apron are so two years ago."

She frowned and wouldn't meet my eyes.

"What?" I asked, fearing my one time stint as a nude model upset her.

"I probably shouldn't tell you this, but Connie has her favorite months framed and Sandy glued this year's calendar pages over the old ones. Cari's talking about doing a new version this year." She bit her lip and I was pretty sure it wasn't because she was nervous to tell me, but to keep herself from laughing.

Resigned, I close my eyes. "How are we going to explain this to Ione?"

"Hopefully the fascination will have died down in five or ten years."

"Stop laughing." I attempted to still my face into a stoic expression reserved for martyred saints.

"Take me to Venice. All that beauty will distract you from your poor decisions in the past." She squeezed my thigh before patting it.

I knew she meant the splendor of the architecture and the magical beauty of the canals, but all I pictured was her, naked and perfect on crisp white sheets.

We parked the car near the airport and hired a private taxi to carry us across the lagoon to Venice. Our driver maneuvered his pristine, vintage wooden boat through the busy water, slipping through the evening gondola and vaporetto traffic of the Grand Canal to deliver us to the private waterside entrance of our hotel.

Upstairs in our room, Roslyn immediately opened the sheer white curtains and then the tall windows facing the canal. Leaning out over the small, Juliet balcony, she happily shouted, "Hello, Venice. I've missed you."

From down below, a male voice returned the greeting. "La bella rossa! Vieni qui e mi dai una bacio."

Another male voice joined the first. "Anchio. Stasera sono tutto per te!"

"Anchio," repeated a few more men before their words turned into a chorus of laughter and insulting each other.

Laughing, Roslyn twisted to face me, her eyes full of questions. "What are they saying?"

"From my limited Italian, I think they're suggesting you open up a kissing booth." I leaned past her so the horny Venetians could see she was taken. To prove my point, I pulled her into my arms and kissed her until her laughter made it impossible. Clapping and cheers drifted up from the water below.

"What was that for?" she asked, breathless and a little dazed.

"Staking my claim, Cara Mia," I softly growled against her mouth. "Easier than running down four flights of stairs to the canal and throwing all of them into the water."

Her hooded eyes widened. "That water is disgusting."

So were the things they want to do to my wife.

"That it is." I gave her another quick kiss to her lips. "Enough with those canal rats, what should we do with ourselves? Overpriced Bellini on Piazza San Marco? Gelato at that little place near the Rialto bridge? Squeezing a quick visit to the Academia? Gondola ride through the canals?"

With each suggestion, I peppered her neck and freckled shoulders with kisses while toeing off my shoes and slowly leading us away from the window. Reluctantly breaking contact with her skin, I yanked my T-shirt over my head.

"Or we could find a little bar and have *cicchetti*." I slipped a finger under one delicate strap of her dress and slid it off of her shoulder, revealing a paler line of skin. Repeating the movement on the other side, I gently tugged her loose dress down her torso until it pooled in a white cloud around her feet. With a kiss to each sun-kissed shoulder, I reached behind her and undid the clasp of her bra. "There's always the option of going to the top of the bell tower for the view."

"This view is my favorite." Her fingers roamed over my chest and abs before she dipped them into the waistband of my shorts. "We could always take a boat to Murano and buy some glass."

My patience evaporated when she palmed me. I spun her around and pressed her back to my front, cupping her full breasts in my hands. "Or we could spend the afternoon making love, tesoro mio"

She responded by threading her hand through my hair and pulling me down for a kiss. "Sono tutta per te."

I'm all yours.

"Sempre," I whisper between kisses.

Always.

A JOHN & DIANE BONUS SCENE

JOHN

"Alene's too young to go to school." I pick up the tiny backpack from the counter and dangle it off of my fingers.

"I know. It's not even preschool and it's only a few hours a couple of times a week." Diane scoops up the pink bag and sets it on the counter. "She has to be three to start preschool. This is more pre-preschool, slightly more than daycare."

I'm not some sort of old fashioned caveman who thinks my wife is the only one who can care for my children. I just hate the idea of my daughter stuck in some germ-infested, viral petri dish daycare where the carpets probably have never been steam-cleaned and she'll be exposed to the nose-pickers and future glue-eaters.

While I glower at Diane, she fills a small baggie with Cheerios and seals it shut. Next she adds apple slices and grapes to a small Tupperware container.

"Stop giving me the stink eye. She's going to have fun." A small line appears between her eyebrows.

"If she's only going for the morning, why are you packing her enough snacks to last a week?" I point at the squeezy tube of bananas and strawberries she's stacked on top of the other food.

"I don't want her to get hangry." The line deepens between her brows.

Leaning my forearms on the counter to bring my face down to her level, I study my wife. Completely focused on stacking the snacks inside of the bag, she refuses to meet my gaze. Other than the furrow in her forehead, her lips are pressed together and her shoulders are tight. In fact, they're locked like she's tense or ready for a fight.

"Hey," I whisper, reaching out to rest my hand on her shoulder. The muscle bunches and releases beneath my hand.

"Don't look at me with those eyes." She lifts her chin and stares up at the ceiling.

Her lower lashes sparkle with tears and her green eyes shine with emotion.

The sound of my children crying is a distant second to seeing Diane cry. My heart gives a tight squeeze in my chest when a single tears breaks free and trails down her cheek. She quickly wipes it away before swiping her fingers under both eyes and blinking back more tears.

"Stop." I still her hands, pulling her toward me by her wrists until I can wrap her arms around my torso. Enveloping her in a hug, I press one hand to the back of her head and kiss the crown. "She's going to be fine."

Diane's sigh blows warm air over my chest. "You're right. She's too young for school. What was I thinking? More and more people homeschool their kids. Makes complete sense. Why should I separate her and Mac? These are the days when they'll form their brother and sister sibling bond for life. And I want to rob them of these precious years together?"

The rest of her words are muffled by my flannel shirt and her soft sobs. More tears spill and create a damp spot I can feel through the thick flannel and my t-shirt.

There's nothing to do but rub soft circles on her back and

whisper how much I love her. No point in arguing until she collects herself enough to let rational thought return.

As far as Alene, I know she'll handle this change better than either of us. Spending time with kids her own age and older will be good for her. Better than hanging out with Mac all day.

At nine months old, he's pretty boring to his big sister except when he farts. That's the most hysterical thing to ever happen according to Alene's toddler cackles. He's other tricks involve food and making a mess. Where Alene is quiet, Mac is a ham. All mischief and fearless confidence.

Diane's breathing evens out and she gently pushes herself away from my embrace. Wiping her eyes again, she inhales deeply before meeting my eyes. "How am I going to handle a full day of kindergarten if I'm a mess dropping her off for three hours?"

"We'll cross that hurdle when we get there," I murmur.

"And what about when Mac leaves for college and the house is empty?" Her chin wobbles.

I glance over at Mac in his high chair next to the dining table. He's smearing sweet potato and cereal puffs around on the try. Every time he bangs his fat fists on the surface, small, orange globs splatter across the plastic and onto his bib. Pretty sure he has some in his dark hair, too.

Patiently, Babe lies in wait beneath the chair. Smart dog knows that when the baby is done eating, that's when the morsels will rain down from above.

Having Babe means less sweeping and mopping.

In her own chair, Alene quietly eats the last of her oatmeal and banana with her tiny spoon. Her dark eyes are focused on us, observing every detail. Her eyebrows pull together with concern just like her mother's.

I give Diane a soft peck to her lips and then pull her into another hug. She arches up and deepens the kiss, her mouth tasting of sweet cream and coffee. Screw school and work and everything else. I want to lose myself in Diane's kisses the way we used to do when we first got together.

I'm only working a half day today and a plan begins to form in my head. Shifting so I can press her against the counter, I cup her ass and give it a squeeze. In response, she moans against my lips.

Giggles pop the bubble that's formed around us.

"Mac mac! Mac mac!" Alene laughs and bangs her spoon on the table.

Diane leans back and twists her neck to check out the kids. "Oh no."

Mac has smeared his face with sweet potatoes, including small bumps of cereal. Babe is busy licking off the mess while Alene joyfully watches.

"Babe, leave it." Diane uses her serious business tone and Babe drops down from where he half stood with his front feet on the highchair tray.

"Don't be mad at the dog. He saved us the effort of cleaning up Mac."

Diane sticks out her tongue. "I'll grab a washcloth for the baby. Will you take care of Alene?"

I release her and she steps around the kitchen island toward Mac.

I walk over to Alene at the table. "How's my favorite girl?"

"Daddy!" She grins at me and my heart melts.

She's too young for school and other big girl stuff like growing up. I get a flash of her future milestones and know it's all going to go by too fast for me.

As soon as I scoot back her chair, she's clamoring off the seat and racing across the room to her pile of toys in the corner. Pulling out a book, she holds it out for me.

With a shake of my head, I tell her no. "Not this morning. We're going to school today."

Her eyes widen and she marches over to the counter

where her Peppa Pig backpack rests. Pointing at the bag, she asks. "School?"

Silently I nod because a lump has formed in my throat.

Still holding the book, she toddles her way back to me. Reaching up her empty hand, she wraps her chubby fist around one of my fingers and then leads me over to her play table near the windows facing the beach.

Diane has disappeared with Mac, probably to give him a more thorough wipe down than Babe's first round. He'll also need a diaper and outfit change before we can leave the house.

Knowing Alene and I have a few minutes to spare, I take the tiny seat in front of me. I'm basically squatting on a small chair, fearing the sound of wood splintering beneath my ass.

She places the book on the table in front of me and then digs through one of her toy bins. With fascination, I watch her sort through various pink and sparkly items until she chirps with delight. In her hand is a pink tiara, her favorite accessory since she received it at her second birthday party.

"Want me to help you put it on?" I hold out my palm.

She shakes her head now and marches over to me, holding it toward my head. "You do it."

This isn't the first time I've worn one of her tiaras or crowns and I know it won't be the last. The damn things squeeze my head and hurt like hell, but I smile and duck my head lower so she can place it on my hair.

Beats anything with glitter. I swear I catch a sparkle of that evil pixie dust in my beard in the truck's mirror most days. I threatened to ban the substance from the house after Mac partially one of Alene's craft projects covered in the stuff.

Turns out, the body passes glitter like it does corn. Intact and easily identifiable.

Tom still laughs about that. Because he's an asshole.

With Hailey expecting their second, it's only a matter of time until one of his kids shits glitter. Or worse.

Mac's happy babbling alerts me to Diane's return. I twist my head to face them and catch her snapping a pic with her phone.

"Ahem," I fake cough.

"It's just for me. I promise I won't share it on the moms' text thread. I learned my lesson the first time."

"Don't make it your wallpaper either. Connie still brings up the shirtless pic of me holding Mac right after he was born."

She shows me the wallpaper on her phone is still the two kids in matching yellow towels with duck hoods. "You're safe. I can't help it if my husband is the hottest lumberjack on this island."

If Alene's going to be at school for a few hours, that will give Diane and I the chance to spend time together. Just the two of us. Preferably naked. We just have to time it with Mac's morning nap. With a glance at the clock on the kitchen wall, I confirm we might be able to drop Alene off, put Mac down, and still have an hour to ourselves. My plant might work out perfectly.

"Time to go." I stand and sweep my daughter into my arms. She squirms and giggles when I kiss her arm and then her belly.

We follow Diane and Mac out to the driveway and commence with the process of strapping the wigglers into their car seats.

Eyeing the cereal and other abandoned snacks on the carpet of the backseat floor, I tell Diane we should let Babe loose in the Jeep to clean it out. Cheaper than feeding quarters into the vacuums at the car wash.

With a laugh and a "maybe," she climbs into the passenger seat.

We're quiet on the drive to the preschool in Langley. Housed in one of the local churches, it's the best program on the south end of Whidbey. And the same school I went to as a kid. I like tradition.

Pulling into a spot, I turn to Diane. "Ready?"

She has her game face on. "No crying at drop off. If the kids sense we're upset, they'll get upset and then all hell will break loose. Tears. Sobbing. It'll be a mess."

"'Ell," Alene repeats from her seat behind me.

Diane's eyes widen. "Great. Now she's going to be repeating that inside a church all morning."

I manage to stifle my laughter by pressing my lips together. "Could be worse. She could go back to using the word that rhymes with truck in every sentence."

"Don't say it!" She clamps her hand over my mouth. "I don't want her to get kicked out on her first day."

We're both laughing now, but at the time, Alene's F-bombs were anything but funny.

"Let's get this over with while we're not sad." Diane opens her door and climbs out. Seconds later she's releases the straps on Mac's car seat.

He rubs his eyes, already looking sleepy.

A bright-eyed Alene grips my sleeve like a vice.

"Want to walk?" I ask her as we make our way toward the side entrance.

She ducks her head into my shoulder and my heart cracks a little.

Walking beside us, Diane has Mac resting on her hip. "You can hold both our hands and we'll do the jumps."

Alene squirms. "Jumps!"

I set her down and then take her hand. Diane takes the other hand. Every few steps we lift Alene up by her hands and let her fly for a few feet before returning her feet to the ground.

Glancing over at my wife, her face lit up with a smile and our son giggling on her hip, I count my blessings. A few years ago, I never imagined this life for myself. Never thought I'd be lucky enough to be loved by a woman like Diane or be the guy who gets to love her every day. Never pictured myself with a kid, let alone two.

And now that this is my life, I'm not going to take a moment for granted.

A TOM & HAILEY BONUS SCENE

TOM

Halloween might be my favorite holiday. No family dinner obligations. Candy everywhere I go. Hailey in some crazy outfit, especially when she wears some sexy version of a regular thing. Like two years ago she dressed as … oh wait. Never mind. That was my birthday. Not Halloween. Move along. Nothing to see here.

"I can't fit into my pants." Hailey points to the gap at the waist of her jeans.

"No big deal. Wear something else. Or one of my shirts. No one will know you can't zip your jeans." We're in our bedroom, trying to get out of the house and down to the Halloween parade. By we, I mean, Hailey, me, and Shaw, who is currently sitting in the middle of the king size, holding court over the remote controls and three pairs of clean socks.

"I'm not walking around town with my fly down." Hailey begins peeling off her jeans. "And your jeans won't go with my costume."

"Wear those black maternity ones you have in the back of the closet. Your ass looks good in those."

She sighs and stares at me. "You thinking my ass looks hot

is exactly why none of my pants fit. I'm barely four months pregnant. This kid is enormous if nothing fits."

"And your boobs have never looked better," I mumble, but not soft enough that she doesn't hear me.

"Thomas Clifford, quit ogling me." With her hands on her thighs, she glares at me. Only she's now in her underwear and a long-sleeve, green T-shirt that only draws attention to her full breasts and the swell of our baby.

The thought of her carrying another baby thrills and scares me. My heart does this weird squeezing thing where I think I might be having a heart attack but then it morphs into a fluttering. No arm pain. I had the doctor in Coupeville check me out. He assures me I'm fit as a horse. Stallion of course.

Shaw bonks me on the forehead with a remote and laughs himself silly. Ignoring the pain, I gently tackled him into the duvet and blow raspberries on his belly. His laughter is best sound in the world.

"Do you have the rest of Shaw's costume ready?" she asks, pulling on a pair of black leggings.

Nodding, I say a slightly thanks for whoever brought back this trend. "Just need to put on his hat once we get to Langley."

"And you're wearing that?" She points to my black jeans and blue T-shirt.

"With my leather motorcycle jacket. The brown one. I was born ready for this costume." I roll to my side and bend my leg, giving her a sexy grin. "Can't you see it?"

She shifts her gaze to the ceiling, but I know she agrees.

"You love it when I wear that jacket. Reminds you of that time we ran into each other on our bikes up at Deception Pass. You had your way with me on a picnic table in broad daylight in front of God and those chipmunks." My grin falls when she chucks a pair of socks at me. "What was that for?"

"You can't talk about blow jobs in front of our son. I'm his mother!" She pretends to be horrified.

"I can't take you seriously in that wig. For the record, I'm not the one who said blowjob in front of the baby." Covering his ears with my palms, I dip my chin and widen my eyes.

"You are incorrigible." Leggings in place, she pulls on a black vest and grabs her tall boots from the closet.

She's right. I am ogling her. I can't help it. She's the most beautiful woman on a normal day, but there's something special about her today that makes her extra hot. Could be the outfit. Could be her baby bump. I'm not going to analyze it too closely. All I know is I can't wait to get her home tonight and show her how grateful I am she's mine.

We park a few blocks from the parade route. The streets and sidewalks are already filled with people in costumes.

"I had not idea this drew such a big crowd." I hoist Shaw into his stroller and get him situated. "Where did all of these people come from?"

"Must've been a recent baby boom." Hailey adjusts his knit hat and then pulls out her phone for another pic. "Smile."

Instead, I snarl. "I'm Star Lord."

Laughing at me, she rubs my bearded cheek. "Oh, okay, Lord."

"You promise you'll keep the wig on for later?"

"I'm just realizing you have a thing for Gamora." She pats her wig. I'm glad she didn't wear the full green face paint. Harder to kiss her.

"Nah, only you." I lean in for a quick kiss.

A car horn honks and someone yells, "Get a room!"

Blinking open my eyes, I glance over my shoulder. "Was that Erik Kelso? Punk ass kid."

"He's over thirty. You're going to have to accept he and Carter are grownups now. Just like you."

I grumble as I push Shaw's stroller down the street.

"Carter and Ashley are parents now," she continues pleading her case.

"All right, all right. They're adults." I cross the street at the corner, using the crosswalk. Like a responsible adult.

The crowd thickens when we reach Second Street, still a block from the parade route.

"Are we supposed to walk in the parade or watch it?" I navigate the stroller through the crowd, using it like a snow plow to cut a path through the congestion.

"You grew up here. How do you not know anything about the annual parade of ghouls?" Hailey follows in my wake.

"Too many kids around and I was probably busy doing other things." Like sleeping off a hangover or catching the ferry home from a night off the island, but I'm too smart to say any of that.

At the corner of Anthes and First, we spot an inflatable T-Rex costume and a guy dressed as whatshisface from Jurassic Park.

"There's Dan." I point them out to Hailey. "And I'm going to assume that's Roslyn inside the costume."

We squeeze our way closer to them.

Roslyn's face is barely visible through the meshed panel of her dinosaur bubble. Waving her little T-Rex arms at us, she greets us with a, "Hi, hi, hi."

"Where's your costume?" I ask Dan. He's wearing brown pants, a brown vest, and a gray collared shirt. Not that different than what he normally wears without the vest.

"Hey, you two are the same guy." Hailey claps in amusement.

Dan eyes me. "I guess we are."

"Where's the kid?" I ask, not spotting a baby strapped to either of them.

Roslyn steps back and reveals a sleeping Ione in her furry dinosaur costume, passed out in her stroller. "Too much excitement."

We shuffle to spread out and claim more space in our section of curb in front of the Dog House. The lights are off inside and I'm guessing Olaf is avoiding this circus.

"Anyone seen John?" I ask our group. "He's probably dressed as a lumberjack. As always."

Roslyn cranes her neck. "I thought I saw some red and black buffalo plaid on the other side of the street."

Sure enough, here comes John, jay walking across the road, dressed as himself. Beside him, Diane is wearing a matching shirt and a bright orange knit cap.

"The kids look adorable," Hailey says with a tone that's almost a squeal of delight. "Look at Mac!"

The baby is wearing a squirrel costume and next to him in the double stroller is Alene, with antlers on a headband and her face painted like a fawn.

"You're a damn woodland fantasy come to life," I greet them with a laugh.

"Who are you supposed to be?" he asks me after we finish our man hug with a back slap.

"I am Star Lord." I spread my legs and put my hands on my hips. "Hailey's Gamora, and Shaw is—"

"Groot!" Hailey interrupts me.

"He's Groot," I finish, half-heartedly. "He is Groot."

"Nice hat," Diane comments. "Did June make it?"

"She did. How did you know?" Hailey adjusts Shaw's bark looking knitted cap.

"She's incredible," Roslyn says. "You should see the sweater she made for Ione." The women continue talking about yarn and knitting and sweaters, but I tune them out.

"Who's dressed as Waldo this year?" I point across the street to a guy standing under the Clyde movie theater sign.

"Looks like Eric Kelso," John answers. "Although I swear we saw a woman wearing the same costume earlier."

Erik spots us and cuts across the street. "Well, look, the gang's all here."

"Where's Waldo?" John asks.

Laughing, he shrugs. "Costumes were Cari's idea. Figured if we lose each other in the crowd, we can easily find each other."

"Shouldn't you be harder to find?" I deadpan.

"Touché."

Langley's downtown is really only three streets and three blocks big. How hard can it be to locate your girlfriend? I don't bother asking Erik this because I don't really want to know.

"Where's your brother and Ashley?"

"They're walking in the parade with the goats this year."

"And the baby?" Diane asks. "Please don't tell me they have a two month old in the parade."

"She's with Grandma," Erik reassures her.

A few moments later, music starts playing and a police officer clears everyone out of the street and onto the sidewalks.

The first group is a den of zombie Scouts. I give major props for lurching in formation. Following them is the mayor and a group of local politicians, dressed as Ghostbusters. At least they're tossing out candy. I catch a mini Snickers and peel open the wrapper.

Next up is the high school marching band, also zombified. I hope something's not in the water.

A random group of dogs in costumes trails behind them. Mayhem almost breaks out when a pirate dog and kid dressed as a teddy bear get a little too close. Evidently, tutus for dogs are a huge business. Whoever came up with that idea is making bank.

A group of witches pretending to sweep the street follow

behind the dogs. They're not giving out candy (sadly), but are handing out voter registration information.

After the witches, comes Carter with his goats.

In tutus and superhero pajamas.

"Hey, look, that one's dressed like you," Roslyn jabs Dan's shoulder with her thumb.

"Batman goat doesn't count," he grumbles.

Langley's a small town and thankfully, this parade is short and sweet. The last contingent rounds the corner up by Village Pizzeria. A vintage black truck leads the way. Sitting on its wooden flat-bed, a band plays music from various horror and Halloween movies.

The truck proceeds a group of puppeteers who hold long sticks supporting the various ghost and ghoul puppets floating above their heads. Among the ghouls, few bats and black cats fly and creep near the crowd.

It's eleven in the morning on a Saturday, but there's something creepy about the way these creatures slink down the street and interact with the crowd.

Older kids squeal and younger ones scream or hide behind their parents. Alene watches everything with huge, round eyes. She's braver than I am.

"Anyone else freaked out by this?" I ask no one in particular.

"Definitely creepier than the annual Sip 'n Stroll," Diane agrees with me.

"Depends on if you get cornered under a kissing ball by the gossip brigade in their ugly holiday sweaters." John shudders, followed by me.

"True. Nothing scarier than that," I confirm. "Still. This might give me nightmares."

The truck pulls in front of us and I spy Jonah behind the wheel. "Why doesn't that surprise me?"

"What?" Hailey asks.

"Jonah's driving the truck. Figures he'd be into this." He's cool, but in a weird way.

"Maybe he volunteered. Seems like something he'd help out with if needed," Dan says.

"I think it's because he'll find any excuse to be in Langley lately." Erik adds his two cents. "He's taken over the place on the corner and I rarely see him at Whidbey Joe's."

"Any particular reason?" Hailey asks, sounding like she already thinks she knows the answer.

"If you mean a certain yarn shop owner, then maybe." He gives her a wink behind his oversized Waldo glasses. He looks ridiculous in his red and white knit beanie with the red pompom.

"Hmm," Diane, Roslyn, and Hailey all hum together.

They may not be dressed as witches, but in this moment they might as well be standing around a cauldron, plotting.

"Jonah's doomed," John whispers, taking a step away from our wives. "They're up to something."

Dan laughs, and strokes his beard. "He could do worse."

"Poor guy." I grimace. "Someone should warn him."

A sharp and definitely female elbow hits me in the ribs.

"Ouch! What was that for?" I turn to see who jabbed me.

Hailey dips her chin and gives me her newly perfected "mom look."

"Yes, my dear, love of my life, wife?" I ask, unleashing the Donnely dimples at her.

"Is it really so bad? This domesticated life?" Hailey asks.

I blink away my confusion. "Who said it was bad? I wouldn't trade my life for anyone else's. I have everything I ever wanted. You. Shaw. Baby two. Future babies three and four." I slide my arms around her and pull her close against me.

"I see what you did there. We'll see after two." Still smiling, she presses her lips against mine.

"Think of all of the family costume ideas you could do." I kiss her again.

"Hmm," she hums against my mouth. "You make a good point."

I keep our kiss PG because we're surrounded by kids and judging parents, but I can't wait to get her home and out of her costume.

A CARTER & ASHLEY BONUS SCENE

CARTER

"What's the turkey drug called again? The one that makes people horny." I open the fridge and try to find something to eat. Our enormous twenty-five pound turkey takes up most of the space in the center. What's not occupied by a giant dead bird is stuffed with vegetables and mysterious containers of pre-made side dishes I've been banned from opening under threat of amputation of whatever digit touched the precious.

Ashley peers around the door at me. "People believe tryptophan makes them sleepy, not horny, but it's really all the carbs and sugars that cause the energy crash after a meal."

I love how smart she is.

"Is that why we have so much kale in here? Or did you buy extra for the goats?"

"I did not buy organic kale for you to feed to the goats. Again. They get enough greens on the job." She slowly closes the door, blocking my view. "I stocked the beer fridge in the garage with sandwich supplies. You should be able to scrounge for food out there."

"Who would I be without you?" I lean close enough to kiss her.

"Some random guy, living in the woods with his brother and a bunch of goats, pining for his true love." She cups my cheek and kisses me back.

"So about the horny chemical in turkey?" I whisper an inch from her mouth.

"That's not a thing." Her hand finds its way down to my chest and begins unbuttoning my flannel.

"Are you sure? Just the thought of it has you stripping off my clothes in the kitchen in the middle of the afternoon. I'd say it's a real thing."

"Rosie finally went down for her nap and we're alone in the house. Tomorrow your family and my brother will be here pretty much all day. By the time your imaginary horny turkey drug kicks in, we'll be too exhausted to do anything but fall asleep at opposite ends of the couch." While she gives this little speech, her hands are trailing down my abs to the waist of my jeans.

"I like the way your mind works. Have I ever told you how turned on I am by your intelligence?" I still her hand when she slips it under my T-shirt.

"Many times. Why are you stopping?" Her voice is breathy and impatient.

"I was just thinking. Wasn't it around Thanksgiving last year that I knocked you up?" I grin down at her.

"I'm not sure of the exact day but it was closer to Halloween."

My smile turns to a frown. "Damn it."

Her eyes search mine. "What's going on in your head?"

"I was trying to change your mind about tryptophan."

"Is it that important for you to be right? My hand is practically down your pants already. I'd call that winning."

She makes an excellent point.

Lunch forgotten, I scoop her up by the hips, encouraging her to wrap her legs around me and carrying her to the bedroom.

Rosalia "Rosie" Kelso is a near perfect baby, but she is not a good napper. Named after Ashley's mentor, Roslyn, baby Rosie wasn't planned. We'd only been married a few months when we found out Ashley didn't have food poisoning after the annual holiday Sip 'n Stroll. Should've realized then that Rosie would be as fierce and independent as her mom. They have the same copper hair, too.

Watch out world. John and Tom's boys are nine months older than Rosie. She's already forbidden from dating either one of them after I caught Shaw Donnely flirting with her at one of those baby social hours. He even has his dad's dimples.

I'm thinking of training some of the goats to be bodyguards. They don't have the ferocious bark and sharp teeth of a dog, but even the little ones can pack some pain with their head butts. Guard goats could be the next big trend.

Our make out session turns into a quickie, followed by nap time when Ashley falls asleep immediately after. My caveman brain wants to be smug about tiring her out, but I'm fighting the yawns too. No one in this house is getting enough sleep these days.

I quietly leave her to nap and head for Rosie's room. Decorated like a woodland wonderland, her little crib is surrounded by more stuffed goats than I knew existed. Turns out when people know you raise goats, they also assume you collect everything shaped like a goat or with a goat plastered on the front. Rosie's too little to play with the herd, including the babies, but give her a few months and I can see her chasing after them in matching pajamas.

Still asleep, she shifts and purses her tiny mouth. I sit on the ground near the crib and lean my forehead agains the corner. This has become a favorite spot of mine. I could stay here for hours, just watching her sleep.

I must doze off because I wake up, sprawled on the floor and Ashley standing at the changing table with a gurgling Rosie.

"Hi," I mumble, rolling to my side and sitting up.

"You can always sleep in the bed, you know. We have all of the fancy baby gadgets so you don't have to keep watch on the floor." She twists her neck to make eye contact.

"I know. I just like being in here. She's so peaceful and beautiful. I struggle to believe she's real sometimes." Most of the time I can't believe I'm a dad.

"I'm going to bring her over to my mom's for a bit while we make the pies for dinner tomorrow. Think you'll manage without us?" Ashley holds up a smiling Rosie.

My heart squeezes at the sight of them. My two loves.

"I'll manage." Standing, I reassure her I can survive without them for a few hours. "I need to talk with Jonah about one of his projects and Cari is bugging me about doing a photo shoot for next year's calendar."

"Next year's calendar? Please tell me Erik isn't planning to do another naked calendar. How many years of staring at your asses can we endure?" She switches her attention to Rosie. "Your daddy and his friends like to run around outside naked. Yes, they do."

"That's not exactly the truth. It's for charity." I remind her of the social benefit besides brightening the lives of lonely women all over the island, and let's be honest, the world. The first calendar went viral and sold out in record time. "Plus, we're thinking about less nudity this year. Maybe do a hot dads theme. Apparently, some women like to look at men holding babies."

Narrowing her eyes, she hands me Rosie. "Let me see this in action."

I hold my daughter and give my wife a cheesy grin, all teeth and bravado.

"Hmm. I can see the appeal. Maybe it would be better if you took your shirt off, too." She gives me a wink. "You know. So you can raise more money for charity."

We're halfway through our first plates of the Thanksgiving feast at our dining table when Ashley brings up her idea for the calendar.

Cari, Erik's girlfriend, and talented photographer, perks up at the idea. "That's brilliant! Dad bods are having a moment right now. We can totally jump on the trend."

"Hey, who are you saying has a dad bod?" I suck in my stomach and straighten my back to show off my pecs.

Ashley and Cari eye my heaping plate of food.

"Keep that up and you'll be in perfect shape." Ashley pats my upper arm and I instinctively flex my biceps for her.

"What if we don't have a kid?" Erik asks. "Not all of us are fathers or have the coveted paunch."

Smug bastard still competes in triathlons. He also probably sleeps at least seven hours a night.

"Can we borrow some kids? There are plenty to go around with the baby boom happening on the island. Between John and Tom, we have a complete season covered. There have to be some moms around here dreaming of their kid's big break that will launch them into being momagers like Kris Whatshername." Jonah brings up a good point.

I'm surprised. I thought he'd be too cool to do another calendar. Unless he's using it as an excuse to find a woman.

"You can't walk into a library and borrow a baby," Ashley chides him. Once a little sister, always a baby sister. "Most women will not hand over their children to a random guy who wants to do a photo shoot with them. Especially one covered in tattoos and piercings."

She's not my mom, but damn if she doesn't have the mom voice perfected.

"Someone could pose with the kids, I mean baby goats. Get it?" I snort-laugh at my own pun.

Multiple sets of eyes focus on me, but no one else is laughing.

"That was terrible," Jonah says, slapping me on the shoulder. "You give me hope."

"I do?" I ask.

"If you can find a woman to marry you and be willing to have your baby, then there's hope for the rest of us poor bastards."

I nod. "Are you thinking of settling down?"

For as long as I've known him, Jonah's always been a lone wolf. To hear him talk about marriage and kids is unexpected, but I guess most of us catch the bug sooner or later.

Cari takes notes on her phone and the conversation switches to the upcoming Sip 'n Stroll. I plan to bring several of the goats. Sandy and Charlene have been crocheting ugly holiday sweaters for them. They even light up—the sweaters, not the goats.

Pausing for a break between dinner and desserts, we flop down on the couches. Rosie is happily being passed between our moms. If they had their way, she'd always be held by one of them. This might be one of the reasons she's reluctant to nap. She'll miss the party.

With a yawn, I tilt my head back so that it rests on the sofa cushion. I could definitely take a nap before round two.

Tryptophan or whatever it's called might not be the horny chemical I'd hoped it would be, but I'm still convinced it makes me sleepy.

"Someone wake me up when the pies are ready," I mumble with my eyes closed. "I have a dad bod to perfect."

OLAF'S CHRISTMAS MIRACLE

OLAF

The Ladies Who Love Decorating Society members have swarmed the streets once again. Like a plague of cheerful locus, they return every year to this location, but instead of stripping off every bit of foliage, they leave behind a crap ton of greenery. They're worse than the seagulls down on the pier. If seagulls shat kissing balls and boughs of evergreen all over the damn town.

Participation is mandatory. A few years ago someone wrote me up for not allowing the windows on my private property to be painted by a bunch of high school students. If I'm lucky, that unofficial citation's been added to my permanent record—along with my detentions in high school, my liquor license, my marriage license, my divorce record, a library book I stole in fourth grade, and the two parking tickets from Seattle I refused to pay out of protest. I hope there's a file at the police station or in town hall. How disappointing if my history of delinquencies is lost forever.

The decorating ladies are not to be messed with. The one time I threatened to close the bar for the evening is brought up every year as soon as November comes around. In some circles, I'm still referred to as Scrooge.

Fine by me.

Finally learned the best way to counteract the women of the LWLDS is to put up my own trimmings before the swarm reaches my corner. I can keep the merriment to a minimum, avoiding all of the bows and, most importantly, the devil's sparkle, aka glitter. Evil stuff gets everywhere, including my beard.

One year, I was finding sparkles in my whiskers well into January. Looked like I'd been kissing a drag queen. For the record, that only happened one time in the eighties, at a club in Seattle. Long story.

John parks his old Ford pickup in the spot right in front of the Dog House. Through the passenger window, I spot Tom and two empty carseats in the back row. Times have changed. The truck-bed is loaded with greenery and what looks like a tree.

Setting down the stack of ones I've been counting, I replace the cash drawer in the register and then head outside to find out what sort of nonsense I can expect.

"Gentlemen," I greet them as soon as they exit the cab. "That looks like a tree back there."

"That's because it is." Tom grins at me. "In fact, we brought two."

"Where you planning on putting two trees? I got enough to worry about breaking fire code with the sippers sipping their one beer all night, I don't need to crowd the space with flammable trees. One of those idiots will knock into it and spill their beer on the lights. Next thing we know it'll spark an electrical fire and the whole place will go up like the dried-out pile of wood it is." I cross my arms and spread my legs to show them I'm not budging. If the building weren't a historic landmark with its iconic red-painted siding and white trim, I wouldn't care what happens to it after the first of the year. Won't be my problem any more. But it's not getting destroyed on my watch.

"You done complaining, O?" John lowers the tailgate. "We're going to set them up outside by the benches."

Narrowing my eyes, I stare at the trees and the spot flanking the door. "Guess that's better than inside."

"Great." Tom hoists one of the trees by its trunk and flips it over his shoulder. "We don't have a lot of time before John needs to pick up Alene from pre-pre-school."

"Next thing you know she'll be in college," I mumble. "They grow up so quickly. Blink and they'll be gone."

"Not so fast. She's not even three." John sets down the other tree and drops two stands to the ground with a loud clank. "I don't want to think about her moving away."

"Everyone leaves the island. Except you bunch." I pick up the end of a garland. "Where's this going?"

"Windows." Tom takes it from me. "Same as last year."

"Maybe I'll leave it up there until next December. Save you the effort and save some trees." I reluctantly help him carry the long garland over to the bench.

"Won't that be a fire hazard?" Tom asks, eyeing the rust on the awning. "You just said the whole place is basically old, dried-up tinder."

"Like your old account?" John chuckles to himself.

"Ancient history," Tom grumbles.

While I watch, the two of them get the garland hung and lights strung around all of the greenery, including the trees.

John stands back and studies their work. "We should've brought ornaments and bows."

"No bows," I snap.

"Lookin' good, Olaf." June from the yarn store next door joins us on the sidewalk. "I have some extra ornaments if you want them. I made way too many this year. Decided on a woodland theme and got a little carried away with felting animals. Turns out you can have too many squirrels."

I don't know what's she's talking about most of the time. She's a nice person, but a little odd. Or maybe awkward is the better word. My tone softens when I speak to her. "That's nice of you, but I like to keep things simple."

Not to say John and Tom aren't good people, but I've never had to ban her from my bar. Or even threaten it.

Smiling, June pats my shoulder. "Simple works. I came over to introduce you to my mom. She's visiting for the weekend."

I notice the older version of June standing a little bit behind her. With similar heart-shaped faces and colorful glasses, there's no doubt they're related. June's mother has her gray streaked dark hair cut to chin length. I'm guessing she's in her late fifties—not that much younger than me. She's a couple of inches shorter than her daughter. Both women appear to be what I like to call voluptuous, but it's hard to tell under their padded coats and enormous scarves. They're sporting knit hats with furry pompoms on the top. Probably handmade by June.

Showing off their good manners, John and Tom both step forward and introduce themselves.

"Are you sure you're not sisters?" I ask with a flirty grin.

"Oh, aren't you a charmer?" June giggles. "Olaf, this is my mom, Lisa Moxee. Mom, Olaf owns the Dog House."

Her mother extends her hand and I reflexively wipe my palm on my shirt before touching her gloved hand. "The pleasure's all mine."

Behind the blue frame of her glasses, her warm, hazel eyes crinkle in the corners. She's even prettier when she smiles. "June was right. You are a flirt."

Tom sputters and coughs; John slaps him on the back.

Ignoring them, I squeeze Lisa's hand and continue to smile at her. "John and Tom would tell you I'm more of a curmudgeon."

One of them snorts, but I can't tell which one.

June laughs. "You do have a certain reputation around town."

I'm still holding Lisa's hand and give it another squeeze before releasing it. "Never you mind them. Are you enjoying your time on the island?"

"Oh, definitely. Langley's so festive and charming. A Christmas village come to life!" Happiness brightens her voice. "I can't wait for the Sip 'n Stroll tomorrow."

The tiny spark of interest inside of me sputters out as she continues chattering with June about all the joys of the season. She could be one an honorary member of the ribbon lovers society or worse, the carolers.

"Mom," June interrupts. "We should let the guys get back to work."

"Sorry. Of course. I could talk about Christmas all year long." She lifts a small bag in her left hand. "Before I forget, I brought you some cookies and fudge."

It's possible I was too harsh in my judgment of her.

"You shouldn't have."

"Everyone's been so welcoming to June since she moved here. We wanted to say thank you. And in our family, we use butter and sugar as verbs in our love language."

I reach for the bag. Lifting it to my nose, I inhale the scent of cinnamon and sugar. "That's very kind of you. Can I offer you a beer or hard cider as a thank you?"

Behind me, I sense Tom and John freeze.

"That sounds wonderful, but we need to run some more errands," June answers for the both of them.

"Can I have a raincheck?" Lisa touches my arm. "I'll be sure to stop by tomorrow evening."

"Of course. I'll be here." I hold up the bag. "Thanks again for the treats."

Lisa pats my arm one more time. "Enjoy them."

With a wave, the two women cross the street.

Peering over my shoulder, John asks, "Are you going to share your goodies?"

"I love fudge." Tom steps closer.

"Back away from the cookies, gentlemen." I tuck the bag close to my body.

Tom chuckles. "If you share, we won't tell everyone how you were flirting with Lisa. Didn't know you had it in you, O."

John moves in front of me, his tone teasing when he speaks. "He makes a good point. Don't want your reputation as the island's grinch to get spoiled. Imagine if people find out you're offering up free drinks to pretty ladies."

"Hey, I have an idea."

"Zip it, Donnely," I practically growl at him.

Laughing, he pulls off his beanie and shakes it. Pine needles drop to the ground around him. "You didn't even hear what I have to say."

"If the idea is you two buggering off and leaving me in peace, I'm all ears. Otherwise, not interested."

"Ah, there's the Olaf we know." John picks up his tools and returns the bag to the truck's bed.

I grumble under my breath. "Fine. You can each have a piece of fudge as long as I get to pretend it's a lump of coal."

Smug grin on his face, Tom reaches for the bag. "Nice to see the spirit of Christmas is alive and well inside of you."

I reluctantly release it. "One. Take one."

As soon as they each have their candy, I snatch the bag away. "Consider that your thank you."

"So what's your brilliant idea?" Tom asks, using a weird voice I suspect is supposed to be mine. "Thanks for asking, O. Here's my thinking. If I met a lady who was obsessed with Christmas and I wanted to impress her, I bet dressing up as Santa for the kiddos would do the trick. Why, Tom Donnely, you're a genius! If only there was a need for someone to play Santa. You're in luck, O! The Sip 'n Stroll is tomorrow night and Chuck Abelhammer has the flu. What a stroke of luck, Tom. I'd be thrilled to help out and you wouldn't even need to alter the suit. You say when and I'll bring the beard and jolly attitude."

"That's bullshit. Chuck's at least fifty pounds heavier than I am. Doesn't even have a beard. What's he doing playing Santa?" I bristle at the idea of him flirting with Lisa.

"He already has the suit." Tom bites into his chocolate and moans. "Wow. This is the best fudge I've ever tasted. Kind of last minute, but we'll ask someone else. Maybe one of the Kelsos could do it."

"Those are your other options? Better off canceling," I huff.

"Carter can dress up some of the goats as elves. Kids love goats," Tom continues as if I haven't spoken at all. "Or we can switch up tradition and have Jonah drive his vintage VW bus through town. Hmm, the dark eyebrows might be an issue."

"Eh, he could spray paint them white," John suggests. "Probably wash out in a day or week or two."

"Santa isn't a hipster at a music festival," I complain. "Your generation is going to ruin Christmas."

Tom lifts an eyebrow in challenge. "Thought you were against all these annoying traditions."

"People like nostalgia." I scratch my cheek above my beard.

"Probably why they keep coming to your bar. Certainly not for your friendly service."

I shoot Tom a look.

"Too far?" he asks.

I continue to glare at him until he holds up his hands in surrender.

"Think of it this way ...," John suggests. "You wouldn't have to deal with the crowd at the bar. Santa usually arrives by boat. It'll be just you and the captain."

"Out on the water there's peace and quiet. No carolers. No Kelsos." Tom nods a couple of times. "No adults in onesies."

He hits on the one thing that drives me crazier than

anything else. "Walking around in public like overgrown toddlers."

"Kids love you." John gets a tender look in his eyes. "Alene already calls you Olaf Claus."

Damnit. That little girl has us all wrapped around her finger. My heart clenches at the thought of bringing a smile to her sweet face.

"You want me to perpetuate one of the greatest lies ever told to children?" I'm still pretending to resist. "Biggest betrayal of childhood is finding out your parents lied to you for years."

The two of them exchange a look.

"It's thirty minutes of your life. Come on, O, do it for the kids. We know you do all sorts of good deeds around here behind the scenes. This is no different. You'll be far enough away, no one will recognize it's you." John makes a good argument.

"Wait. I thought we wanted June's mom to see him dressed as Santa so he can ask her if she's naughty or nice." Tom scrunches up his forehead. "What's the point if she doesn't know it's him?"

John elbows him.

"What? Isn't that the end game?" Tom jokes.

"Life isn't always about a girl," John scolds him.

The creases in Tom's forehead deepen. "It's not? Hailey's my everything. I don't know what I'd do without her."

He's completely serious. Before we all stand around in a circle on the sidewalk, sharing our feelings, I need to put an end to this conversation.

"I'm too old for this nonsense and it's too cold to stand around out here debating something that's never going to happen." I glance at the pine debris on the sidewalk. "I need to get a broom and clean up this mess before people track pine sap all over my floors."

"You're welcome," John tells me.

"Thank you for your unsolicited assistance. Feel free to come by on the twenty-sixth and take it all down."

"So that's a no on Santa?" Tom's a dog with a bone.

Alene's happy face flashes in my mind, along with memories of my own boys when they were little. The hope and excitement of Christmas in their eyes. The awe when they saw my ash-covered boot prints from the fireplace to the tree. Their joy while they unpacked their stockings and opened their presents. Those were happier times.

The angel on my shoulder makes a rare appearance. If this is going to be my last Christmas at the Dog House, I should make it a memorable one. This time next year I'll be fully retired and hopefully soaking up some winter sun in California. Dan and Jonah will have to deal with the Ladies Who Love Decorating Society and their holiday antics.

Dreams of poolside naps filling my head, I find myself saying out loud, "Fine. What time do I need to be ready? And who's going to watch the bar while I'm gone?"

Tom's mouth drops open. "It's a Christmas miracle!"

John fights a grin. "Who's moved from the naughty to the nice list this year?"

"Ha ha." I stroke my beard for a moment. "I only trust you two, Dan, Jonah, and Ashley. No Kelsos. That's it. Falcon's already been hired to watch the door. If he doesn't forget. And I want Tom to use his boat. The fewer people who know about this, the better."

"We'll handle the details. I'll pick you up at five." Tom holds out his hand. "Thanks, O."

Grumbling, I shake on our agreement. "This gets out, you'll both be banned for life."

"Santa!" a single high-pitched voice calls out from the railing at the edge of the bluff.

"SANTA'S HERE!"

Evidently, I've been spotted.

"Santa!"

"Santa!"

"SANTA! SANTA! SANTA!"

"SAAAANTAAA!"

Wow, that last kid has a set of lungs on her. Future opera singer.

More small bodies crowd against the metal like a tiny pack of hyenas gathering around a recent kill. Hyenas wearing padded coats and pompoms on their heads. Baby hyenas strapped into strollers and sitting in wagons. Through the openings between the rails, chubby arms extend toward the water. Adults create a line behind the smaller humans. The carolers break into a round of "Here Comes Santa Claus."

A deep, primal fear wraps around my chest and squeezes.

"You going to glare at them or wave?" Tom steers his boat closer to the shore. "I'd suggest waving and smiling."

"Who can see my smile through this thick, fake beard?" I stroke the silky material—a last minute decision to protect my identity. The round glasses don't even have lenses in them but they add to the illusion.

"Good point." He slows, leaving barely a wake behind us. "Maybe shout out a few ho, ho, hoes instead. Give them what they want. You're making memories that will last a lifetime."

Standing on the stern of the Master Baiter, illuminated by strings of multi-color lights and a bright spotlight, I wave my arm over my head.

High-pitched cries of joy ring out from above us.

I do it again and more voices join in the shouting. The crowd swells and a few people run down the stairs to the grassy area behind the seawall. Waving and running along the path, the group of kids try to keep up with our boat.

This is what Jagger must feel like. Or the Beatles arriving

at JFK to hordes of screaming fans. I know, I know, not *quite* the same, but let me have my moment.

This isn't going to become tradition.

One and done.

And if all goes right, I'll escape tonight with my secret intact.

The plan is to dock in Tom's slip in the marina, ditch the red suit and fake beard before catching a ride up the hill in plain clothes.

It's not Christmas Eve. Santa's only doing a drive-by tonight. More of a cruising the neighborhood but too busy to stop. Right now, Santa's got too much on his plate for more than a few waves and a couple of ho, ho, hoes. I'm giving this gig too much thought as I stand on a fishing boat, waving like a fool.

"They're all loving it," Tom shouts from his spot in the captain's chair. "Should we go back around one more time?"

Mine arm is tired and starting to ache. "Nah, they've got an eyeful. That's enough. Let's stick to the plan."

"Aye, aye, Santa." Tom gives me a two-finger salute.

Once we're around the bluff, heading toward the harbor, I drop my arm and rub my shoulder. "Damn. How do those beauty queens keep it up for an entire parade?"

Tom releases a snort. "For one thing, they're a quarter of your age."

"Watch your math, Thomas Clifford." I glare at him while unbuttoning the red coat.

"Age isn't an excuse. Queen Elizabeth is older than you. Maybe you need more practice with your technique? We could sign you up as fair marshal."

Ignoring my glare, he maneuvers the boat around the pier.

"Quit calling me old," I mutter under my breath.

"Sorry. Must be the Santa suit. Reminds me of Pop and how he used to dress up as Santa for the Donnely family party."

"Clifford was a good man."

Tom's voice goes soft. "He was. And a helluva lot more cheerful as Santa than you."

"I'm here, aren't I? I should get some bonus points for agreeing to your nefarious scheme."

"Bringing joy to dozens of small, sweet, innocent kids?" Tom steers us into his slip and cuts the engine.

Faint Christmas music echoes off the quiet of the water. A couple of sailboats have lights strung up their masts, but here, down the hill and away from downtown, the harbor is peaceful.

A beeping sound, like toy horn, disrupts the stillness.

"What in the damn world is that?" I squint down the row of boat slips toward shore.

A pair of small headlights flash over the water as a golf cart comes zooming around the corner before stopping near the end of the dock. Lights and garland drape the canopy and a red ball of light glows on the hood. Squinting, I make out a pair of antlers strapped to the sides. It's not a golf cart, it's a Christmas abomination.

"Is that your ride?" I glower at Tom.

"I suspect it might be yours." He finishes tying off the line around a cleat near the bow.

"Hell no. I agreed to the boat. That was it." Forgetting I'm still in the Santa costume, I attempt to cross my arms over my padded middle and can barely touch my elbows.

"You could stay here. Wouldn't be the first time a man slept on the boat to avoid someone. In my case, it was usually a woman, not a crowd of happy children."

"I'm well aware of your days catting around this island."

He stares up at me from his spot on the dock. "You staying? If so, I'm going to take your ride."

Bastard has the nerve to walk away, boots clomping down the dock, with the sack of wrapped presents slung over his shoulder.

I rub my gloved hand over my face. "Mother Mary and Joseph, bet you never imagined malarkey like this nonsense."

By the time I scramble off the boat and get myself to dry land, Tom's sitting in the passenger seat, grinning like a fool.

Carter Kelso is in the driver's seat, looking even more stupid with his toothy smile than Tom.

"Oh, hell no. I'll walk up the hill." I stomp around the golf cart.

Leaning out the open side, Carter tries to stop me. "Oh, come on, Santa. We'll do a quick loop through town and drop you off. Keep the beard and glasses. No one will guess it's you."

"That's what I told him," Tom gloats. "Totally against character. He'll be hiding in plain sight."

"Then one of you can wear this cockamamy costume." I continue making my way around the cart.

Carter puts it in reverse and backs up along side me as I walk. The warning beep, beep, beeping grows more annoying by the second. "How can we sweeten the deal? What will make Olaf happy? Tom can name his next kid after you. Olaf Donnely has a nice ring to it."

"Hey now. Use your own kid as a bargaining chip. My daughter isn't going to be named Olaf." Tom slaps his hand over his mouth. "Shit. Not supposed to tell. Forget I said anything."

My eyes widen but I keep my mouth shut. Tom raising a daughter is going to be fun to watch. Then I remind myself I won't be around as much. Not like Tom and John are going to come play pool every week at my house.

We're at the bottom of the steep hill leading up to First Street. Carter circles around and comes up beside me, facing the right direction now. I really don't want to huff it up this damn hill. This suit was fine on the water, but it's getting kind of warm now.

Abruptly halting, I lift my gaze up to the clear winter night sky. When I exhale, my breath is visible.

"Fine. We drive down First. You take the left on Anthes and drop me off at the Historical Society. I can ditch the suit and walk back to the Dog House from there. Under two conditions."

"We're all ears." Carter gestures to the place where his normal, human ears should be. That's when I notice he's wearing pointed elf ears. In fact, below his jacket I see what appears to be green and white striped pajamas.

Boy can't be normal if he tried. Last year he and his brother and a bunch of hooligans dressed up like snowmen from *Frozen*. Yes, the one that shares my name. Year before, there was more striped pajama nonsense. You'd think they'd grow of out wanting to look like a fool. Married. With a daughter. Still an idiot. Guess somethings never change.

"Don't stop for any reason. Don't let them mob us. I don't want to be torn to shreds by a pint-sized mob on a sugar high, looking for their next candy cane."

Both men laugh at me.

"I'm serious."

They barely contain themselves.

"May I continue?" I don't wait for them to settle. We'd be here all night. "Second, I ride in the front seat next to Carter. Too exposed in the back. The sack of toys can go there." I listen for the sound of children's footsteps running toward us.

Tom relinquishes his front seat. "Where am I supposed to ride?"

"You sit in the back up the hill, but once we hit the library, flank the golf cart like the Secret Service does. Make sure no one gets too close."

Tom's laughter bursts out of him. "You're hysterical."

"Still serious."

Carter is staring at me with his mouth open. "I never knew you were afraid of kids."

"I'm not. I hate crowds." I blow out a breath and make sure my suit buttons are closed.

Carter reaches inside of his jacket and pulls out a flask. "You should take a shot."

I accept it from him and unscrew the cap. "What is it?"

"Local whiskey."

"Moonshine?" I sniff the contents, sending a burn of alcohol fumes into my nose.

"No, legitimate and legal distillery."

I eye him, but take a long sip. The liquid goes down surprisingly smooth. "Thanks."

"Ready?" Carter asks, slowly accelerating.

"I regret every decision that led me to this moment. Let's go." I adjust my hat and glasses.

Tom slaps my shoulder. "Remember to be jolly."

"Ho, ho, ho," I say, drily.

The streets aren't officially closed for the evening's festivities, but traffic is lighter than normal. Our little cart weaves a path down the street uninterrupted. Carter honks the horn and I wave to the kiddos, who keep to the sidewalks thanks to their parents' vigilance. After spotting Hailey with Shaw near the the yarn store, Tom wanders away, leaving us exposed.

We almost make it to the Dog House and the left turn to freedom before chaos breaks out.

Baby goats dressed up like elves are frolicking in the middle of the damn intersection. Erik and Cari chase the little ones around, grabbing for their leashes. The whole mess looks like a weird production of the *Nutcracker*, mainly because Erik has enlisted the help of the mouse king and snow queen from the local dance studio.

The cart comes to a halt. Carter abandons me to help with the goats. And that's when the shouting begins.

"Santa!"

"Santa!"

"SANTA!"

Traffic is at a standstill. Everyone is gathered at this end of the street to watch the impromptu goat ballet. Slowly at first, kids abandon their distracted parents on the sidewalk and cautiously approach the cart.

"Santa?" An adorable little girl with dark hair and wide eyes stands in the middle of the road. She's dressed in a fluffy pink coat and matching boots.

"Lizzy!" a blond man calls out before scooping her into his arms. "What did Daddy tell you? Never step off the curb without us!"

"Is he the real Santa?" she asks, still staring at me.

Emboldened by her, a few more kids come closer, surrounding the cart, but keeping a respectful distance. For the moment.

The crowd shifts and I spot the familiar red hair of Maggie Marion. She joins the man with the pink fluff ball of a daughter. Recognition sparks in her eyes as she studies me.

I tap my finger to my nose—like the mobsters do in *The Sting*—to let her know I know she knows, but to keep quiet.

"Of course he's real," she tells the little girl. "Diane is going to die when she sees this. Where is she?"

"Right here. Alene wanted to come say hi to Santa." Holding the squirming toddler in her arms, Diane steps beside her.

When she spots me, Alene does a forward dive, nearly toppling out of her mother's hold. "Olaf Claus!"

"Holy Christmas miracle," Diane says loud enough for me to hear. "I can't believe my eyes."

Tom approaches, holding Shaw. "Look, it's Santa."

Hailey joins them. "Quick, can we get a photo with Santa?"

Next thing I know, Tom's thrusting his one-year-old son at me. "Here."

Old instincts kick in and I adjust the little guy in my arms so he's comfortable.

"You're a natural," Hailey tells me as she snaps photos with her smartphone.

"You were born for this." I swear Diane wipes tears from her cheeks. "This is the sweetest thing ever."

A line begins to form behind them. I spot Dan and Roslyn with ridiculous grins on their faces. He dips his chin in acknowledgment.

My cover has not only been blown, Olaf Claus is about to be memorialized in hundreds of snapshots.

"Oh, hell no," I mutter to myself.

Ditching the cart, I stand and hand Shaw back to his dad. "Santa needs to go feed his reindeer! Ho, ho, ho, and a Merry Christmas!"

I pat a couple of kids on their heads as I weave through the crowd toward the Dog House.

"Daddy? Why is Santa going to the bar?" a little voice asks.

Crap. Plan foiled.

I reach the sidewalk and spot Jonah inside. He gives me a wave and a thumb's up. Falcon's perched on his stool. The lights on his green Christmas sweater complement the trees and garland. At the moment, as strange as it all is, he's the most normal thing about this scene.

"Ho, ho, ho," I shout, navigating the crowd as I move toward the yarn shop. "I have to pick up a present for Mrs. Claus!"

People move out of my way and salvation is a few feet away when the door to the shop opens and Lisa exits. She's changed from earlier and is now wearing a hand-knit sweater that resembles my Santa suit. The only difference is hers has a frilly collar and cuffs instead of the fake fur on mine.

"Hi, Santa!" she greets me with the same warm smile as before. "I was just coming to see you."

"It's me, Olaf," I whisper to her.

"Of course it's you." Her smile doesn't waver as she tucks her hand in my elbow.

"Look! Santa and Mrs. Claus are standing under the kissing ball," someone shouts, and I'm not certain it isn't Diane. Maybe Roslyn. I add both of them to the long naughty list I started earlier today.

Glancing up, I spot the mistletoe orb directly above our heads.

"Don't feel obligated," I whisper to Lisa. "It's just a silly, old tradition around here."

"I like traditions." She stares up at me, her glasses reflecting the white twinkle lights in the shop's windows. Without hesitation, she stands taller and presses her lips to my cheek.

It's a good thing I'm still wearing the fake beard and wire-rimmed glasses. Otherwise she could probably see my embarrassment. Been a long time since a woman has kissed me.

"Thank you," I tell her, my voice tender.

"Merry Christmas," she replies.

"Merry Christmas," I say softly before I raise my voice to address the crowd. "Merry Christmas, one and all!"

From the youngest voices to the oldest, the sentiment is echoed up and down the street. This is the spirit of the season. We're no longer random strangers, but friends and neighbors sharing a moment of community. My cynicism fades as I enjoy the moment of happy camaraderie.

It truly is a Christmas miracle.

AN ERIK & CARI CHRISTMAS BONUS SCENE

ERIK

"I'm not sure I'm ready for kids." Cari falls on her back in the middle of our bed.

"The goat or human kind?" Exhausted, I flop next to her.

"Both. Who knew goat wrangling was so tough? I swear the one in the Olaf pajamas looked me straight in the eye and challenged me to try to catch her." She laughs, sounding bewildered by the mayhem we caused at the Sip 'n Stroll tonight.

I'm still not sure how it happened, but we lost control of the herd. The twelve goats of Christmas somehow slipped out of our grasp. First one, then another two, until we had more goats off leash than on. At some point, I was on my hands and knees, crawling around in the street. A couple of the goats decided to climb on me for an impromptu goat yoga session.

"You know someone got it on video, right?" Rolling over, I poke her hip.

"Of course. It's you. It'll probably be viral by tomorrow. Should you let your buddy Gomez know? He'd love an exclusive for his website. I'm sure he misses you."

I groan and bury my head into her side. "No. Please, no."

"Come on. It would be great press for Carter's business

and we could get a mention for the new calendars. Think of it the money we could raise for the foundation."

"We've already sold more calendars online than we ordered. It's only been two weeks since you came up with this crazy idea. The second printing won't be ready until after Christmas."

"What can I say? I'm brilliant. Although I never thought we could get everything organized and shot so quickly."

"Makes no sense to me. We're not even naked in this year's calendar. All of us are wearing flannels or T-shirts and jeans. What's so special about that?"

She shifts to her side. "Doesn't surprise me. Women are more about the fantasy than just naked flesh."

I scrunch up my forehead. "Explain the appeal to me again."

"Hot men holding babies? It's primal, evolutionary. Even if the man and the baby aren't ours, we like to fantasize they could be." She scrapes her fingers through my hair.

"So somewhere in Nebraska or Michigan, a woman is staring a picture of John holding Mac and having dirty thoughts?"

"John, Tom, Dan, Carter, Jonah ... you." Her fingers still. "I really didn't think this concept through."

"You should deal with the inappropriate emails and customer service calls." I shift closer to her. "Some of those women have very, dirty imaginations. Jonah's going to need a bodyguard."

She laughs and her thigh bounces under my cheek.

"I'm not kidding. After what happened on Black Friday and now all the women with their tattooed DILF fantasies, the guy needs back up. There could be backlash when they find out he's not even a dad."

"What's the opposite of a backlash? Forward lash?" Cari smirks. "I think he's going to be very popular with the ladies next year."

"Poor guy."

"Jonah can hold his own." She yawns and shifts again until her head is resting on her pillow.

I join her and she drops her head to my shoulder. Pressing a kiss to her temple, I share something that's been on my mind for months. "Do you think about us having kids? Human ones, not goats."

She twists her upper body away from me to stare into my eyes. "Do you?"

"Asked you first."

"I do, but I'm not convinced it's not a side-effect of the baby fever going around the island. I feel like we're too young, but that's obviously not true." Her brows pull together and then relax. "Don't laugh, okay? I'm totally guilty of fantasizing over your calendar picture. It's my phone's lock screen. And it's not even my baby. She's the daughter some random client of June's. I can't even remember her name. But you're holding her and kissing the top of her head. It does things to me."

My brows lift at her confession. "What sort of things?"

She ducks her head into my neck, muffling her words when she speaks. "Makes me want to jump you and demand you impregnate me."

"Excuse me?" I ask out of surprise.

"You heard me. I can't control it."

"Why would you want to?" I'm still stunned. "Is this why we've having sex all of the time?"

More than seeing, I feel her nod against me.

"I'm not complaining. Just so you know."

"We were going to travel the world together, visiting all of your partner coffee farmers and lying on remote tropical beaches." Her voice waivers.

"No reason we can't still do that. Dan and Ros travel with Ione. And most of our farmers have kids. The more the merrier." I reassure her.

"But what if we can't get pregnant?"

Her shift in thinking gives me whiplash and I don't know what to say.

"It's not a guarantee. Some people can't have kids. Like thirty percent. It's a really high number. Odds are against us."

Inhaling deeply, I pull her closer, wrapping my arm over her shoulder. "If it doesn't happen for us, we'll be okay. There are other ways to become parents. Or not. No matter what happens, it won't change my love for you, Cari."

"Love you, Erik Kelso," she whispers against my skin.

In this moment, I have everything I want right here in my arms.

"You sure you can handle the Christmas rush?" I close my laptop and stare at Jonah. It's the twenty-first of December and our flight to Albuquerque is tomorrow.

"Yeah, we're ready for the last minute coffee buyers on Christmas Eve. All of the extra beans you roasted earlier in the week are packaged and ready to go. I think the crew can take care of the extra six people showing up here the morning after Christmas. Most of the early birds will be lined up at Walmart in Oak Harbor or off island for the post Christmas sales." He shoves his chair away from his desk across from mine, bumping into a stack of boxes. Our office at Whidbey Joe's is more chaotic than usual with all of the new Naked Whidbey calendars.

"You plan on bringing the coffee truck to the madness again?" I ask.

A slight shake of his head followed by a full body tremor tells me he probably still has PTSD from the mob scene on Black Friday. "I, I … I wasn't prepared. I never thought they'd try to climb inside the truck with me."

"You were bringing coffee to the under-caffeinated.

Always lock the doors." This is zombie apocalypse 101. I might get mocked for my horror movie obsession, but I've learned valuable life skills.

Unlike Jonah. By the time he'd returned to headquarters, he had three different color lipstick kisses on his cheeks and one sleeve of his flannel was torn at the shoulder.

"Lesson learned. No good deed goes unpunished." He shakes out his hands. "I should get that tattooed on my arm. Or forehead."

I'm not sure where he'd put another tattoo on his forearms, but I'm against face tats. "Uh, you might want to rethink that."

He scrubs his hands over his face and beard. "I need something to remind me to not care so much about stuff that's none of my business."

I wait for him to elaborate, but he doesn't. Instead of asking for further explanation, I tell him, "Thanks for handling Christmas. I appreciate it. Gives Cari and I the time to spend a few extra days in New Mexico with her family."

"No problem. I didn't have plans except, hanging around with Carter, Ashley and Rosie."

"Crazy how everyone has kids now but us." My talk a few weeks ago with Cari comes to mind again. We haven't discussed the kid thing again. Part of my mission during our visit with her family is to ask her dad for his blessing. Carter and Ashley eloped, but I want to be more traditional when I marry Cari. Becoming her husband isn't something I take lightly.

His brow lowers as he frowns. "Yeah, I guess. You're paired off, though. I'm the only guy still flying solo."

"You're the unicorn."

"Magical?"

"Uh, that too." I realize too what I was about to say is kind of mean.

"Oh. Got it. I'm guy left off the ark when everyone pairs up two by two." He nods in confirmation.

"What do I know? I'm just your business partner. You could have a secret family off the island for all of the time you spend over there." Someone take away my shovel so I can't dig this hole any deeper.

"When would I have time? Between the roasting business, Fellowship of the Bean and the coffee huts with Ashley, and finishing the new place in Langley, I can barely find time to eat and sleep. All work and no play makes for a very dull Jonah. I haven't been to a concert or a show in Seattle in months. All I do is work, work, work."

Behind him, the tower boxes sways and tips precariously.

"Watch out." I jump from my chair and catch the top box before it topples over and gives him a concussion.

"Thanks." Jonah stands and helps me rebalance the stack.

"Death by Naked Whidbey calendars would definitely go in the police report hall of fame." I set the box on his desk.

"Is this all we have left?"

"Yep. I'm going to have to place another order. It's insane."

"Brilliant to have June carry them at the yarn store. She's already sold an entire box. If someone asks for a baby blanket pattern or yarn for booties, she mentions the calendar. She's brilliant." Lost in thought, Jonah taps the cardboard.

I let him have his moment.

"Right, enough about her." He straightens up. "I'll be taking off for Baja once you get back. Really looking forward to having a few days solo to start the new year. Need to get my head on straight."

He's been working non-stop for months. "How's the new space in Langley?"

"Good. Pinball machines have all arrived. Shelves are built for vinyl and books. I'm interviewing staff after I get back from Baja."

"It's going to be great."

"We'll see. I'm used to being in the coffee hut. Not sure how I feel about managing a big project like this."

"With Olaf finally retiring, Dan will be officially taking over the Dog House. He'll be available to give you advice or help out. We all will. The island needs this place, especially the teens. I would've loved a hang out space like this when I was in high school."

"Yeah, me too." He meets my eyes and nods.

"Plus, you'll have the added bonus of being across the street from June."

"Eh, not sure that's a good thing."

"Why not?"

"She's not speaking to me right now." He shrugs and then stands.

"What happened?" I'm being nosey and I don't care.

"Long story. You need to get out of here and get ready for your trip." He ends the conversation by walking toward the office door. Stopping in the doorway, he says, "Merry Christmas and Happy New Year to you both"

Before I can react, he's gone.

"Merry Christmas!" I yell back, but I'm not sure he hears me and I'm left wondering about the mysteries of Jonah's life.

I hope the new year brings good things for all of us.

A JONAH AND JUNE HOLIDAY BONUS SCENE

JONAH

If anyone is wondering *Can you have too many twinkle lights?*, the answer is absolutely not according to June.

Gazing down the row of white tents in Seawall Park, the aforementioned lights sparkle in the pale, late afternoon. For a Saturday in December, the weather is dry and mild—an early Christmas miracle it's not cold, gray, and rainy.

Local crafters fill the narrow strip of land below First Street. Normally, the park would be empty this time of year, which makes it the perfect location for a winter market to expand the annual sip 'n' stroll downtown without blocking the parade route. The view over the water to the snow-capped mountains is a beautiful reminder of how lucky we are to call Whidbey home.

June wanders through the vendors, greeting people with hugs and friendly waves. Since we started Craft Whidbey on her property, she's become the ambassador of all local artists, even joining the local business council with Dan and me.

Spotting me, she grins and weaves her way to where I'm standing near the entrance to the market.

"Hello, handsome." She kisses my cheek as I wrap her in a hug.

"I missed you." Inhaling her warm, familiar scent, I take a moment to enjoy the peace being in her arms brings.

With a laugh, she leans back, her hands interlocked behind my head. "We've been in the same place all day."

"Not together. I've barely seen you outside of working this week." I sound like I'm pouting, because I am.

"After tonight, we have nothing to do but take a long winter's nap and enjoy time together." To punctuate her meaning, she gives me a soft kiss.

She's lying of course. We'll both go back at it on Monday and work long hours through Christmas Eve. Such is the life of small business owners, but we will make the most of our two days off. Carter and a very pregnant Ashley are hosting Christmas at their house this year. Eric and Cari will be there too, along with the four dozen tamales Cari and her mom will bring.

"Earth to Jonah." June taps my nose. "Where'd you go?"

"Sorry. Was thinking about tamales," I confess with a guilty smile.

With a laugh, she pokes my chest. "You're obsessed."

I shrug. Not going to deny the truth. "I love their New Mexico tradition. I might have to hide some to freeze for later."

"Good thing I already asked for an extra two dozen."

My smile turns into a grin. "Have I told you lately how much I love you?"

Twisting her mouth, she pretends to think. "Not since this morning."

"I love you." I seal the words with a kiss.

"Get a room!" I swear the voice belongs to Eric Kelso, but when I open my eyes, I don't spot him.

"Who's the polar bear?" Gesturing over her shoulder, I point at the lumbering figure in the white fleece costume.

The enormous bear head hides the identity of its occupant behind a white mesh square in the neck. With the red Santa hat, the creature stands close to seven feet tall.

"I thought you hired him," June whispers, not making eye contact with me. In fact, I'd go so far as to say she's looking anywhere but at me.

Ducking my head, I bring my face into her line of sight. "Why would I pay someone to dress up like a bear for our market?"

Her attention flits to my face and then behind me. "I don't try to second-guess your decisions. Maybe you wanted to bring the charm of the Rod and Gun Club taxidermy to the streets."

I steal a quick kiss, tasting peppermint and chocolate on her lips. "I appreciate the vote of confidence. However, I think the gun club aesthetic is better kept indoors."

"Oh, I don't know. Antlers and taxidermy seem to be on trend." Laughing, she points at her hand-knit Christmas sweater decorated with a buck head, its antlers draped with garland. It matches the dark green one I'm wearing. Yes, we're that couple.

"If some weirdo has crashed our event, I want to know." My shoulders tense at the thought of a creep lurking around the kids.

June's hands come up to my shoulders and she gives me a gentle shake. "Loosen up. It's probably someone you know having fun. He's not bothering anyone. In fact, the little ones seem to love it."

True enough, the bear is surrounded by a tiny army of sugar-amped, sticky-fingered children.

"Where are their parents?" I grumble. "This is Dateline 101."

June cups my jaw and scratches my beard. "Okay, Scrooge, what's up? We're not hosting a party. We're in Langley at our first winter market. It's not like all these people are crowded into our living room, so what's with the bah-humbug attitude? Are you playing the role of Olaf this year?"

Leaning into her touch, I kiss the edge of her palm. "Nothing. Nothing's wrong."

"Spill."

With a sigh, I lift her hands and hold them in both of mine. I'm about to speak when Sally envelops me in a cloud of floral perfume. Given her giggling, the peppermint on her breath is probably from schnapps.

"There you are! Connie, I found him!"

"Sandy, Jonah's over here!" Connie squeezes around her friend to hug me too.

I'm the awkward filling in a tipsy granny sandwich.

Sandy, the third wheel on their tinsel-covered tricycle, joins their group hug, patting me on the top of my head. "Thank you, thank you. This is wonderful."

"Uh, you're welcome?" My arms are trapped by my sides, but I manage to wiggle my way out of their hold.

"Ladies." June's voice interrupts the cooing. "Maybe give Jonah some room to breathe?"

"Oh, sorry. Of course, of course." Sally gives my bicep a final squeeze.

"We're having the best time." Connie's glassy eyes meet mine.

"And we've had a cup of delicious holiday cheer in the warming tent." Sandy's words run together in a happy slur.

"The mulled wine." Connie explains.

"And by a cup, she means three." Sandy wiggles her fuzzy-red-gloved fingers.

Nothing like overserving at three in the afternoon. I'm not sure who's bartending in there right now, but I can't imagine it's Dan. He came up with the idea to bring together the local breweries and wineries in a festive beer garden at the far end of the market.

"Jonah, you're a genius." Connie opens her arms for

another hug, but I grab her hands in a double high five instead.

I search for June's face and mouth, "Help me," over the top of Connie's head.

Laughing, June shrugs. No help whatsoever.

"Did you see our sweaters this year?" Sandy opens her coat to flash us. *Naughty* is embroidered across her chest.

"And it says *Worth it* on the back." Connie shimmies her jacket off her shoulders to reveal the rest.

"You three inspire me," June remarks with a giggle. "Major points for embracing the holiday spirit."

Once we extricate ourselves from the overzealous trio, I tug June by the hand into the narrow row between two tents.

"Too many people?" she asks, a sympathetic smile tugging at the corners of her mouth.

I nod.

"This is a good thing. Everyone is loving it." She sweeps her arms around, gesturing at the crowded stalls. "It's a huge success."

Her grin soothes the tension in my shoulders. "I'm happy about that, but I didn't anticipate all the hugging."

I don't mention the pinching because I'm trying to block out that experience.

"Come on, we'll go find Dan and get ourselves some of that holiday cheer. We've earned it." June entwines our fingers and gently pulls me from our hiding spot.

"Jonah!" Maggie Marion greets me from inside the candle tent.

She's someone I'm actually happy to see. Her partner Gil joins her along with their dog, Biscuit, who wags his tail when he sees me.

"Maggie, Gil, this is June, my wife." My chest still fills with pride whenever I say the word.

Maggie's blue eyes crinkle as she shakes June's hand. "You own the yarn store."

"I do. You look familiar."

"I bought your cross-stitch kits last year for Christmas gifts. My friend Selah is around here somewhere. She doesn't craft, but loves anything to do with the downfall of the patriarchy."

"Someone call my name?" A woman in a leopard coat and black knitted hat with the world's largest pom-pom steps up beside Maggie.

"Speak of the devil," Gil jokes. Since he and Maggie got together six years ago, he's gone more salty than pepper in both his hair and his neatly trimmed beard. I like his style and decide I need to ask June to make me a cardigan à la Kurt Cobain.

"I own that." Selah smirks at him.

Maggie makes the introductions and the women chat about the long tradition of subversive crafts.

June's eyes widen when a tall Viking joins our circle.

"Kai Hendricks," Gil informs us.

"Nice to meet you." June reaches out and pets the man's cream-wool-covered forearm.

His smile freezes in place for a moment, his eyes following the path of her hand.

"Your sweater—is this a handknit Gansey?" Her voice is low and a little husky.

I could be jealous my wife is fawning over another man right in front of me, but I know her well enough. It's the sweater that has her full attention.

"Yes?" he answers.

Blinking herself back to the present from wherever her knitting fantasies just took her, June drops her hand as pink spreads across her cheeks. "Sorry. I haven't seen a sweater like this in person."

"My grandmother made it for me, many years ago. I think it's a little tight, but Selah insists it still fits." His loving gaze connects with hers.

"Like a glove," Selah purrs as she tucks her hand around his elbow.

The sexual tension between them surrounds our little group in a charged haze.

"Well, enough about yarn." Maggie breaks the awkwardness. "We're going to the beer garden to find Quinn and Ryan."

Selah rolls her eyes. "I heard all the parents are gathered there, using the fence as a pen for their children to run amok. Doesn't the rule about no one under twenty-one allowed apply to the under-four-foot crowd as well?"

Her voice holds disdain, which makes Maggie stick out her tongue. "We'll find you a corner seat with the other curmudgeons."

"Speaking of," June pauses, catching my eye. "My mom texted earlier from the ferry. She and Olaf should be here by now."

Scanning the crowd, I search for the Santa lookalike and my mother-in-law. Two years ago, Olaf dressed up as jolly old St. Nick himself. At least he nailed the old part.

I miss his constant stream of good-natured complaints from behind the bar of the Dog House. Never thought I'd feel that way, but absence does strange things to a man's heart.

"Maybe he's in the polar bear costume," I joke but June doesn't laugh. Huh.

The sound of children singing draws our attention to the far end of the park.

"Isn't the one in the pink faux fur our Lizzy?" Selah asks.

A dark-haired girl leads a line of kiddos marching through the crowd, adults clearing a path for them. Among the pack of little ones are Alene and Mac Day, Ellie and Shaw Donelly, and Rosie Kelso toddling and trying to keep up. The polar bear dances at the end of their tiny conga line.

"What are they singing?" Gil asks. "Or should I say screaming."

My ears strain to discern meaning amidst the high-pitched word soup.

"'Let it Go'," Maggie declares.

"Still?" Selah asks. "Will it ever stop?"

"You sound just like Olaf." June laughs.

"The snowman?" Selah gives her a confused look.

"No, the old bartender at the Dog," Maggie corrects her friend.

"Poor man. My sympathies." Selah frowns. "Oh look, now it's a full-on parade."

A group of elves dance through the crowd, followed by a whole herd of reindeer-onesie-wearing adults.

John and Diane walk over to our group. He's dressed in his usual flannel and boots, but his wife is wearing a red sweater trimmed in white fleece that matches her Santa hat.

"Not sure I'm a fan of the onesies," Gil says, and John nods in agreement.

"I think they're adorable. So comfortable, especially when you're pregnant." Diane casts a quick look at June.

"Speaking of, where are Tom and Hailey?" June asks, ignoring Diane's not so subtle hint.

We haven't told anyone yet, and June's not showing unless you notice her fuller breasts and the roundness in her face. I wonder if women have a sixth sense for knowing when other women are pregnant.

Part of my mood today is fear that June is overdoing it. This market has been a lot of work, and after losing an early pregnancy in March, I'm allowed to worry about the woman I love more than anything in this world.

We'll be in the second trimester at New Year's and plan to share the news then—just to be safe.

Tom and Hailey, who is pregnant with their third—and, according to her, final—baby, approach us. She's in a Santa onesie, her round belly stretching the fake black belt.

"Who's in the bear suit?" Tom asks. "I spotted both Kelsos, so it isn't one of them."

"My guess was Olaf," I tell him.

"Wrong." June points out her mom and her boyfriend—man-friend? Acquaintance? I never know what to call him now.

"Darn it." I resign myself to go up to the bear and ask as soon as the impromptu dance party parade ends.

"Anymore guesses?" June asks, pointing at the tall figure, who has somehow grown even taller since I last looked.

As it turns out there's no need to ask his identity.

Not when I see the unicycle the polar bear rides in a circle around his tiny legion of followers.

"Don't tell Carter," I say with a laugh, knowing it's my old business partner inside the costume.

"Too late." June points at my brother-in-law. He's scooped Rosie into his arms and scowls at Falcon. "Guess some things never change around here."

There are some parts of life I wish I could freeze forever, and moments like this are top of the list: laughing with friends, creating new traditions while enjoying the old, and the simple joy of being together.

After the market and sip 'n' stroll wind down, June and I hop in the VW to lead a line of cars south from town to the Craft Whidbey property for our official after-party.

An enormous pyre of wood looms in the dark of the field, flanked by the vintage trailers lit with old-fashioned Christmas bulbs. The dry wood alights with ease, roaring to life and soon crackling with flames and creating a circle of warmth.

Standing and sitting around the fire are my favorite people. This community of friends and family is my whole world, and I wouldn't trade this island life for anything.

"It's snowing!" June points to the sky.

Fat flakes drift down through the trees, swirling and dancing in the air.

Oohs and aahs, the kind most often heard at firework displays murmur through the crowd.

Wrapping my arms around June, resting my chin on her shoulder and placing my palms on her belly, I kiss her neck by her ear. Her gloved fingers slip between mine.

"Merry Christmas, to all," I whisper, saying a little prayer that we'll all be gathered here together again next year.

THANK YOU

Thank you for reading this Very Merry Wingmen collection of holiday shorts. Please consider leaving a review on your retailer of choice, Goodreads, or BookBub.

Wish you all happy holidays and an amazing New Year!

OTHER BOOKS BY DAISY

Wingmen

Ready to Fall

Confessions of a Reformed Tom Cat

Anything but Love

Better Love

Small Town Scandal

Wingmen Babypalooza

The Last Wingman

Love with Altitude

Next to You

Crazy Over you

Wild for You

Up to You

Modern Love Stories

We Were Here (prequel to Geoducks)

Geoducks Are for Lovers

Wanderlust

Tinfoil Heart

Park Ranger Series

Happy Trail

Bewitched Series

Bewitched

Spellbound

Enchanted

Charmed

Wicked Society

Get Witch Quick

Someday my Witch Will Come

Four Witches and a Funeral

Want a reading list?

www.daisyprescott.com/books/

To keep up with my latest news and upcoming releases, sign up for my mailing list.

www.daisyprescott.com/mailing-list/

ABOUT DAISY

Daisy Prescott is a USA Today bestselling author of small town romantic comedies. Series include Modern Love Stories, Wingmen, Love with Altitude, as well as the Bewitched and Wicked Society series of magical novellas. Tinfoil Heart is a romantic comedy standalone set in Roswell, New Mexico.

Daisy currently lives in a real life Stars Hollow in the Boston suburbs with her husband, their rescue dog Mulder, and an indeterminate number of imaginary house goats. When not writing, she can be found in the garden, traveling to satiate her wanderlust, lost in a good book, or on social media, usually talking about books, bearded men, and sloths.

Mailing list
www.daisyprescott.com

Printed in Great Britain
by Amazon